About the Author

Born of an Italian war bride in 1948 at Newcastle upon Tyne, he
lived in Naples, Italy with mother and younger sister for a short
time before returning to England. Attended Gateshead Boys'
Grammar School and was the youngest interpreter in the 1966
World Cup. In 1974, he was awarded a LLB(Hons) and went on
to be called to the Bar of Gray's Inn. Youngest head and founder
of Barristers' Chambers in London and was later admitted to the
New York State Bar. Lived in the US with his wife and six sons
for many years before returning to England, where he now
resides with his wife and one son in Hamstreet, Kent.

The Valletta

Ben Conlon

The Valletta

Olympia Publishers
London

www.olympiapublishers.com
OLYMPIA PAPERBACK EDITION

A CIP catalogue record for this title is
available from the British Library.

ISBN: 978-1-80074-950-4

This is a work of fiction.
Names, characters, places and incidents originate from the writer's
imagination. Any resemblance to actual persons, living or dead, is
purely coincidental.

First Published in 2023

Olympia Publishers
Tallis House
2 Tallis Street
London
EC4Y 0AB

Printed in Great Britain

Dedication

To all those who I love and have ever loved.

Acknowledgements

Much appreciation and thanks to my wife, soulmate, and best friend, Loraine, who as always was a great help and support throughout. I would like to thank Lynn Robson for her help in the early stages of this book. Many thanks to my sisters, Rosaria Todd and Christine Rogers, and my good friend from primary school days, Ian Oliver, for their helpful critique.

Chapter 1

San Gennaro

Captain Vincenzo Gennaro Falcone, decided that it would be best if he joined the Medical Corps before he was conscripted by the Italian Fascist Government. By, doing so he was able to make his own choice of what he wanted to do, and so he enlisted in the Medical Division of the Tenth Army, shortly after Italy declared war on the Allies.

Non-political, Falcone was of a minor landed family who owned vineyards, and a Villa at San Giorgio a Cremano, just south of Naples, in the District of Portici. They also owned two apartment blocks palazzi on the fringes of Piazza Mercato, in the heart of Naples, which had proved to be a wise investment by his grandparents, just before the turn of the century. It now comprised a dozen large flats, one of which was kept free for Falcone family use whenever they were in town.

Falcone's wine, borne from the fertile volcanic foothills of the menacing Volcano, Mount Vesuvius, had been served on the tables of Italian aristocrats from before Cavour's reunification. Papal recognition for the contributions and services made to the Roman Catholic Church by this respected Neapolitan family came by way of a papal knighthood. Don Mimmi (the Neapolitan nickname for Domenico) Falcone, the Capitano's father, now became Il Cavaliere Domenico Falcone. Italians, especially those from the south, love titles. They collected and used them as much as they could, and Mimmi was no exception.

Vincenzo, lovingly shortened to Enzo by the family, was the only son of Mimmi and Adelina, Lina for short. Uncharacteristically less spoilt than most only sons in this genre of Italian, *'Mezzogiorno'* society in the south, he wanted for nothing and received the best. Privileged, he received the best education available at the private Roman Catholic schools that educated the children of the wealthy. At this time these renowned schools exercised an overt strictness, perfected by the Nuns and Monks over centuries, which would these days be regarded as abuse.

Overall, Enzo came out relatively unscathed. To his father's dismay, he did not want to take over the family business, instead he wanted to study medicine. His parents' respect for the profession helped to soften the blow. The family business still needed to be continued, and Mimmi ensured that his progeny spent time in the vineyards and taught his son, the art of winemaking

The father and son reached a compromise. Mimmi was still a healthy man in his early forties and expected, based upon his father and grandfather having lived into their late seventies and eighties, to live into his late seventies at least. Enzo would go away and qualify as a doctor but would spend his vacations working with his father. This way he would learn to manage the businesses and, eventually, when he inherited the vineyards and other property they owned in Naples, he could employ others to manage for him.

Seventh September 1929 was Enzo's twenty-first birthday. The Falcone clan, uncles, aunts, cousins, their spouses, offspring and in-laws, spent the whole of the month of August on the island of Ischia. Along with Capri and Proceda, Ischia made up the three islands located in the bay of Naples. Unlike most islands, Ischia was very fertile. The island's volcanic spas and springs made it into one of the first tourist venues, claiming the patronage of a number of historical Roman Emperors.

The Falcone family had acquired a cliff-top property on Ischia soon after the Great War and a moderate vineyard, with sea views across the bay towards Pozzuoli to the Northeast of the Bay of Naples. The land terraced in gentle steps down onto their private beach where they constructed a small boat landing from a natural hollow in the volcanic rock face. Adjacent to the San Francesco beach, a couple of kilometres from the growing village of Forio, the family built a substantial villa on the lowest terrace, just above the beach.

Enzo and his parents loved this place. They would remain in residence well after the rest of the family had left. One rule his parents insisted on, however, was that they had to return from Ischia to be at their apartment in Piazza Mercato, for the festival of San Gennaro on nineteenth September San Gennaro is the Patron Saint of Naples and the Neapolitans. Enzo was confirmed on this day by the Cardinal of Naples in 1917, when he was nine and given Gennaro as his Saint's name.

Birthday celebrations lingered a few days, but the annual Falcone family 'get together' on Ischia slowly dissipated. Everything secured and locked up, Enzo and his parents boarded the small steam launch that always came to get them after the summer, to take them back to the main port in Naples.

The Faculty of Medicine, University of Florence, beckoned. The day before he left, Enzo and his parents took Holy Communion at mass at the Cathedral of Naples. Once again, they witnessed the miracle of San Gennaro's blood bubbling, as the

Cardinal held up the small glass vial of red liquid within a golden cross, walking among the throng, muttering Latin prayers and chants. The congregation stretched out to touch the cross. Those who succeeded in their attempts, immediately collapsed to the ground, made the sign of the cross, and began another more intense round of incomprehensible mumblings.

Now, twenty-four hours later, Enzo was boarding the sleeper to Florence at the Central Station, Piazza Garibaldi. Mama and Papa Falcone were inconsolable, weeping at his imminent departure, as two porters loaded his luggage onto the train. It was the first time he had ever been away from home or been separated from his parents. His mother wanted to make sure that everyone in the station knew of her pending loss.

It seemed an eternity before the train was to depart. His loving parents had now become an embarrassment to him, they refused to budge when he suggested that they go home. As diplomatically as possible, he tried to signal and mime to his father to take his mother and just go, *"Please go. Papa!"* he pleaded.

Papa would have none of it. Indignant at his son's request, he made matters worse by explaining to his spouse that their son had asked them to leave.

"What? Are you ashamed of us now? My God, I never thought I would hear those words come out of my son's mouth. Ashamed, he is," his Mama continued to rant.

Enzo shook his head in disbelief, looked up toward the heavens, and said out loud, *"Please, San Gennaro, ask God to tell the driver of this train to get a move on."*

"Another miracle, two in two days!" he said to himself, as

the train tooted its imminent departure. Doors slammed shut, and his parents stood back from the carriage when the guard's whistle blew. The train chugged along the platform and picked up steam as he waved to his sobbing, distraught parents.

The train rapidly accelerated to cruising speed along the contour of the plains north of Vesuvius towards Rome, then northeast, on towards Florence. His fellow travellers had all witnessed the earlier pantomime, his mother playing the star role, telling everyone her son's life history and plans. Hardened travellers, heading north to work, adopted him. When he arrived at his destination, they accompanied him; made sure he got a porter to carry his luggage and got him a taxi. They then said their farewells and departed, going their various ways.

The degree of Doctor of Medicine from the University of Florence necessitated three compulsory academic years to be studied, plus three years of practical training in a recognised teaching hospital or under the direct supervision of a certified Professor of Medicine. Enzo had made a pact with his parents that he would complete the practical part of his degree in the local hospital at San Giorgio, under supervision as approved by the Royal Medical Board. Like his father, Enzo was practically minded and had a focused perspective on life; he saw no point in first studying Literature and then becoming a doctor. Go direct. Study medicine.

The University of Florence was, all in all, a good experience for Enzo and widened his horizons. He enjoyed the culture; made new friends from other parts of Italy, even met some English, American, French, Spanish, and other foreign students. This was a much different world to what he had been used to at home. There were girls and he had a few flings, but nothing serious and certainly nobody his parents should know about.

Enzo kept his focus on getting through the academic phase of his training. With that completed, he was back home and working through his final year at the Casa Di Cura in his hometown of San Giorgio a Cremano.

Professor Antonio Rossi, an eminent teaching clinician and a Medical Board approved teaching supervisor, was being privately paid by the Falcone family to get Enzo through his clinical exams. Toward the end of his final year, Rossi sat his prize student down to establish which specialised field of medical practice Enzo preferred. Without hesitation Enzo told Rossi, *"Anaesthetics."*

Pleasantly surprised, Rossi enquired further how Enzo had come to this choice. Using the typical logic of his father, Enzo explained to Professor Rossi why he was choosing this road, *"Just as there will always be a need for barbers to cut hair, anaesthetists will always be needed for surgery. The relief of pain, control of consciousness and support of the vital functions of life; these are all the fundamentals of medicine. Modern anaesthetics are still in their infancy with a vast capacity to expand; I want to be part of it."*

Enzo had given no prior hint of this interest to Rossi, who agreed with all he said. He advised, *"Enzo, if you are serious about this, then you must go, and get experience. I have contacts in St Bartholomew's Hospital in London. They have the most advanced techniques in that discipline of medicine, as well as continuing research in that field. I can arrange for you to go there. You need to spend at least a year specialising in this field. It's a sound choice, and we have very few anaesthetists in Italy trained to cope with the modern demands of surgery."*

"But Professor," Enzo argued, *"I speak no English and have never been beyond Florence."*

"Don't worry, Enzo," Rossi placated, *"Medicine, like Law, has its own language which transcends linguistic barriers. Anyway, there are a few Italian doctors already working and studying at St Bartholomew's, you will pick the language up in no time. It will be a good experience for you."*

Chapter 2

Prisoner of War

Enzo had been expecting, and indeed, hoping for surrender, weeks before the inevitable capitulation of the Tenth, to the Australian Troops in North Africa. As a doctor, he had been immediately commissioned as a Captain into the Medical Corps of the Italian Tenth Army, who were fighting the British and Empire forces in Tunisia and Libya. A patriot of Italy but not a supporter of Mussolini or Fascism, he saw being a doctor as a means of keeping under any political radar. He did not want to be in the army but made the best of it. He was a medical doctor first, above all else! More than that, he was one of the few consultant anaesthetists in Italy. He had trained for two years at St (Bart's) Bartholomew's Hospital, London. During that time, he learnt to read, write and speak English fluently. Enzo had promised himself that he would do his best never to fire a shot at anybody. He was to be a healer and not a killer.

Captain Falcone's Field Hospital consisted of twelve tents. Two were operating theatres and recovery areas, two for emergency intake, and the rest for the recovering wounded. Enzo and a couple of fellow doctors were provided with a caravan in which to sleep. The tents each held up to thirty beds. When the surrender eventually came in early February 1941, it was surreal. The magnitude of the number of Italian troops that just gave up was so great that the allies had difficulty coping. None of the

Italian Medical Corp had been armed and the wounded being tended, were not a threat. Hence, Enzo's Field Hospital was left to its own devices for several days.

Eventually, a platoon of Military Police under the command of a young subaltern appeared, accompanied by a captured Italian Major as his interpreter. Using the existing Tannoy system, the Major announced that the walking wounded and sick would be transferred to transit Prisoner of War Camps in Egypt. Medical staff and the bedridden would be transferred to a hospital ship at Tobruk and transported to England.

Lists of all patients were to be supplied to the Officer in Charge of the Military Police within forty-eight hours by the officer in command of the field hospital. All captured Italian military personnel would continue to comply with their existing chain of command, who would in turn take its orders from the British High Command.

A second announcement followed, requesting that all those who spoke English came forward. About a dozen or so complied, including Enzo. These were to be utilised by their captors as interpreters to assist with the marshalling and documenting of the many tens of thousands of captured Italian troops. Out of these few who came forward, Captain Falcone was the only medic who spoke English. As the one in charge of the Field Hospital, that was where Enzo had to stay. The other volunteers were casually marched off, away from the Field Hospital enclosure, towards the general Italian captive population now housed in a makeshift tent city, behind a perimeter of coiled barbed wire, five foot high.

Weeks passed by in the hot sticky desert conditions of north Libya. Only the occasional breeze from the Mediterranean Sea gave any relief during the day. Nights were freezing and the days so hot that eggs could be fried on pans that had been left out in the sun for just a few minutes. Sand got everywhere.

Frequent sandstorms made things worse and the impact of the grains of sand against the skin hurt As the Italian bedridden wounded improved, they were transferred to 'Tent city'. Other beds became vacant as a result of death, either from wounds suffered, subsequent infection, or one of the many diseases prevalent in that part of the African continent. Beds never stayed empty for long, once disinfected, cleaned up and remade, another wounded or sick soldier arrived. This time they would be the sick and wounded of the captors, who eventually became the majority. By the time the hospital ship arrived in June 1941, Enzo found himself in charge of a field hospital full of the wounded and sick of his captors. His surgical, medical and nursing staffs were supplemented by Allied medics, and Enzo was promoted to the rank of Major by his surrendered General. He was the only qualified anaesthetist in the facility but, as in all battlefield hospitals, he had to deal with conditions not yet written about in medical books. English was spoken throughout the working day. Only on a rare break with his remaining Italian medics was he able to return to his mother tongue.

The hospital ship was a converted Italian cruise ship, MS Principessa Emilia, she had left Genoa with her aristocratic and rich passengers a few days before the outbreak of hostilities. She had been anchored in the Port of Valletta, Malta, when the Royal Navy boarding party took possession of the vessel, such was the patriotism of the Italian crew that they cheered and applauded their captors as they came aboard. They turned it into a real "Italian Boarding Party" and, like many Italians, this crew had no stomach for the war, proclaiming their feelings by shouting: "*Our Mad Leader*" or "*That Shit Hitler*".

So, party they did; captors, some passengers, and Italian crew alike. There then followed various diplomatic manoeuvres to repatriate the various VIPs of enemy and neutral countries.

The MS Principessa Emilia, built in 1927 at the Monfalcone shipyard, on the Adriatic, and launched by her namesake Her Royal Highness Principessa Emilia di Savoia, on 5 October 1927. It became the Flagship of the Brancaleone Line of luxury cruise ships that roamed the Mediterranean and occasionally crossed the Atlantic to destinations in South America, Caribbean, and New York. The target clientele was the wealthy 'B' list European Royals, rich aristocratic, nouveau riche industrialists and bankers. Anyone else who had the money and knew the 'right people' could get on the waiting list of this floating prestigious palace.

A 24,000-ton twin screw diesel generating 20,000 horsepower, with a maximum speed of 21 knots MS Principessa Emilia was 632ft long and 79.7ft wide. Eight passenger decks, fifteen hundred passengers and four hundred and fifty crew. Four classes of passenger travel and accommodation aboard: three hundred and twenty First Class, four hundred and ten Second Class, two hundred and seventy-six Third Class and five hundred Fourth Class.

Since its launch, the 'Emilia' had built a reputation of being luxurious and extremely popular amongst the elite that regularly sailed. Some made it their floating home, others boarded for the 'season', the rest just came for the cruise and boast of having been on the 'Emilia'. Borne from all this came a perceived arrogance of the Brancaleone line, Ship's captain, and officers, most likely inspired by that of VIPs who frequently populated the ship's passenger list.

Mussolini and Hitler were allies but the former did not join in the war after Poland was annexed by Germany. Nevertheless, these were dangerous times. Mussolini with typical rhetoric boasted that Italy had nothing to fear. Such propaganda that followed, combined with the attitude of the Brancaleone Line, meant it was 'business as usual' to the Captain of the 'Emilia' and its patrons. Above it all living in a parallel world they boarded the liner for the last time. Conversion to a hospital ship took several months, and the Italian crew remained with the ship. Command was taken over by Officers of the Royal Naval Auxiliary, flown into Malta from Portsmouth. The refit and conversion complete, medics began to arrive from various military and naval medical units. Major Alan Russell was a career army medic, whose promotion was accelerated due to shortage of qualified medic officers. Alan had joined the Royal Army Medical Corps as a Regular, subsequent to completing a two-year residency in orthopaedics at Bart's. Three months of compulsory officer-training followed, and then he was commissioned as a first lieutenant. After a short time, he was promoted to Captain and was now a Major in charge of a medical contingent aboard the newly named His Majesty's Hospital Ship (HMHS) 'The Valletta' which now docked just north of Tobruk, where mines had been removed and other submerged hazards made safe. Orders were given to Enzo to select and prepare the patients for embarkation within twenty-four hours. A fleet of ambulances and other vehicles would pick up the ninety-two sick and wounded for transportation to the Valletta.

Even though the British Navy dominated the Mediterranean, there were still lurking Italian naval forces and German 'U' Boats active in the area. Although the Valletta was clearly marked with a red cross as a hospital ship and should not be attacked, it was still felt prudent that it should be escorted as far as Gibraltar. There was only a three-day window, no time was wasted, and contrary to many instances in the North African theatre, this operation went like clockwork.

After a few days in harbour in Gibraltar being refuelled and restocked, the Valletta was escorted back to England by the Home Fleet. It had come to meet the hospital ship once it was west of The Straits, on a heading north to England.

Despite being a POW, Major Falcone was treated like any other medical officer aboard the Valletta. He wore no uniform and was either in surgical greens or a white lab coat over his khaki combats and tee-shirt, indistinguishable from the other doctors.

Bart's was a big place, and it was not surprising that Major Russell had only a vague recollection of his Italian, counterpart a sentiment reciprocated by Enzo. Both had the discipline and experience learnt whilst in that hallowed institution, which enabled them to get along professionally and, with this common ground, a friendship began to grow.

Whilst at Bart's, Enzo spent the best part of his time in theatre, masked and gowned, attending to the anaesthetics in every type of operation; whether Cesarean amputation, appendix, resetting a fractured limb and so forth; he had to be there as the anaesthetist. Alan's only recollection of ever meeting Enzo was in the 'theatre' at Bart's when the Italian had been the duty 'Gasman'.

He was assisting his Consultant, Mr Rix, reset a fracture of some kind and remembered being told in good humour, before entering the operating theatre, "If you smell garlic when we go in it's because our Gasman is an Eyetie."

Enzo was already fully masked up, as was Rix and his Registrar Alan, when they entered the operating theatre and greeted each other. At no time did either of these two medical Majors ever actually see each other without a mask, before the Valletta.

The Ship's destination was not disclosed until English soil was in sight. It took no great intelligence to work out that the port

23

of disembarkation was to be Southampton. Commander Butler, the hospital ship's Captain, summoned Enzo to his cabin. Norman Butler had received orders from the Ministry of War in London, which he had to read and then give to Enzo.

"Major Falcone, these orders were wired to me a short while ago," Norman said as he handed Enzo a brown envelope containing a copy of his transfer to Camp Eden. He continued, "They are as follows: You will be taken by military police escort to Eden Prisoner of War Camp, near Malton, in North Yorkshire. This Camp is a facility especially provided for Italian prisoners of war. You are required to take charge of the camp hospital, the medical facilities, and all Italian medical staff. On arrival you are to report to Major Percy Logan, Camp Commandant. Sorry Enzo, but there is still a war going on. I would have preferred you stay on board and continue your work with us."

Disheartened and saddened by this unexpected development, Enzo put on a brave face, "Cannot complain, Norman. No danger of being sunk by the Italian or German Navy in Yorkshire!" Enzo said.

Butler had already poured out two glasses of naval rum in anticipation that he might need something to soften the blow he had to deliver.

"Here, Enzo, pick up your glass of rum with the compliments of the crew of Her Majesty's Hospital Ship the Valletta!" Butler encouraged.

Together they raised their glasses and toasted,

"The Valletta!"

Chapter 3

Camp Eden

Major Logan had served in the Durham Light Infantry; he was wounded in his right knee as he got out of the trenches to lead another suicide attack against the Hun, somewhere in Belgium, in the "War to end all Wars", as he would frequently say.

Percy Logan and his ebony carved walking stick were called back into service by some genius in Whitehall's War Department, a clear sign of how desperate things had become. The man loved being in charge. Incapable of making instant decisions, a past master at the 'Blame Game' and just as good at 'Pass the Buck'. Percy now found himself Commandant of the Eden Prisoner of War Camp, near Malton, North Yorkshire, in charge of forty assorted Home Guard-types. They had the job of containing five hundred and seventy-five officers and men of the Italian tenth Army, which had surrendered to the Allies not far from Tobruk, in early February 1941.

"Next stop, Northallerton," shouted the guard as he made his way down the corridor of the train, crowded with all types of military personnel of various ranks.

Enzo's uniform, now long gone, had been replaced with a generic khaki overall on top of which he wore an army overcoat without insignia and a brown beret. He got off the train with his escort, who handed him over to the contingent of two sent to pick him up from the Eden Camp.

Percy Logan had never met an Italian before being made Commandant. Most of his life had been spent pig farming in the Yorkshire Dales and he had only gone out of England to serve 'King and Country' in the 'War to end all Wars'. His Italian inmates caused little problem and looked after themselves. Any issues were generally as a result of football matches, they had organised or card games that had got out of hand.

"Welcome to Eden Camp, Major Falcone. I have a copy of your orders and you will be taken to the hospital compound. Please settle in as best you can and I will be around tomorrow, about noon, to formalise matters."

"Seventh September 1943, I am now thirty-five, single, stuck in a Prisoner of War Camp in a foreign country surrounded by complete strangers. By this age, my father had been married to my mother for twelve years and I was ten," muttered Enzo to himself. *"How much longer? How much longer, San Gennaro?"* He demanded of his patron Saint as he sipped the illegal self-brewed wild blackberry wine, which one grateful patient had given to him as a gift.

Next morning, eighth September, the Camp loudspeaker system requested attention for an important announcement by Prime Minister Winston Churchill to be broadcast at eleven-hundred hours. It was the worst kept secret and despite being expected, brought about delirious celebrations. Italy had surrendered and joined the Allies against the Germans. France continued to be occupied and forces loyal to the fleeing Mussolini were being pursued and hunted by the Italian National Forces.

Based upon these facts there was now no immediate prospect of Enzo or anyone else being returned home. They were no longer prisoners, and the camp was to be vacated. Polish troops would soon occupy Camp Eden in preparation for the Normandy landing. The Italians were gradually integrated back to reformed Italian Regiments.

Enzo was summoned to Percy's office, where the Commandant provided him with more instructions by saying, "Now we are both on the same team, Enzo, your talents can be put to better use. There is absolutely no chance of you going home for some while. The War Department has issued a request for me to have you transferred to the Royal Victoria Infirmary at Newcastle-upon-Tyne. Here is your travel warrant and orders. Gather up your belongings, I have arranged for you to be driven into Darlington to catch the fifteen-hundred hours to Newcastle."

In silent acquiescence, he took the brown envelope, thanked Major Logan, and left.

"*What have you done to me now San Gennaro?*" the voice in his head asked.

The steam train, much the same as the one he travelled on from Southampton, began to slow down as it came to the Gateshead side of the High-Level Bridge, spanning the River Tyne and carrying the rail track into Newcastle Central Station. The steam driven 'Swing Bridge' built by Armstrong, who also built the High-Level Bridge, lay to the east, parallel to the New Tyne Bridge, (replicated in Sydney Harbour). None of this meant anything to the Italian Major who was seeing Newcastle, a place he did not want to be, for the first time. A place, however, that would impact his life forever. Even the banks of the River Tyne, scarred by recent bombing attacks on the city shipyard went unnoticed.

The Royal Victoria Infirmary lies just beyond the northern side of the Haymarket, overlooked by King's College, part of the

University of Durham, later to become the University of Newcastle -upon- Tyne.

Enzo was met by a medical orderly in the uniform of the Royal Army Medical Corps (RAMC) and taken to the hospital's residential wing called 'Surgeon's Quarters.' This was to be his home for the duration. He was led to a room on the second floor, which comprised no more than a hospital bed, bedside lamp and cabinet, desk, chair, wardrobe, and a chest of four drawers. There was a light above the mirror over a small washbasin. Toilet and bathroom facilities were to be found at either end of each of the three floors; consequently, room twelve, being situated in the middle, gave him a choice. He was told, when exiting the building, that his keys were to be left with the porters at the Porter's Lodge at the front entrance. It was now ten at night, and he was exhausted. He just wanted to collapse in a heap on the bed.

The Orderly turned and handed him a brown envelope which contained a folded sheet of paper.

"Last but not least, Dr Falcone. Here is your rota. It will be explained to you when you report for duty on Monday. In the meantime, you will be on call. If you leave the hospital premises, notify the Porter on duty."

This was only Friday night, and he did not need to report for duty until Monday morning.

"*Another miracle, San Gennaro? Grazie,*" Enzo thought.

Chapter 4

Leazes Park

The various blends of gold, yellows, greens, browns, and reds of autumn hues were to be seen in the scattered leaves all about. Last night's sleep was one of the best Enzo had ever had and one he would remember all his life. So deep was that slumber, he had no sense of his own existence on planet earth, until he reluctantly awoke from his surreal and pleasant unconsciousness. Voices could be heard up and down the corridor outside his room, but no-one came to disturb him or get him out of his bed. He looked at his watch and refocused his hazel eyes, now slowly adjusting to the daylight he was letting into his room, from the curtains he had drawn open. It was ten to twelve, almost midday. Never in living memory had he slept so long or so late. Stretching, he looked out across the hospital building and could see a park with a pond, people walking about, mostly in uniform. Groups of recovering wounded being wheeled around, others on crutches or walking sticks supervised by a couple of nurses with their white butterfly headdresses and warm navy-blue military topcoats.

Enzo began to take stock of his situation. He had been given another set of civvies by the quartermaster at Eden Camp before his departure comprising, a suit; three shirts, white, blue, and khaki; underwear, two pairs of socks; a pair of shoes, boots and woollen gloves. His overcoat and everything else had been issued when he had first arrived in North Yorkshire. Bart's Medical

School tie, and the shaving kit ensemble his parents had given him were his only real possessions. All the other bits and pieces he had picked up along the way. The camp paymaster, complying with the requisition slip issued and signed by Major Logan, paid Enzo two pounds and five shillings, which he signed and acknowledged to be payment for his work as a doctor for the next week.

Two pounds of that money was in his wallet on his bedside cabinet and the five shillings, made up of two half-crowns, in the trouser pocket he had slung on the floor as he collapsed into bed the night before. He checked his wallet, removed the notes, and put them in his drawer. Five shillings was more than enough, free food and board was being provided at the hospital, so there was little else he needed.

It was incomprehensible to Enzo that he was able to have a hot bath in the bathroom at the far end of the corridor, let alone shave and dress without seeing anybody. Next time he was going to try the bathroom at the other end.

Meals were to be taken in the hospital refectory. Enzo checked out at the Porter's lodge, handed in his keys, got directions to the park, and told the porter he would be back later that afternoon. More out of curiosity than hunger, Enzo ambled over to the hospital eating place. Nobody really noticed the tall, olive-skinned, dark curly-haired Italian with hazel eyes, other than to acknowledge him. He took a metal tray and ordered tea, sausage, chips, beans, and toast. He found a corner next to a window where he could look outside to the park he had seen earlier from his bedroom, watching his new colleagues as he ate.

"Excuse me, is that a park over there or part of the hospital?" he asked the woman clearing the tables. Enzo's accent threw her momentarily before she replied.

30

"No, that's the Leazes Park, pet."

The word "park" was the only thing he understood from her reply. Not having heard Geordie spoken before, he assumed that she might be one of the many foreign domestics that staffed hospitals, as he had noticed when at Bart's. He thanked her, and once she had cleared where he had been sitting and moved her trolley away, he left the refectory.

The sun was as high as it was going to get, on what had started as a crisp mid-September morning; the mild ground frost which looked like white glitter on the fallen foliage, had now all evaporated. To people in this part of the world, this was a nice warm day. For Enzo, who never got used to the English climate, it was anything but warm. He pulled on his gloves, fastened up his heavy overcoat, pulled up his collar and walked out of the main gate of the hospital.

Determined to exorcise the draw of Leazes Park, he crossed the road behind another flock of shepherded patients on to the path, which led by the pond. Oblivious to the people around him enjoying this fresh new freedom, he became aware of the couples linked hand in hand or arm in arm, sitting on park benches, throwing crumbs to the quacking ducks and the silent stealthy white swans selectively picking at the larger morsels. Enzo wandered around the pond and noticed a large stadium towering to the south of the park. He made a mental note of this observation for future enquiry in his next conversation.

Almost three quarters of the way around the outer circumference of Leazes Park Pond, he saw a tarmac footpath wind off into a more densely treed area of the park. In a paved clearing beyond it he could see a disused bandstand, a very poor contemporary mock Tudor single story structure. Smoke rose in

31

a short vertical plume out of the chimney which, in Enzo's mind, meant that there was a good chance of a nice warm open fire. His guess was that it might be a small cafe like those he had seen in the London parks in his Bart's days. This hunch was confirmed as he drew closer and saw *'the insane English'* coming from the building eating ice creams!

"They are all mad here! It is so fucking cold, and they are eating ice creams. I don't understand how they can do it!" he muttered into the space ahead of him, shaking his head in disbelief.

People were sitting inside having afternoon tea and scones. Enzo was more interested in the blazing coal fire which, like a magnet, pulled him to it. The table closest to the fireplace looking out of the cafe door was his, even before he crossed the doorway. As if in a trance, he aimed for his target and stood guard over *'his table'* while he warmed himself up at the adjacent fireplace. Suitably reheated, he sat and gazed into the flames and began thinking of when he might get home.

"Pot of tea and scones, sir?" she asked.

No reply.

"Would you like to order a pot of tea and scones, sir?" the woman repeated with more volume and authority in her voice.

Enzo turned around and saw a young woman in her early twenties, long brown curly hair held up in a fashionable hair net. She wore a mauve blouse and dark grey skirt past her knees, a folded tea towel over her left shoulder and a blue and white striped apron tied securely around her waist. Notepad and pencil in hand, at about five foot six, she seemed to tower above him as he sat giving his order. For Enzo, there was immediate chemistry but nothing obvious from her.

"Yes, thank you," he answered.

She took his order and headed off back behind the counter. Enzo watched as she moved, hoping that he might see some reaction. Again, nothing! He turned back, stared into the flames, and returned to his thoughts of home as his tea and scones were prepared.

"Mama, where has Papa gone?" He heard, spoken in Italian.

"Angela he's at home and will be back shortly," was the response from Mama.

It had been years since he had heard the voice of any Italian woman. These voices were not only speaking in Italian, but they were in a Neapolitan accent. It sounded so good to hear, he cried, sobbed, as he looked to the ceiling. Nothing had fazed him; despite all he had been through. He had a warm personality and made friends easily, never really becoming nostalgic but rather focusing his mind on the job in hand and the work to be done. Now, the first time he got to wind down and relax, he found himself sobbing like a baby, simply because he had heard the voices of two Italian women.

"Totally absurd!" he scolded himself.

Angela returned, placing the pot of tea and scones on his table. She was puzzled, his head was turned away, tears rolling down his cheeks as he tried to take back control of his long-pent-up emotions.

Concerned at her customer's obvious distress she gently asked Enzo, "Is everything all right, sir?"

Chapter 5

Inquisition

Embarrassed and sniffing back his tears, wiping his eyes, and blowing his nose on his only handkerchief, he turned and got up to leave, speaking to her in his mother tongue,

"Please forgive me Signorina when I heard you speak Neapolitan with your mother it just set me off. It has been a long time since I have been home and heard the voices of Neapolitan women. I was just feeling sorry for myself and being very nostalgic. I was overcome. How much do I owe you? I must leave! I have made a scene. Please, I am so very sorry."

The woollen gloves, hat, and scarf he had put on the table, were swiped onto the floor at Angela's feet as Enzo picked up his overcoat to put it on. She stooped and picked them up and ushered Enzo to the counter.

"Signore, please, there is no need to apologise. Come with me and meet my mother. It has been many years since we have had a chance to meet anyone from Napoli. Both my parents will be very pleased, none of us have been back since my eighteenth birthday just before the war," she responded.

Angela, now carrying Enzo's gloves, hat, and scarf, had reached the counter hatch only a couple of yards behind where he had been seated.

The native dialogue between Angela and Enzo had not escaped the attentive ears of her mother, Gilda. Her curiosity had brought her from the kitchen at the back of the cafe-cum-ice cream parlour, to the front. If Angela had not invited him back, Gilda had every intention of doing so. She knew straight away by the way that he spoke that he was an educated man and any man from Napoli, who was educated there, probably was from a good family with money.

Angela was now twenty-three and single. Not a good age to be single in her book. Gilda had already been married a couple of years and was expecting Angela.. The war had spoilt it all. Angela had been taken back to Torre del Greco, a short train journey south of Napoli, for her eighteenth birthday, just before the war in August 1938. Angela had been born in the flat above the family Trattoria. When she was five, Bernardo and Gilda di Carlo sold up and emigrated to England with Angela and her elder sister Teresa. When Teresa was eighteen, she was taken back home and returned on her own the following year in 1937 to spend the whole summer with her aunt. In accordance with local custom, family connections and tradition, Gilda's sister Pia acted as matchmaker and found Teresa a good husband. Her parents intended to do the same for Angela. Aunt Pia had targeted one of her son's friends as her next matchmaking victim. As in Teresa's case, letters and photos had been exchanged but the outbreak of war had stifled Zia Pia's matchmaking plans.

So, when Gilda clapped eyes on Enzo, he had no idea what she was thinking. Angela was now inadvertently luring the distraught, unsuspecting, eligible, and lonely 'Paesano' into her mother's den. He would probably not have cared if he had known, and even in normal circumstances would have been a willing victim. Now, at his age, thoughts of settling down and finding a wife had come to the fore of his thinking. Time and time again he had been asked by his mother, *"Would she ever see grandchildren?"*

His studies and his profession, then this war, had all been exceptionally good alibis for him. Anyway, he had not wanted to be tied down, he liked being free to do as he wished, and he was having a good time until the war broke out. But now he wanted a soul mate; not just a wife who would provide offspring, tend to his needs, and keep house. His parents had married young and, even though in love, it was only later that they became soul mates who knew instinctively the needs and thoughts of the other. Bottled up in the recesses of his mind there were stored his own desire, to someday seek out that ideal mate.

However, none of this crossed his mind as he went through the door behind the counter, being opened by Gilda. Enzo was confused and completely puzzled by his sudden breakdown; there had been times before when he had felt more nostalgic than today, even tearful but then had not broken-down sobbing like a baby, as he had just done.

"Come in, Signore. Can I offer you a nice Neapolitan espresso?" Gilda asked as she sat him down by the small fireplace in the back shop, which kicked out a nice comforting heat. Gilda invited him to remove his overcoat, which she gladly helped him take off, and hung up on the door which led to the backyard of the cafe. Enzo, now more composed but still embarrassed, again apologised to his hostess.

"I just do not understand and cannot explain, Signora. You and your daughter have been so kind," Enzo apologetically repeated. It was then he realised that Angela had not come into the back shop. Gilda, who missed nothing, caught his silent observation with her built-in radar.

"Angela is out front seeing to rest of our customers and

clearing up before we close. It is now five minutes to four and we close at four."

He got up from his chair, thanked Gilda, and motioned toward his coat.

"No. Please sit down and drink this nice hot cup of espresso I have made you. My husband Bernardo will be here shortly to take me and Angela home. He would love to meet you, so please just stay," she entreated.

Enzo took little persuading and returned to his place at the small square folding multi-purpose card table that had been opened by Gilda in his honour.

In her calculating mind, Gilda knew that Angela would be out in front of the shop until at least ten past four. Bernardo always came in through the backyard at his usual time of a quarter past, she would lock the back door and tell him to use the front. Then she could tell Angela to wait at the front door to let her father in and explain to him that there was a visitor. This would give Gilda between fifteen to twenty minutes to interrogate this ex-Prisoner of War.

Angela just got on and did what her mother asked. No fool, as far as her mother was concerned, she knew exactly what her mother was likely to get up to. Without making any attempt to rescue him she got on with her chores and closing shop. This inquisition would get all the answers a mother needs to establish if the subject could be considered as a potential suitor for her daughter.

Softly, softly Gilda began, *"How long have you been here in Newcastle?"* she asked.

"I arrived last night by train from Darlington and was so tired after the journey I went straight to bed and slept until about midday," Enzo explained.

"And are you staying nearby?" she enquired.

Keen to cooperate with his interrogator Enzo broke every rule in the book and volunteered much more information than was requested. *"Before the armistice I was at the Camp Eden Prisoner of War Camp in North Yorkshire. Once we surrendered, we were all released. I was ordered to the Royal Victoria Infirmary here in Newcastle,"* Enzo volunteered.

A cold shudder went through Gilda's body as she reasoned to herself, *"God, he must be sick and dying. That is why he broke down."*

She just had to follow this up!

"Are you recovering from some wound or illness?" She leaned forward to ask, in a maternal tone and touching his hand.

Realising that his answer about being ordered to the RVI had been taken the wrong way, he became even more open and told her everything. Suitably impressed with his very candid and detailed voluntary statement, Gilda moved to the bottom line. *"When I saw you so upset, I felt so sorry for you, Dottore. I thought you were missing your wife and children!"*

Still not appreciating the real purpose of his interrogation by Gilda, what came next was the only real information that she had wanted to glean from him.

"I only wish that I were, Signora. I am not married. Even worse, there is no-one in my life. How could there be?" Enzo smiled.

Gilda's heart leaped and she said a silent prayer, *"Thank you Holy Mary Mother of Jesus, and all the Saints for this miracle that sits here before me!"*

Her excitement almost bubbled out into open speech. She wanted to hug him. He would be the ideal husband for her Angela.

"Maybe they will not like each other?" she questioned herself. *"No, this was meant to be, meant to happen. Please Mother of Jesus make this work!"*

Enzo, oblivious to it all, and now at ease, sipped his espresso and gazed into the crackling flames.

Chapter 6

Claremont Terrace

Thinking that the warped back door had stuck again, Bernardo rattled and pushed at it.

"Gilda, what's wrong with this door? It does not open," he asked in a raised voice.

She remembered that she had locked it and answered, *"It's locked. I am coming, a little patience!"*

Gilda got up, unlocked, and opened it. Enzo stood up in anticipation of an introduction. Bernardo came straight in, closed the door behind him and took off his cloth cap.

"Who have you got here?" asked her husband.

"What do you mean?" Gilda said with an attitude, as if she did not know what he meant.

"And who is this?" he asked his wife, looking towards Enzo.

"Do not be so rude! Watch your manners!" In her best formal Italian, she scolded her husband, fearing that he might scare off this potential suitor. Gilda pushed Bernardo over to Enzo then presented him. *"Dottore Falcone, this is my very bad-mannered husband of more than thirty years, Bernardo Di Carlo."*

He dutifully offered his right hand to the visiting doctor. Continuing Gilda added, *"Bernardo, this is Dottore Major Vincenzo Falcone who has just been transferred to work in the Royal Victoria Infirmary. He is a Consultant Anaesthetist who*

40

studied in Florence and London. He is an only son, and his parents own a vineyard and property in Napoli. He arrived only last night!" She paused for breath, marked with a deep sigh.

Both men shook hands and greeted each other. Angela, having realised her father had come in the back door, joined the party. During the handshake, Gilda took hold of Angela by the arm and brought her over to Enzo, formally introducing her daughter.

"This is my youngest daughter, Angela, who you have already met. We have two. Her sister Teresa is two years older, married, in Italy and has one beautiful grandchild. Angela is still a Signorina," Gilda emphasised.

"Mama, please! You are embarrassing Dottore Falcone!" interjected Angela embarrassed and shook Enzo's hand.

On the contrary he thought. Enzo was flattered that Gilda had sought fit to present her daughter to him in this way. In the world that they all came from, such an introduction by the mother, in the presence of the father, could mean only one thing; the mother, Gilda, approved of him and sanctioned any relationship which may develop. If her father disapproved, now was the time to say but Bernardo said nothing. This could only mean consent and there was no protest from Angela, false or otherwise.

When he first came into the cafe and sat down by the fireplace waiting to be served, he was attracted to her. He watched as she dealt with other customers, the way she smiled and moved about the room; he admired her good looks. Before any of this happened in the back shop, he had planned to return to this cafe in the park, in the hope of seeing this waitress again and maybe ask her out. Now this!

"Thank you, San Gennaro, another miracle!" Enzo

proclaimed to himself.

Still in full flow and unable to contain her excitement, Gilda announced even more information gleaned from her interrogation of Enzo. *"Il Dottore Falcone originates from San Giorgio a Cremano."*

Enough said. Bernardo and Angela knew that her cross-examination of the unsuspecting Enzo had been successful. There was no need to say that he was also single and what was on her mind. If he had not ticked all her boxes, she would not be acting in this way.

"Dottore, Angela is a midwife at the RVI, she comes here to help out at weekends," voiced an immensely proud mother.

Enzo looked Angela directly in the eyes. He gave a smile indicating he was not only impressed with the appearance of this young lady to whom he was being introduced, but also, as a doctor, he appreciated and respected the work of midwives.

"So, you will be colleagues and working together, Dottore," continued a less than subtle Gilda.

"Mama, of course not! It is only in emergencies that anaesthetists are involved and by that time doctors and surgeons will have taken over from the midwives," blurted Angela, irritated at her mother's comment.

Enzo diplomatically intervened in this potential domestic spat, *"If it were not for midwives none of us might ever make it into this world. I am sure that our paths will cross in the hospital now that we have met."*

This intervention by the good doctor defused the potential conflict between mother and daughter.

Bernardo took command. *"It is time that we locked up and left ladies. Dottore, will you walk with us back home and join us for an evening meal? Please, it would be an honour and a great pleasure! I will not take 'no' as an answer!"*

Both Angela and her mother could have been knocked down by a feather. Such invitations to come home for a meal, only ever came from Gilda herself or after getting her consent. Bernardo knew that, on this occasion, he was on safe ground.

The Di Carlos lived just over a quarter of an hour's walk from Leazes Park; east of the hospital, looking on to the Town Moor. They resided in a three-bedroom, end-terraced house; one of the blocks of six, on Claremont Road, behind the Hancock Museum. Being located at the end of the terrace allowed the Di Carlos' extra garden at the side of the dwelling, in addition to the couple of square yards at the front of the house, and a bit greener at the back.

The house was rented from one of the patrons of the Royal Station Hotel where Bernardo worked as head waiter. Bernardo used every inch of arable garden he had at the house. The old shrub patch at the back of the cafe he also cultivated and was growing potatoes, carrots, courgettes, and other root crops. Indoors, in the cafe and at home, he put his 'green fingers' to good use, growing garlic, herbs, and tomatoes. Gilda preserved surplus produce for special occasions and winter months. This evening was going to be one of those *'special occasions'*.

On his wife's express instructions to Bernardo earlier that day, the minestrone was on a low simmer, and he had put the dough in the airing cupboard to rise for Gilda's return. When she got back, she would bake fresh hot bread to go with the soup. As a head waiter, Bernardo had access to a wide range of alcoholic beverages, which he tucked away for later consumption.

Now, just coming up to a quarter to five, they had to get back or the minestrone would burn. The sun was just setting and the temperature dropping as Bernardo snapped the last padlock. The women went about checking and packing their handbags, pulling up their collars and wrapping up in their scarves. Normally, daughter and wife would link on to Bernardo's arm as he proudly walked them home, deep in conversation or even occasionally singing some Neapolitan Air. It would never happen again. By the following weekend Angela and Enzo would be arm in arm. To an outsider it would look as though it had always been that way.

The autumnal wind had picked up during the day; underfoot the leaves were still crisp, and foliage was reduced to about one third of the summer canopy. The quartet headed back along the route Enzo had taken a couple of hours earlier. Ahead of him he saw the stadium that had been at his back when he had walked up the path. It had a high wall and the tell-tale signs of flood lights.

"What is that place?" he asked Bernardo.

"Hallowed Ground for the people of Newcastle," Bernardo replied proudly. *"Saint James' Park, home of Newcastle United. Like we Neapolitans, the people here, called Geordies, are mad about their football and this team. Because of the war everything has stopped so no real football is played. Once the war is over it will start again. I watched them until all matches were suspended. They play in black and white stripes and are nicknamed the 'Magpies'."*

Gilda had heard enough from her husband. He should be finding out more about her *'catch'*. Instead, football! Football!

"Enough, Bernardo! I am sure Il Dottore does not want to hear about you and your football!"

Angela joined in, *"Give it a rest, Papa, I am sure Il Dottore is not the least bit interested!"*

44

With a shrug of his shoulders and raised palms he acknowledged the admonishment from both wife and daughter and shut up. Enzo was quick to his host's defence. *"You are mistaken, Signora! Football is my sport too. I used to play and before the war, when I was at Bart's I played for the hospital team. I have also seen Arsenal play Newcastle. I would go to watch matches whenever I could! "*

She just could not help herself. Gilda looked up to the Heavens and beseeched the Madonna, *"Not another one! Please!"*

They all laughed.

"Right, we have arrived!" Bernardo announced, as he opened the wooden gate to the footpath, which led to the front door of number six Claremont Terrace.

"Ladies first," he insisted. Enzo followed Bernardo's wife and daughter down the short path. As Gilda was about to turn the key to unlock the front door, Enzo raised up both his hands in a gesture as if to signal a halt to an advancing truck, which got the immediate attention of the others.

Gilda's heart sank for a second time, thinking the worst, *"He does not like us and is not going to come in!"* She convinced herself.

Not knowing what was coming next, all three of the Di Carlos were focused on Enzo, who announced, *"Before we go any further, I will only set foot in your home on one condition."* The trio looked at each other wondering whether they had done something to offend him. He laughed. *"My name is Enzo. Please stop calling me Dottore. To you I am Enzo."*

He did not notice Gilda's immense sigh of relief and her thanks to the Madonna and Child. Angela, never slow on the uptake, took that cue and reciprocated her own terms, *"Then*

Enzo, you must stop calling me Signorina. My name is Angela!"

Absolutely delighted at what she had just witnessed, Gilda opened the door and hugged everyone as they entered, including Enzo.

Chapter 7

Minestrone

Although the Di Carlos had made their house in Claremont Terrace as Italian as they could, it was still an English house of the late Victorian era. Enzo had never been inside any family dwelling in England. When he was at Bart's he was in hospital accommodation and his only other experience was Eden Camp. His instant impression of Six Claremont Terrace, after the quick tour that Bernardo gave him, was that it was small in comparison to back home at San Giorgio. The rooms were, however, cosy, and functional.

Gilda had wasted no time checking the simmering minestrone. Before he had left to go to the Cafe, Bernardo had stacked the fire so now the red-hot coals heated the whole house and the black iron box-oven adjacent to the fire grill. The smell of yeast from the rising dough combined with that of the vegetable soup brought back to Enzo memories of his mother's winter meals. Gilda divided the kneaded dough into four greased bread baking tins on a metal tray. Angela opened the black iron door of the oven using a tea towel while her mother slid the tray onto the middle shelf and clanged the door shut.

"Just twenty minutes, that's all it needs," Gilda declared, *"Bernardo come and help me in the kitchen!"*

The man looked puzzled for a split second, until he saw his wife's coded signal that told him she wanted Angela and Enzo left on their own.

"Angela, go get our guest a drink, set the table and call me when the bread is done," Gilda ordered. Having made her instructions clear, she smiled at Enzo and bundled her husband ahead of her into the kitchen.

"Please sit down," Angela invited Enzo to take her father's favourite armchair nearest to the fireplace. *"What can I offer you to drink, would you like Vermouth as an appetiser?"*

Enzo. completely taken by surprise, accepted. *"Of course, but how?"*

Angela sensing her guest's curiosity interrupted and went on, *"White, red, sweet or dry? No, don't worry, it's not black market. My father as Headwaiter and Maître d' at the Royal Station Hotel oversees buying all the wine and liquor. As a perk of the job, he gets samples, gifts and surplus from the various merchants. Apart from the odd glass of wine with a meal, we drink very little as a family. When Papa brings it home, my mother stores it for special occasions like this evening."*

She went over to a dresser occupying most of the wall opposite the fireplace, reached up and opened the top right section. There displayed for all to see was the evidence of what she had just told Enzo, a cabinet full of bottles.

"So, Enzo, what can I get you?" she asked.

He stepped forward and, without intending to, brushed up against Angela, pointed to a bottle of Cinzano Bianco, and got it down.

"A glass of this would be nice. I cannot remember the last time I had a glass of Vermouth," he told her as he handed Angela the bottle.

"I will join you. Let me get the glasses, you open the bottle," she instructed Enzo, as she reached for two glass tumblers from

another section of the same dresser. Angela then poured the drinks and told Enzo to sit down in the armchair.

"Can I not help you set the table?" he asked.

"Enzo, thank you for the offer but you are our guest and anyhow you do not know where things are kept. So please just be a good guest and sit in the armchair," Angela graciously replied.

He surrendered into the arms of the waiting armchair, took a sip from the glass he cupped in both hands. Enzo let the sweet tingle of that first sip of Vermouth linger on his taste buds for as long as possible. It had been a long while since he had tasted such delicious nectar.

Angela had made her mind up that she liked what she saw in Enzo. By the reaction of her parents, they did too. They could not all be wrong. Enzo was much more *'simpatico'* than anyone else she had met.

"I bet they have not shown you around the hospital yet Enzo?" Angela enquired, taking the initiative.

Not the type of conversation opener Enzo had expected. He would soon come to find out Angela had a knack of doing the unexpected and speaking her mind. He replied, *"No, not yet but I have to report to the Hospital Administrator and Head of Surgery at nine o'clock on Monday morning. I had planned to ask the porter at the Porter's Lodge to give me directions to the Administrative Block."*

"Unless you have something better to do, I could show you around tomorrow?" Angela volunteered.

Her suggestion came as a pleasant surprise to Enzo. *"No. I have nothing else to do, but is it not Sunday?"* he quizzed Angela.

"Exactly! What better time to show you around? We can go after Mass, at noon. I will meet you downstairs at your Porter's Lodge. I know where that is!" "

Enzo saw no problem in agreeing with this *'fait accompli'*. *"Noon it is then"* he confirmed.

"Angela! The bread, check and see if it is ready," shouted Gilda from the kitchen. Her dutiful daughter checked and reported that it needed about another five minutes to be done.

"Another five minutes to ourselves," Enzo thought to himself.

"What made you want to be a midwife, Angela?" he asked.

"Just as people will always die and need undertakers, there will always be birth. Dying is much easier than a baby being born and a mother giving birth. In my book, midwifery is the oldest and most respected profession. Midwives will always be needed," Angela explained.

That unexpected response from Angela seemed to mirror his philosophy on life, heightening his interest in this beautiful young woman, which prompted Enzo to comment, *"Apart from the obvious, medical dimension to our work, there are some other aspects of our respective professions that we have in common. You bring babies into the world, and I bring patients 'back' into the world from unconsciousness and the brink of death."*

"I'll drink to that, Enzo. Salute!" Angela replied, taking the last sip of her Vermouth and Enzo followed suit. Suddenly, remembering her baking duties she exclaimed as she dashed over to the oven, *"Ahh! The bread, Mama, the bread is done!"*

Enzo was quick to get up and go to her aid. He took the tea towel from the table, opened the oven door, and proceeded to remove the four freshly baked loaves of bread. Gilda entered the room; saw the crouched duo working together to deliver the loaves from the red-hot womb of the oven. She glowed and beamed a smile to her husband to come and observe the natural chemistry between their daughter and Enzo; a man who had been a stranger to them all just a few hours ago. She had prayed that the bread in the oven would work as a catalyst to bring these two together. Gilda saw that prayer being answered.

"Good! Give me the bread and we can all sit down and eat. Please, Enzo, take your place at the table sitting opposite Angela. Me and my husband will sit in our usual seats, also opposite each other," Gilda directed.

Bernardo poured out the red wine, Gilda sliced one of the newly baked hot loaves, while Angela ladled out the first bowl of minestrone to Enzo. They all sat, wished each other *'bon appetite'*, and tucked in. Silence prevailed as the wine, soup and bread were consumed. At the end of the meal, Angela made it her business to take care of Enzo and collected his empty bowl and spoon first, for delivery to the kitchen with the rest of the dishes. On her return she announced to her parents that she would be meeting with Enzo the next day at noon, to show him around the hospital.

Without thinking Gilda asked her daughter, *"What about Church?"*

"It will be after Church, Mama," answered Angela.

Enzo interposed, *"If you do not mind, I would welcome a chance to come to Mass with you all. It has been a long time!"*

It was agreed. They would meet Enzo at the main gates of the hospital and then proceed to Saint Mary's Cathedral for the half past ten Mass. Bernardo and Gilda would walk on home whilst Angela would take Enzo for his tour of the hospital. Afterwards she would bring Enzo back home to have Sunday lunch *'in famiglia'*.

The evening meal over, Enzo parted from the Di Carlos with hugs all around. He made his way back through the park, revisiting the events of the day. He had arrived in Newcastle alone and a stranger and now he felt destined to be there. He reached his accommodation block; signed in at the Porter's Lodge and, not wanting to sleep-in the following morning, he requested an eight-thirty wake up call.

Chapter 8

The Monsignore

Mass was over by a quarter to twelve and the congregation slowly filed out of their pews into the centre aisle of the Cathedral. The '*Monsignore*', as the Di Carlos preferred to call Canon Wilkinson, still in his Mass vestments, stood outside at the entrance of the Cathedral in the fresh autumn morning, thanking and shaking the hands of his flock as they filed out.

The Di Carlos were his only Italian parishioners and he always stopped them for a quick chat, providing him the opportunity to practice the Italian he had picked up as a young priest studying in Rome. The Monsignore greeted the group of four.

Enzo took the initiative and introduced himself, "Doctor Vincenzo Falcone, I have just been transferred to the RVI and arrived here in Newcastle on Friday night. I was incredibly lucky to meet *Signore* and *Signora* Di Carlo and their daughter only yesterday. They invited me to come with them to Mass this morning," Enzo shook the priest's hand.

"Welcome to our Church. I compliment your English. I only wish I spoke Italian like you speak English. Please, do not be a stranger!" acknowledged the '*Monsignore*'. All four exchanged the usual niceties with the Canon who wished them, "*A good day and Bon Appetite.*"

Apart from the few words Enzo had spoken to Angela when

ordering in the Cafe less than twenty-four hours earlier, he had spoken no other English in the Di Carlos' presence.

"I did not realise that you spoke English so well, Enzo!" complimented Bernardo.

"I had two years working and studying at Bart's Hospital in London. Then when we surrendered in North Africa I had to act as interpreter. On the hospital Ship I worked with English doctors and tended to English-speaking wounded. In fact, I have spoken more English in recent years than my mother tongue. That is probably what got me so emotional yesterday when I heard Angela speak," explained Enzo.

Gilda told Angela and Enzo that she and her father would be popping into Bernardo's place of work on leaving the Cathedral. The Royal Station Hotel was situated not far away, on the opposite side of the road. An excuse obviously contrived to let Angela and Enzo have time alone.

"Remember we eat at half past two. Do not be late!" Gilda reminded them as she hugged them both, as did her husband. She then took Bernardo's arm and turned left out of the gate.

If Angela had been a man, Enzo would have had no difficulty in understanding this instant feeling of friendship, but she was an extremely attractive woman which added another dimension. There was chemistry between them, and he was struggling to understand this sentiment. Having slept on it, discussed it with his inner-self and with no help from *'San Gennaro'*, he persuaded himself to act on his instincts. If he were right, what was to come would be fate and meant to be. He never wanted to be an *'if only'* man, preferring not to have regrets. She might be the love of his life and she might not, he had to find out.

Angela was in a similar dilemma about her feelings towards

Enzo. Her mother had reminded her time and time again how, at her age of twenty-two, she was already married and pregnant. Of course, she wanted to meet the right man, settle down and marry, but it was not that easy with the war on and no eligible men on the scene.

During times of war life was different; people live for the moment with the shadow of death influencing every decision or commitment. Like Enzo, Angela decided to have the courage to act as she felt. She liked the man; she was attracted to him and wanted to get to know him better. Without any hesitation or ceremony, she naturally did what her mother had just done with her father and, taking Enzo's arm, turned right and headed off towards the RVI.

To the outside world nobody would have ever known that these two were out together for the first time.

"Angela, I am very curious about one thing, and I am sure that it may take a lot of explanation, but it is something I find very hard to understand," Enzo asked gently, tapping her linked arm with his other hand.

"Well ask and I will answer if I can!" she replied.

Enzo posed his question, *"It was my understanding that all Italians living here were interred once Italy allied with Germany and declared war on England. The cessation of war between Italy and the Allies only a few days ago, got me released. You and your parents do not give the impression of having been interred. Can you explain?"*

Angela gave an understanding smile and pointed to a bench in the Bigg Market, saying, *"Let us go sit down over there. It is not that complicated but there is a lot of background to explain for you to understand."*

The couple reached the seat and sat down without breaking

the linking of their arms. Angela began to tell the story in full:

"As you will have already understood, my parents are both from Torre del Greco and, like many families back then, those who were unrelated became related through marriage. My mother is five years younger than my father who was born in 1896 and fought in the first war. She was the daughter of his mother's closest friends. When war broke out, she was thirteen and my father nearly twenty. He was gone for most of the war; my parents obviously knew each other as children and their friendship developed through correspondence encouraged by both mothers whilst he was away. By the end of the war, my mother was no longer an adolescent teenage girl but had grown into a very eligible young lady. To the delight of both families my parents married shortly after my mother turned eighteen. With the help of both of my grandparents, they opened a small trattoria in the piazza opposite the Vesuviana station. Teresa, my older sister, was born in 1920 and seventeen months later I came along. Our Trattoria was doing well and had a regular clientele. My father was popular and became active in local politics. He was a reluctant politician and had no ambition to move up the ladder. Eventually, despite his young age, he was persuaded to run for mayor and was elected as an independent for a four-year term. This was about the same time that Mussolini became Prime Minister. My father said that he had met 'that jumped up corporal' when their regiments were in transit during the war. He said that he was arrogant and pompous but, more than anything else, it was Mussolini's square chin and beady like eyes that stood him out from the others. For the first years as mayor, father coped well and had a great deal of support. In the north of Italy, the Fascists were gaining political momentum and that were gradually moving south to the Mezzogiorno region. My father

was not happy about how things were developing. Enzo, you understand I was far too young to know all that was happening, I am telling you what I later found out!"

"No, of course, I understand. Please go on, Angela." Enzo nodded.

"I think it must have been about 1930 or thirty-one; a new family moved down from Milano, the Pollo family. He was an engineer with the National Railways and had been put in charge of the network south of Napoli by the Fascist Government. He bought a large Villa on the seafront four teenage sons and two married daughters, all living together. Independent in mind, and his politics, the Fascist doctrine was an anathema to Papa's beliefs. For my father, the arrival of the Pollos was the beginning of the end; unless the growth of fascism was stemmed, Italy was doomed. It was about this time that my father had a visit from an old army colleague who had emigrated to England after the War. Initially living in Southampton, he met an English woman from Newcastle, they married, and he moved north with her. Marco, my father's friend, took up a job as a waiter in one of the hotels. He was well-paid, and now managed the hotel bar. Marco got my father interested, especially when he told him that there was a shortage of people with his culinary skills and wine expertise. Marco had come to introduce his new wife to his family and spent a weekend on the beach with us."

"Does he still live here in Newcastle?" enquired Enzo.

"Oh yes. He now runs the Jesmond Park Hotel just outside the city. He was also not interred! Marco told us he would keep a look out for a job in Newcastle for my father." Angela looked up and saw that the clock in the centre of the Bigg Market showed twenty-five past one. *"Oh my God, Enzo, Look at the time! We will never get back in time to eat. We had better leave now!"*

Time had flown, Angela stood up, agitated, and for the first time broke the link she had with Enzo since the Cathedral. Enzo stood up and resumed the link. Quietly and calmly, he told her, *"Forget the hospital tour. I have plenty of time to find my way around. I can listen while we walk."*

What took place next came totally unexpectedly. They kissed and embraced.

Enzo looked into Angela's eyes and said, *"Angela, I am not going to apologise for what I just did, it was nice, very nice. We must have been lovers in another life who lost their way and have just found each other again. I have no explanation for my conduct but do not regret it."*

He kissed her again, this time on the cheek.

"Enzo, I do not want you to regret it. It would diminish what has just happened. Let's just have the courage to see where it leads," Angela responded, a little out of breath. This had been a spontaneous bonding and meeting of their souls, they looked into each other's eyes, kissed, and set off walking towards Claremont Terrace. Reaching the house, they stopped at the gate and kissed again.

"Enzo, when we go in, I do not want us to act like nothing has happened, but I also do not want to overreact. We are adults, and my parents are not fools, they will know that something has happened between us just by looking at me," Angela explained.

"I know exactly what you mean. I could not hide it either," agreed Enzo, taking her in his arms once again and kissing her passionately on the lips.

Angela, glowing with happiness, knocked on the door. Gilda answered, the tears welled in her eyes when she saw her youngest daughter standing there, arm in arm with Enzo. She knew instinctively they were made for each other and more than this;

they were in love.

"Come on in, you two! We are about ready to eat," proclaimed joyous tearful Gilda, silently congratulating herself that her plan was going so well.

Chapter 9

Corporal Square Jaw

Rhubarb crumble and wartime ice cream from their *'Cafe in the Park'* was the only English dish worth being included in an Italian Sunday lunch. The rhubarb was grown by Bernardo, as was most of the food at the table. Gilda had learnt the recipe for crumble from Marco's English wife, Irene.

'Primo piatto' comprised fried peppers in garlic from that year's harvest, then the *'Secondo piatto'*, fresh home-made lasagna containing the week's ration of corned beef and a tomato *salsa* with basil and garlic; all supplemented with the crusty bread, baked the night before, and washed down with Bernardo's home-made blackberry wine. Conversation at the table was relatively subdued as the food was good and bellies needed to be filled. What was said came mostly from Bernardo, who offered his observations and advice to Angela and Enzo. *"War gets people to focus on the things that really matter in life, but it can also distort reality. I can see that there appears to be relationship developing between you both and I welcome it. Be mature, have the courage to let whatever feelings you have develop naturally."*

Angela got up from her place, kissed and hugged her parents. Enzo beamed and took another mouthful of his host's excellent blackberry wine.

"Did you have a good look around the hospital, Enzo?" enquired Gilda.

"No, we sat and talked in a small piazza on the way back from church," replied Enzo.

"It was in the Bigg Market, Mama," interjected her daughter.

Angela turned to her father explaining, *"Papa, I started to tell Enzo how we came to be here in Newcastle and why we were never interred, but I did not get very far when we realised the time. I told him what you and Mama had explained to Teresa and me, as we were too young to remember or understand."*

Bernardo nodded and asked, *"How far did you get with the story?"*

Enzo answered, *"Please, Signore Di Carlo, it was very interesting, I apologise for any intrusion or discourtesy."* Before he had a chance to finish what he had to say, Gilda piped in:

"No offence taken. After the grilling I gave you, you have a right to know about us. Now, you men, go make yourselves comfortable in the armchairs beside the fireplace, Angela and I will clear the table and make coffee. We have heard it all before and my husband will enjoy giving you the history."

Taking their cue from Gilda, the two men got up and did as instructed. Seeing the men sitting relaxed in the armchairs facing each other, Angela smiled at Enzo who smiled back. She got on clearing the table with her mother, making frequent trips back to see how the two men in her life were bonding.

"So where did she get up to with our story, Enzo?" Bernardo asked, easing further back in his armchair.

"Marco and his English wife had just visited you and discussed the prospect of coming to work here in Newcastle," Enzo replied, now just as comfortable as his host, cradling the half inch of red wine still left in his glass.

"Yes. That's right. Marco did set me thinking, and I was

61

tempted," Bernardo said, picking up where his daughter had left off. *"Marco was brought up near Piazza Carlo III in Napoli. It was around 1912 we were both conscripted and hit it off the day we met at the barracks. From then on, we looked after each other and shared everything.*

"After the war he got work as a waiter on the Ocean Liners. Somehow, he met Irene on one of these ships. They married after living a short while in Southampton; Irene's father found Marco a job in Newcastle where her family lived, so they moved north. After their son Michele's first birthday, Marco came to introduce his wife and son to his family. So, he visited me at Torre del Greco.

"Our regiment was joined with northern regiments. Mussolini was the corporal that was pushing us around for about a week, until we were transferred. You know what we from the south think of Northerners? Instant dislike! He, Mussolini that is, could see that, unlike the others he pushed around, we did not take him seriously. We would just ignore and laugh at him. Incredible! To think he was made Prime Minister!

"Marco told me to get out and come to England where he said life was much better. The girls were very young, and I still had another two years to run as Mayor. Gilda got on well with Irene who had begun to speak some Italian. Their son Michele was a couple months older than Teresa. Marco and I agreed that he would start looking to find a suitable job for me. Both Gilda and I saw a great potential, but I would see out my term as Mayor.

"If we had any doubts about moving to England, the arrival of the Pollo family and the growth of Fascism in the south was the push we needed. Alberto Pollo was a poor imitation of 'Corporal Square Jaw', that's what Marco and I called Mussolini to his face! It would really set him off and he would give that

glare, which intimidated everyone, including the officers. Marco and I, we just laughed at him and called him 'an arrogant half piece of shit'. Told him he did not have the balls or the height to be a 'full shit'."

Gilda had walked into the room. "You!" She pointed to her husband. "And that other fool Marco, together, they'd get us all shot. Fancy that! Of all the people in the armed forces, those two idiots pick on a man who ended up being dictator of Italy and they both think it's funny. What cretins!"

Enzo could not resist a laugh, when Bernardo chuckled at his wife's outburst. She continued gesticulating with the wooden ladle she was drying. "Not so funny, you two!" added Gilda, pointing the ladle in their direction, continuing to make her point. "This is the same Mussolini who has people who disagree with him murdered. Il Duce decided to come and visit the Pollo family when he came south for a rally of Fascists in Napoli. Bernardo was Mayor and was to act as host!"

Shaking her head in frustrated anger, she retreated with her daughter back into the kitchen, muttering curses blaming Marco and her husband for all her woes.

"Enzo, we just had to leave and get out of Italy," continued Bernardo. "I received a formal letter from Il Duce's office which told me that he was coming south for a fascist rally in Napoli, and he would spend time in the region meeting with some of his appointees. Alberto Pollo had been recently appointed regional director of the railways and had been selected for a half day visit. As Mayor I had to make all the arrangements for the visit and greet him from the train. Mussolini was so impulsive, he was unpredictable. The letter gave me just under six weeks' notice.

"Gilda and I decided that we needed to leave. I contacted Marco and explained what had happened. He told us he and

Irene would put us up and he would find me work. Our parents and families were very supportive and understanding; they took over the running of the Trattoria. My deputy, Luigi, who had begun to have fascist sympathies, knew nothing of my plans to flee with my family to England. He was looking forward to Il Duce's visit.

"We were to leave by train the week before the visit. Luigi would be in charge. I would tell him that I was visiting family and I would be back the day before Il Duce's arrival at Torre del Greco. I had made all these arrangements with Luigi on the Monday, ten days before the visit and three days before we were due to flee. The very next day, Luigi came into my office very excited. A military courier on a motorbike had delivered a letter addressed to me personally from Mussolini. I broke the red seal and I read it out aloud, it said:

'Dear Mayor,

I believe that we served together for a short time in the war when our regiments were in transit. As you know I will be visiting the Pollo family.

It will also be a pleasure to meet with you and your family during that time. Perhaps we may be able to reminisce about the time we spent in service together.

Sincerely,

"Corporal Square Jaw"'

Luigi was very impressed; he thought it was great that 'Il Duce' was so familiar with me. He had no idea of the history behind the name. I took the letter back home to Gilda and showed it to her. It was what they call a 'no-brainer'! We had to leave. I got the tickets changed at Thomas Cook's and we left the next evening on the couchette to Milano."

Angela had been listening throughout from the kitchen, preparing coffee and slicing the Panettone baked earlier in the week. She shouted from the kitchen, *"Enzo, he still has that letter locked away."*

The ladies brought in a tray with coffee and Panettone, placed it on the dining table and served the men. Angela passed Enzo his coffee and cake; Gilda attended to her husband. Both women then served themselves and sat on the arms of the armchairs in which Enzo and Bernardo were respectively seated.

Like everything else, coffee was hard to get during these times but not for the head waiter of the Royal Station Hotel. Not the best espresso Enzo had tasted, but better than any other provided since he was last home.

Bernardo continued:

"We were met at Newcastle Central Station on Easter Monday 1925, at three o'clock in the afternoon. The journey had taken five days and five nights. I have never been back and will not return until Mussolini and the Fascists are gone. Gilda and the girls have been back many times before the outbreak of war. Teresa married out there just before the war. As soon as this is all over, we intend to visit her and see our grandchild for the first time, please, God!"

Chapter 10

Category 'C'

It was now almost six o'clock; even though the RVI was only a short walk away, Angela expressed concern that Enzo should not be late in returning to the hospital. The next day was to be his first as the newest member of the surgical team. She too had to report for duty at the other end of the hospital in the labour ward.

Bernardo had never told the full story to anyone outside the family except for Marco, who knew most of it anyway. Enzo did not want to go anywhere until he had heard it all, so when Angela interrupted her father, alluding to the lateness of the hour, Enzo told her firmly that he would like her father to continue; he never liked to leave anything unfinished.

"Signore Di Carlo, did it take long for you to get a job and what about the language? You spoke no English?" Enzo asked with interest.

Before he continued his account, Gilda had returned from the kitchen with two glasses of Scotch whisky for her guest and husband.

"Marco and Irene" – Bernardo explained – *"lived with her parents in Gosforth, two miles north of where we are now, on the other side of the city. Mr and Mrs Robson, Irene's parents, had a large three storey Victorian house just off Gosforth High Street. Mr Robson owned two public houses and had just bought the Jesmond Park Hotel, which is where Marco and Irene lived, in*

the manager's accommodation. He let us have three rooms on the third floor, two bedrooms and a small sitting room. There was also a small bathroom and separate toilet. We took all meals together and the women shared the housework.

"Marco managed the restaurant and bar at the hotel. I worked with Marco, at first in the kitchen, but as my English improved, I was moved to the bar and eventually to waiting on tables. Mr Robson gave me full board with my family; five shillings a week and I was allowed to keep any tips I made. This was a great help and an excellent start for us in this country. The girls began to pick up the language very easily and Michele became like a brother to Teresa and Angela. John Robson, Marco's father-in-law, would have meetings every two or three months in one of the private function rooms at the back of the Jesmond Park Hotel. This was a Masonic Lodge meeting."

Bernardo reacted to the confused look on Enzo's face, adding:

"No, I am not one. They do everything in secret and although we served the masons who were there, we were not allowed into the room once the door was closed. One of them, dressed in his apron and wearing white gloves, would sit on guard with a sword outside the door. His job was to stop anyone not a mason from entering. They all dressed in black suits, white shirts and black tie, very smart. Different types of aprons and collars to signify rank. After their secret meetings, they would come down to the main bar and mix.

"This 'Lodge', as they called it, seemed to have some very influential professionals and businessmen, doctors, lawyers even a judge. Marco and I got to know them quite well. One night, after the bar had closed, Marco and I joined John and some of his Masonic friends for a chat. They were interested in the *circumstances which led to me coming to England.*

"Marco had always joked about 'Corporal Square Jaw' every time he saw Mussolini's picture in a newspaper. Now I had to tell them my story. As it happened, one of the masons there turned out to be a barrister who became a judge, and I would have contact with him in my next job. They had no idea what was happening in Italy and what 'Square Jaw'' was doing. In early January 1931, we were still living with the Robsons. Marco and I managed the hotel in shifts, and he also helped manage his father-in-law's other two pubs.

"One day John told me to stay behind at the hotel after I had finished my shift, at three o'clock that afternoon. He was prompt and came with Marco and two other men. One was this Barrister-mason, who I have already mentioned, and the other I had never seen before; he wore pin-stripe trousers, ,a waistcoat, black jacket and tie. John introduced me formally to the Barrister who I had known as just 'Mr Sharp'. His full name was Norman Sharpe KC and the other man, also a mason, Max Ridley, Managing Director of the Royal Station Hotel which is considered one of the best in this region. The Head Waiter, or Maître d'hôtel, was to retire in Easter and they wanted me to replace him. I would start the following week and understudy him until he left. I would be paid Two Pounds Ten Shilling a week, with perks.

"They had come to me because the Hotel was also the venue for several Masonic table lodges, which meant at least two such meals every week. As I had experience in the catering of such functions, I was best suited to take over the job. I was taken completely by surprise at the offer being made but there was more! Mr Sharpe explained that he had been recently elected Leader of the North-eastern Circuit; that is one of several Court

circuits in which English Courts are divided. All Barristers join at least one of these in order to practice in these regions; they are supervised by Judges from London, who are assigned to them. The barristers elect a Leader and one of his jobs is to hold a 'Bar Mess' where they all meet at least four times a year and must organise dinners for the visiting judges from London. These are always held in the Royal Station Hotel. The Bar Mess appoints its own butler, who has traditionally been the Head waiter/Maître D'at the Royal Station Hotel. His job is to preserve and replenish the Bar Mess's wine stock, stored at one of the old cells at Moot Hall – the Assize Court, near the High-Level Bridge. That job would pay me fifty guineas a year, plus gratuities given at each Mess and Dinner. Mr Indigo Soames had occupied that position for twenty-five years and would be retiring to the Isle of Wight. Consequently, he would be vacating the tied terraced house owned by the Royal Station Hotel, which would be available for me and my family. Upon my appointment being confirmed, my pay was to be increased to Three pounds a week, but ten shillings per week would be deducted for rent and utilities. In other words, I gained a house and lost nothing."

"So, you have been here ever since Easter 1931. Over twelve years?" confirmed Enzo.

"Correct! I remember thinking, 'Thank you, Corporal Square Jaw!'" Bernardo laughed and continued. "I got to know many of the Masons very well; Judges who came up from London and all the local Barristers, as well as many others, but I never joined the Freemasons. I was never asked, nor did I ask. I suspect it was because it would have interfered too much with the work, I did for them. Norman Sharpe KC. became Sir Norman and a High Court Judge. Another Circuit Leader was elected, Maurice Jackson KC, also a Mason.

"As Mussolini became more and more in the news, my story became more known. By the time war broke out, there were very few people who knew me and had not heard my story. Italy declared war on the British Empire after it allied with Hitler's Germany. Me and my family, Marco and his family, became classified enemy aliens in danger of being interred. The Royal Station Hotel was no longer open to the public but was to be used for visiting Military and Government personnel. It was, however, allowed to continue with its other business such as Masonic and Legal Bar functions.

"Churchill passed an Order which required that all Italian nationals were to be arrested and. interned After a protest in Parliament, Churchill relented, and three classifications were created. 'A', those considered to be a serious threat to the realm and had to be interred. 'B', Italians who had only recently come to England and posed no threat. These aliens could remain at liberty with supervision by reporting weekly to the Police and had restrictions on their movements. Category 'C' were Italians who posed no threat; lived for some time in the country; integrated into the community did not support the Fascist regime and who had left Italy because of some realistic perceived danger to themselves or their family. People in this classification were allowed to just continue as they did before the war."

"Ah, I see, therefore, you were all given a Classification under Category 'C'!" Enzo deduced out loud.

Almost at the end of his saga, Bernardo went on:

"But, Enzo, in order to be classified we were all subject to arrest. We then had to give proof to a tribunal who would give us a classification. For me, Mario and our families it never happened. In my case, The Chief Constable of Newcastle City Police, who had known me for years through his Lodge meetings

at the Royal Station Hotel, came to see me at work. He handed me a very official looking 'Brown Envelope' with a red seal on it. I opened it and took out a certificate, which declared me a Category 'C' alien, by Order of the Honourable Mr Justice Sharpe, High Court of Justice London. Marco got the same. We were all issued with our ID cards."

"Fascinating, Signore Bernardo," commented Enzo.

"Look at the time! It is almost ten o 'clock, and you need to get back, Enzo!" Angela announced as she got up from the arm of the chair.

"Signora and Signore Di Carlo, thank you for such a very pleasant weekend. I have one, very important, request of you both. You may have both noticed that just in these two days I have become fond of Angela, and I believe it is mutual," Enzo said, smiling towards Angela who corroborated his statement by linking his arm and sidling up closer to him as well as making obvious nodding gestures to her parents.

"Out of respect to you both, can I have your consent to go out with her and visit her here, with you both?" he asked.

"Enzo, nothing would give me and Bernardo greater pleasure," Gilda enthused,

"We will expect you here for dinner tomorrow. Plan with Angela to meet at the hospital tomorrow, when you get finished and come back together. Bernardo and I will expect you. Let this become your home."

Bernardo had retrieved Enzo's overcoat and was helping him put it on. Checking he was well wrapped up, Gilda, proud of her 'catch', gave the type of hug that he only ever got from his own mother. Kissing him on both cheeks she bade him, "Good Night."

Bernardo gave Enzo a fatherly hug and discreetly left with

Gilda, leaving the couple alone in the hallway. Enzo took Angela into his arms, little was spoken but much was said; they lingered there for a short while, controlling their passion; they had one final full kiss goodnight. She watched him walk all the way down the terrace and around the corner out of sight. Then, and only then, she closed the door and retired.

Chapter 11

A Pint of Guinness

Even though they worked in the same hospital, their meetings were infrequent. Most of Enzo's time was spent in the operating theatre, whilst Angela would be either out on call or in the delivery suite. Whatever spare time they could get, they spent together. It was not long before Enzo's room became their oasis of love and passion, where they were able to sneak off to be as one.

Some evenings and every fourth weekend when they were not working or on call, they spent time as a family with Gilda and Bernardo. The last weekend in November was to be their first weekend off together. On arrival for the evening meal that Friday night, Angela's parents sensed an air of excited tension about the couple as they came into the living room. Her father was sitting in his usual place by the fire and Gilda was putting the finishing touches to the table set for four. Normally, Angela would come straight over to her parents, hug and kiss them both. Not this night!

Her parents glanced at each other wondering what was going on but not sure whether to ask. Angela began:

"Mama and Papa, Enzo and I have been seeing a lot of each other and..."

Enzo held up his hand, which had the desired impact of stopping Angela before she could ruin the agreed script. He began:

"Signore and Signora Di Carlo, something happened to me when I first saw your daughter, whatever it is, it's clear to me now that she is the missing link in my life. We are soul mates and love each other. I cannot imagine continuing without her. In the short time I have known you both, you too are now part of my life. I ask for permission to marry your daughter."

No verbal response to his question was ever given but the effervescence of emotion, especially from Gilda, the tears of joy, hugs and kisses which flowed, were obvious demonstrations of joyous consent.

Once the excitement had dissipated, the four all sat down to eat. Enzo and Angela had a provisional plan to discuss with her parents. Arrangements had been made for all four to meet with the *Monsignore* that Saturday morning. The couple would become formally engaged at Christmas and marry at Easter. Gilda was delighted and again burst into tears.

"Enzo sitting next to his future mother-in-law tried to comfort her.

"Please, Signora, I do not like to see you cry."

Bernardo in mock anger but in a serious tone, admonished Enzo, *"That will be enough of that. From now on you will call me Papa and my wife Mama!"*

Angela went straight to her father and threw her arms around him, prompting yet another lachrymose interlude.

"Thank you! It will be a great honour to show you both that respect."

Talk about the practical issues followed.

Even though the War had ended between Italy and the Allies, Germany and forces loyal to Il Duce were continuing to fight in Northern Italy. Air raids on London and the main cities had all but ceased. Many US, British Empire, Free French, Polish and other forces were beginning to collect in England. It became more apparent that there would be a new front and invasion of the French coast soon.

Although a Medic, Enzo was still an Italian army officer. Experienced in commanding and running a field hospital, he had been recently advised by Allied Command that he would be needed to participate in any invasion. This potential call to arms had precipitated the nuptials. Enzo did not think that there was any prospect of invasion until the following summer of 1944. They both wanted to be married by that time. An Easter wedding at Saint Mary's was agreed. If things were to move faster than they expected, it could be brought forward.

"Son, you will both move in here and live with us. Bernardo and I will have no argument from either of you!"

This matriarchal decree from Gilda, was a given. Accepted without protest.

"What of your parents, Enzo?" asked Bernardo.

"I have had no contact with them since before I was taken Prisoner of War. I do not know if they are alive or dead. Now, even though we are allies, communications between here and Italy are impossible. After the Armistice there is no way of repatriating Ex POWs. Those with professions such as mine, with skills and trades, have been used for the war effort. I can see no prospect of getting in contact with my parents until after this war has ended. Even then it will take time to get everything back to anything near normal." Enzo pensively explained.

"Did you tell the Monsignor why you wanted to meet with him?" Gilda asked her daughter.

"No, Mama. He was not there so I spoke with his housekeeper who checked his diary and booked us at four

o'clock, before he takes confessions," Angela retorted.

"That will be handy; I had planned to take confession tomorrow, for communion on Sunday. Now we can all go together. Take communion for the first time as a family. I can give thanks to Our Lady for this blessing!" her mother explained.

Smiling in acquiescence, Bernardo kept silent. Regardless of what he thought, he would just do as she wished, it was futile to do otherwise as she would just get upset.

Not being British Citizens meant that getting wed was not going to be as straightforward as they imagined. A process of certification was needed but they reckoned there was plenty of time until Easter. Bernardo had enough connections to be able to lubricate the wartime bureaucratic machine. A combination of his own efforts and that of Enzo's future father-in-law should ensure an Easter wedding.

That was the plan as far the Monsignor, Enzo and Bernardo were concerned, but only a small part of the plan that Gilda and Angela were devising. Wartime rationing, restrictions and other curtailments of normal society, were mere hurdles in these women's minds when it came to organising a wedding. And of course, Angela agreed with her mother that 'Aunty' Irene would have to be involved.

Mass the next day ended about the usual time, the Monsignor, in his customary place, spent more than the allocated thirty seconds of chat with the foursome when they were leaving the church. Arrangements for the Easter vows being the main topic of discourse.

Gilda then told her priest, "It has been a long time since you came for dinner *Monsignor.* Next week at Mass tell me when you can come. I will make a nice Italian meal and we can talk about the wedding too!"

It was not too often that the *Monsignor* was ever asked to a parishioner's home for a meal, but Gilda was one of those few who felt duty bound to entertain him at least twice a year. The food was always excellent, and he had no hesitation in accepting.

"Thank you. But there is no need to wait for me to tell you next week, I can tell you now! Once I have tended to my after-Mass duties next week I will be free. If that is not too little notice, I can make it then as I am covered for evening Vespers," the Canon Wilkinson proffered.

Seizing the opportunity to get things rolling about the wedding arrangements, Gilda agreed, "This will be the first time that you will be dining with us on a Sunday. Every other time was during the week or a Saturday. You must excuse me and Angela from Mass that morning. We will need the time to prepare!"

Canon Wilkinson laughed with the others, and remarked, "I am sure that the Good Lord and Saint Mary will understand. I will also say a special prayer."

With that, the two couples headed off to Claremont Terrace, the Di Carlos leading the way. That next week Gilda occupied herself with not only planning the forthcoming Sunday meal with the *'Monsignor'* but wasted no time in enrolling Irene into plotting the *'Festa'* she was going to throw for the engagement at Christmas. The Easter wedding was the main item on the agenda.

Irene and Marco had always looked upon the Di Carlo girls as the daughters they never had. She had missed out on being involved in the planning of Teresa's wedding in Italy. Gilda knew Angela wanted 'Aunty Irene' to be involved. If Enzo and Angela had any real say, they would have happily gone off and got married with the minimum of fuss. That was not going to happen! Respect had to be shown and tradition followed, both families would expect no less.

The only time Gilda could get to talk about her planning was at the evening meal. By midweek Bernardo had had enough of his wife going on about what she was going to cook for the *'Monsignor'*.

"Hell, woman! It is not the Pope who is coming! You do this every time you invite him. Thank God it only happens a couple of times a year!" he complained.

Gilda with overt contempt plonked his plate on the table.

"Stupid ignorant imbecile!"

She called him and proceeded to ignore him for the rest of the evening, taking every opportunity to let him know the type of 'doghouse' he was in.

Following Mass, Enzo and Bernardo were expected to come straight back home with their guest. Of all Sundays to come back late this should not have been the one. The *'doghouse'* awaited both men when they decided to turn up later than Gilda had instructed. She had expected them back about an hour earlier when Angela went to answer the front door. Gilda could be heard ventilating some choice Neapolitan expletives in the background. The door was opened to three men, one was in a black suit and wore a dog collar.

"How nice to see you, Monsignor," Angela greeted their guest in a voice just short of a shout, so that her mother would hear and defuse her tone.

Gilda got the message; wiped her hands on her apron as she took it off, threw it onto the kitchen table, adjusted her hair and then greeted the three arrivals with a very special welcome for the *'Monsignor'*. She could not, however, help herself and gave her husband a withering stare, which said *'I will deal with you later!'* Enzo followed Bernardo's lead and said nothing. The *'Monsignor'*, practised in being the cause of these predicaments, acted as defence counsel for all three. In his polite melodic Irish brogue, he eloquently mitigated and accepted full blame for any perceived disrespect.

"I am sorry if we are late, Signora Di Carlo. It's all my fault! I asked yer man here and Enzo to wait until I had finished seeing the congregation out. I needed to talk to both in private, especially Enzo. Ye know about the things needed to be done. The paperwork, all that sort of stuff ye wouldn't want to be bothered with over the meal. So, I suggested we went somewhere quiet on the way back, where we could talk. The publican of the Haymarket Pub is one of me parishioners who also knows yer man. That was as good a place as any on the way here, so I took them into the Snug. We had a pint of Guinness each, , to celebrate Enzo's good fortune. Poor man never had a Guinness before! Sure, there's a first time for everything. Here we are then, and that food smells good."

All acquitted. The good priest led his new disciples over the threshold to eat.

Chapter 12

Fenham Barracks

No-one would have imagined that there was a war in progress on New Year's Eve, 1943 in the Di Carlo household. *Zio* Marco and Aunty Irene were happy to hold the engagement party at the Jesmond Park Hotel, which was later in the evening than expected. Angela had been delayed with an emergency premature delivery.

Engagement rings were not easy to get in these times but, through the Masonic connections, Enzo secured a suitable small solitaire diamond from Abe Green, a Jewish jeweller who had a kiosk in the Cloth Market. Abe gave Enzo a good discount as he bought the wedding rings at the same time all for £20. Angela surprised Enzo with a silver fob of a bear.

"To signify the strength of our love!" she told him.

Canon Wilkinson assumed the role of Maître d' and Master of ceremonies. Food was consumed amid laughter and speeches, interspersed with toasts for the couple's long and happy union. He blessed the couple followed by yet another toast.

By the end of 1943 the Allies had begun to consolidate their position in all active theatres as well as now having much better organised human and material resources. There was great anticipation that 1944 would be a significant year towards ending the War. The Italian Navy having escaped the wrath of the Germans, sailed to join the British Fleet controlling the

Mediterranean. Former Italian POWs were separated out and those who continued to have Fascist sympathies were interned. The rest, who wanted to cooperate with the allies, were used and even given the option to join the Allied forces.

When Enzo had been given his transfer orders to the RVI upon his release from Eden Camp, he had to sign a *'Declaration of Co-operation'* as well a document which required him to acknowledge Italy's surrender to the Allies. He had been told by the commandant that the order which he was given would be temporary and subject to change.

Now eighth January, three months later, he was engaged to be married in a place he would never have imagined being. He signed out at the Porter's Lodge that morning, on his way to prep the morning operating list, when the porter called him back to the desk.

"Doctor Falcone, Sir, there is a letter here for you."
The Porter was waving a brown official looking envelope at him. "Hand-delivered this morning by an Army dispatch rider. Can you come and sign for it please?" asked the Porter.

Enzo retraced his steps, took the unexpected correspondence, looked at it, confirmed it was for him, and then signed for it as instructed. Thanked the Porter. Looked at it again for some clue or vision of what was inside. He decided, best not to open it until later when he was to meet with Angela in the hospital.

By chance they had both completed their morning lists early, Angela was already at the table waiting for Enzo, as he walked through the swing double doors. Enzo sat down after a mutual hug and kiss. Took out of his inside pocket the letter and opened it. Read it quickly to himself then handed it to Angela to read. It was not good news!

"What does it say? What is wrong?" he asked.

"I am not sure what this means but you are requested to appear before an Army Board on Monday, 10th January, at nine a.m. at Fenham Barracks here in Newcastle. That is just the other side of Leazes Park where we have the Cafe."

Puzzled, she re-read the correspondence on the Ministry of War headed paper.

"What else does it say?" he wanted to know.

"Not much else. You are to be dressed in civilian clothes and it is signed by someone called Colonel Aldridge," she retorted, still staring at the page.

She passed him the letter which he read and nodded silently to himself.

Then he asked her:

"I will have to arrange cover for that morning. Can you come with me?"

"I should be able to but what does it mean? Do you have any idea, Enzo?" she enquired.

"No. I cannot even guess. But we will know in about forty-eight hours."

Fenham Barracks was no more than a short walk from the RVI. Angela met Enzo at the Porter's Lodge at eight that morning. Arm in arm they speculated as they walked. Arriving at the main gate in good time, Enzo produced his letter to the guard. He read it and beckoned the duty sergeant who checked his clipboard.

"Both follow me this way, sir," the sergeant requested.

Led across the corner of the nearest end of the quadrangle, half-packed with military vehicles of all description. The other half echoed with the castrated yell of some drill sergeant putting recruits through his unique form of sadistic square bashing.

Entering the main block, the NCO pushed open a heavy oak-panelled Victorian door and clipped to his escortees, "This way please, sir. Madam, I am afraid you will have to wait in the waiting room here on the right."

Enzo kissed Angela. She went into the waiting room and sat down.

Down a short corridor, which came to a 'T' junction, Enzo's escort came to a halt. Firmly gave two solid knocks on a door to the left.

An authoritative educated voice of an officer beckoned from within, "Come in, Sergeant!"

The sergeant opened the door, ushered Enzo in, saluted, span around right, took two smart strides over the threshold out and closed the door behind him.

An old functional office about half the size of the Di Carlos' dining room; lit by high windows akin to those found in police cells. Horrible dark green tiling rising about four feet from the concrete slab floor and dirty cream speckled paint to the ceiling. Enzo saw the Crown and two pips of a full Colonel on the epaulettes of the lead officer sitting with two others. They all stood to greet him. This Colonel had to be the author of the letter that had summoned him to this meeting.

"Good morning, Dr Falcone and welcome. Let me introduce Major Rich to my left and Major Jackman on my right."

Introductions and niceties complete, Aldridge continued and got straight to the point.

"Your transfer here to the RVI was always going to be temporary and short term. There have been a lot of discussions and re-organisation going on with the new Italian High Command. It has been agreed that all Ex Italian POWs can be recruited into any of the Allied forces of the countries where they

83

were being held. Your service as a medic is exemplary within your own army and, I see, when captured you took charge of the field hospital, which catered for both your own wounded and ours.

You served on the hospital ship Valletta until landing here in England and whilst at Camp Eden, you organised and ran the hospital for your fellow POWs. I also note that since the Armistice you have been at the RVI here in Newcastle. Before the war you completed a residency at Bart's, London, and worked as Consultant Anaesthetist before enlisting in the Italian Army. You now hold the rank of Major. You are single, recently engaged to a lady from a respectable Italian family living here in Newcastle. Have I missed anything out Major Falcone?" he asked, putting down his manilla folder.

"No, Colonel, you have been very thorough. It surprises me, yet does not surprise me, that you know of my engagement," observed the attentive Enzo.

Aldridge picked up his file. "Angela Di Carlo, twenty-two, younger of two sisters; father, Bernardo married to Gilda. He virtually runs the Royal Station Hotel, where I happen to have been billeted for the past six months."

"I see, Colonel. Can you tell me why I am here?" Enzo enquired.

"Of course, Major, with the consent of your high command, you are being transferred with immediate effect to the Royal Army Medical Corps with the rank of Lieutenant-Colonel. The hospital ship Valletta is being refitted and is in dock at Liverpool. That refitting will take another eight weeks. It will then sail for Naples via Malta repatriating Italian Prisoners of War and sending medical reinforcements. Field hospitals will need to be set up on the outskirts of Naples. You will be ordered to join the ship two weeks before departure, which is expected to be no later than 1st March and take command of the medical reinforcements. You will receive further orders before arriving in Naples."

"What about my wedding plans for Easter, Colonel?" asked Enzo in a subdued voice, stunned by what he had just been told.

"Yes. Good question. We have thought of that too! It is of course a matter for you and your intended, but we have taken the liberty of speaking to Canon Wilkinson. A special marriage licence will be obtained, and he is able to marry you at eleven-hundred hours on Saturday twenty-two January. It gives you just under two weeks to get organised and just over two weeks before you have to report."

This was the sugar on the bitter pill he had been given. He knew that Angela would agree to the marriage being brought forward but would not be happy with everything else. It was war! Neither of them had much choice in the matter.

Having paused for thought, Enzo requested he have a few minutes to go and speak to Angela in the waiting room.

"A good idea. We will take a break now. When you return, please bring the future Mrs Falcone with you. It would be nice to meet her, and she may have some questions," the Colonel instructed.

Enzo thanked Aldridge. Got up, left the room. Angela, who was looking out of the window watching the square bashing, turned as he opened the door and asked, *"Have you finished? What was it all about?"*

Not knowing any other way to break the news to her but be direct, Enzo blurted it all out like a machine gun volley and ended with the, punchline *"Please, will you marry me on Saturday twenty-second January?"*

"Of course, I would marry you now if we could!"

He pulled her towards him and kissed her tenderly.

"The Colonel has asked that you come with me back into the meeting. Do you mind?" Enzo asked.

"Why should I mind? I am to be your wife. I wanted to come with you when you first went in!"

The meeting resumed. Angela presented well and impressed Aldridge and his two wing-men who had contributed little throughout.

By half past ten they were walking back through Leazes Park to Claremont Terrace. Focused on the fact that they would be married sooner than they had expected, all concerns about everything else that was to happen were put aside. Now they had to break the news to her parents.

Chapter 13

Best Eytie Gasman

Enzo would move from the hospital accommodation into Claremont Terrace. Bernardo would redecorate Angela's room and a new matrimonial bed would be bought as a wedding present.

Everything about the wedding went as smoothly as could be expected. The reception was held at the Jesmond Park Hotel. Not the big affair that Gilda and Aunty Irene had planned but the best that could be done in the circumstances.

Bernardo had arranged for the newlywed Falcones to spend their first night as husband and wife in the Empire Bedroom Suite. Breakfast would be served in their room the next morning up to eleven and only when called. At noon they were to take the train to Wylam Village, in Northumberland, where they were to spend the rest of the week at the Ship Inn and enjoy time together on honeymoon, returning the following Saturday.

Friday, following his interview at Fenham Barracks was to be Enzo's last day at the RVI. Colleagues and staff threw an impromptu party to say farewell to Enzo.

His management, organisational and interpersonal skills had been recognised as greater talents to be harnessed and utilised in this final build up for the war effort. The subsequent rebuilding that inevitably follows war, needs good professional administrators who cope well in crises of all kinds, having a full grasp of their responsibilities and how best to execute them efficiently. Enzo had been one of the chosen few to be entrusted with the rebuild.

Southern Italy was chaotic at best, even before the war, now after the Allied Invasion and the armistice the whole of the Mezzogiorno and Sicily was in a complete state of collapse. Epidemics were becoming a greater danger day by day. There were many wounded on all sides and many homeless due to intense bombing. Medical facilities were minimal and badly organised.

With the authority of his military rank, his team and facilities, Enzo was expected to set in operation field hospitals where needed and re-organise the existing medical infrastructure. It was to this new world that his colleagues raised their glasses, toasted and bade a fond farewell to:

"The Best Eyetie Gasman Ever!"

A week after his meeting with the Aldridge trio at Fenham Barracks, Enzo was back again for a full week of briefing. He also had to be measured up by the Quartermaster who would order his new British Army uniform.

Colonel Aldridge and his two majors took turns in setting out Enzo's role. His responsibility would be to take charge of all civilian, military personnel and facilities from Benevento to the North of Vesuvius, to Salerno in the south. This was a region whose topography and geography Enzo knew very well.

Six of the trucks parked at the barracks had been allocated to his new medic company. Upon his return from honeymoon, a platoon of his newly formed company from Catterick would spend the next week loading these trucks and being briefed. Once loaded they would leave for Southampton for embarkation on a ship bound for Naples.

Italian POWs that were being repatriated on the Hospital Ship HMHS Valletta had all been documented. On board there were seven hundred and fifty officers and crew with seven hundred Italian military personnel to be returned home.

For this trip, the Valletta would carry no wounded or sick. Its role was to transport the Italians who would relieve Allied troops on the ground and supplement the shortage of specialist medical staff needed in that operational zone. Upon arrival in Naples, the Valletta would remain in port for the duration, serving as a floating military hospital catering to military and civilian needs. Once docked in the Port of Naples a skeleton crew would remain with HMHS Valletta serving as headquarters to units under the command of Lieutenant-Colonel Falcone RAMC.

Departure from Liverpool was scheduled for early March, for a journey via Malta that would take up to three weeks, including refuelling for two days at Gibraltar. At sea, Enzo was to brief and organise his units ready for deployment on arrival. Six field units, plus headquarters staff who would remain on board. Some would be administrative staff, but the majority would be medical and surgical personnel to staff the hospital ship. Once in harbour and after the repatriation was complete, the Valletta would get another refit to provide for more beds and two additional operating suites.

Several weeks earlier in a bomb-proof room somewhere in the Ministry of Defence a secret committee had made this plan. Enzo and his staff were ordered to liaise with the Italian military in situ and civilian authorities. Co-ordinate, collate and secure storage of medical supplies in addition to maximising available manpower.

Under constant fire and bombardment in North Africa, Enzo

as a young Captain had to run a mobile field hospital for hundreds of thousands. Improvising as he went, with no support or planning and somehow managing to achieve the needs of each situation he encountered. What was being asked challenged Enzo in a different way. It opened a new dimension to exercise and apply the intellect with which he had been blessed.

Even though the Mediterranean was now completely rid of enemy shipping and under control of the Allies. The obvious *'perils of war'* were a real concern to the newlyweds and Enzo's new in-laws.

The Valletta would sail from Liverpool, down the Irish Sea south past Land's End, where it would be met by the Home Fleet escort. Travel as part of a larger convoy under escort as far as the Neutral Spanish and Portuguese Bay of Biscay. The Italian Navy would then lead the convoy to Gibraltar to refuel before they sailed on to Naples. The south of Italy was now occupied by the Allies and all enemy hostilities had ceased.

It was all happening far too quickly for the newlyweds. This was a leap year, and so they had an extra day together before Enzo had to board the train that would steam its way on a twelve-hour all-stopping wartime trip over the Pennines, to *'Scouseland'*.

These last few months had been idyllic. His in-laws had always made him comfortable when he was courting Angela, providing him with a family, respite and home cooking. This became even better when he married Angela and became more *in famiglia*. Not having to get up and leave for his lonely room at the hospital, he had the love and companionship of his wife, the warmth and passion of her body in a comfortable bed. No responsibilities and more! This was the lull before the storm, things were about to change again for Enzo.

Shortly after midnight his Liverpool bound train would leave platform three and only God knew when he would be back again. Emotions and tensions began to show when he came back the day before, fully kitted-out in his new uniform of a Lieutenant-Colonel in the Royal Army Medical Corps. Enzo looked so smart and impressive when he arrived home; it brought a flood of tears from Gilda when she opened the front door to him. Initially, taken aback, not realising that the Army officer standing on her doorstep was her new son-in-law. She burst into tears when she recognised him. Hugged him so tightly that he nearly lost his balance and fell backwards out of the doorway.

Angela tried in vain to control her emotions as they arrived at the station for Enzo's departure but became increasingly clingy and hung on to the last moment. Inevitably, she broke down and sobbed as the train pulled away. Papa Di Carlo held out, right up to when Enzo boarded the carriage at the platform. He and Gilda retreated after their good-byes, to give the newlyweds space and time. Just before they walked away Bernardo grabbed his son-in-law and gave him a bear hug, then backed away

This was never going to be the most comfortable of train journeys. At least Enzo's rank merited a first-class compartment with five other officers making the compartment's full complement of six. For obvious reasons Troop trains always travelled at night. First light was not until after seven, by which time the train would be too far inland for German fighter bombers to risk a daytime attack. By this time the war had reached the 'End Game' and the Luftwaffe were concentrating on the Russian Front and trying to hold back the Allies' advance up through the 'soft underbelly' of Italy.

Before he left for the station, Bernardo had made sure Enzo had a good alcoholic 'nightcap' that would send him off to sleep.

Shortly after the six occupants of his compartment had met and greeted each other, they were all comatose. The booze, clickety-clack of the rail track and rock of the train, soon cradled Enzo off into a deep slumber.

He woke up Liverpool was not far now! The passengers began to prepare for the mass exodus onto the platform when the train arrived. Kit bags, suitcases, haversacks and holdalls began to appear. Enzo had a small holdall and briefcase which he carried. His trunk had been delivered two days before his departure and was already on board the Valletta in his quarters. Even though the first-class compartment had a door which opened directly onto the platform, the passing throng of disembarking passengers only permitted cautious exit.

Enzo saw no point in making any effort to leave until all had become quiet and subdued. He was the last to get out. He donned the braided cap of his rank, fastened his overcoat, opened the compartment door, and backed out. He was reaching to lift out his holdall, when he became aware of someone gently pushing past him to get a hold of the bag.

"I'll get that for you, sir!" a voice stated.

Enzo turned and saw an RAMC Corporal pick up his bag, come to attention, and salute him.

"Corporal Proud, sir. Ed Proud. Pleasure to meet you, sir!"

The Corporal was a stout man with auburn hair and freckles, who in peacetime would probably have a more substantial belly than he was currently sporting. Distracted by this encounter Enzo was not aware of the two officers standing behind Corporal Proud.

"Welcome to Liverpool, sir,"

Synchronised male and female voices rang out.

Proud put down the holdall and introduced the lady officer

first, "Sir, this is Major Elizabeth Kirby in charge of the nurses."

She smiled, shook Enzo's hand and spoke.

"Betty to you, sir."

Classical Matron! With the handshake of a vice. He thought to himself Could be a formidable ally or foe.

Betty, pulled rank and took over the Corporal's introductions, "May I introduce Major Roger Hill who is the Adjutant and with me, second in command. He gets called Rogge, and of course you have met your batman, Corporal Proud."

Bespectacled Major Hill shook hands with his new CO but knew his place. When Betty was there, there was no doubt as to who got the attention.

Enzo thought it prudent not to lift the barrier of formality at this early stage and thanked them for coming to meet him.

His Batman picked up the holdall and led his three officers to the car allocated for use by his CO. Proud then chauffeured them to the Valletta, docked west of the Liver Building.

Chapter 14

The Command

Betty Kirby was born just after the turn of the century. Born and bred in Chester she had gone into nursing after the first war and did all her training at the Chester Royal Infirmary. After a broken engagement, she decided to dedicate herself to her chosen profession but was still open to the occasional discreet affair.

The retreat from Dunkirk had brought with it numerous injured and wounded that needed to be treated and nursed back to health. The War Department had to source and enlist experienced medical and nursing staff to cope with the consequences of this massive carnage. Assistant Matron Kirby was one of the many who answered this call and was duly commissioned as a Captain into the Queen Alexandra's Royal Nursing Corps. Dropped into the deep end, Betty was sent to organise and manage the care of the rescued troops in the various field hospitals set up around the coast of Kent and Sussex. This is where she remained until recently promoted to Major and assigned to be one of a medical command team headed by Enzo. This nursing Major had, over the years, travelled extensively throughout the Empire with various medical teams and units but spoke only English.

It had never crossed Dr Hill's mind that as Chief Public Health Officer of Wigan, in his late forties, married with three married daughters and soon to be a grandfather for the first time, that he would ever be of any use to the military. After qualifying in Medicine at King's College, London, he knew he was not cut out for hospital life. Nor was general practice to be his niche, but he was tempted to apply to an advert as a Medical Officer in his hometown of Southend-on-Sea in Essex. The job description did not involve direct contact with patients or practice of medicine. He was to be an organiser, regulator, administrator and develop bean-counting skills, all of which he mastered in the context of public health.

Between the wars, he climbed the ladder by spending no more than a couple of years at different local authorities. For the past five years he had become Wigan's youngest Chief Medical Officer, where he had created a well-oiled and efficient model that had got him onto one of the Ministry of Health advisory panels and monthly trips to Whitehall. In October, he was in London on one of these trips, when he was summoned to the Ministry of Defence. In short, they told him that Allied troops, who were now occupying southern Italy, were potentially being exposed to typhoid, cholera and other waterborne diseases due to the collapse of the infrastructure, bad sanitation and no structured public health. He had been selected to be commissioned as a Major to join a task force that would be sent to Naples. That appointment came into effect on first January 1944.

Roger and Betty had only joined the Valletta during the previous week. They had been fully briefed in Whitehall. Their orders included fully discussing the operation with Enzo, working out its implementation, logistics, deployment of personnel and other matters pertinent to the execution of the entire 'Plan' whilst en route to Naples.

Corporal Proud had started life as a junior footman, Sir Norman Richard, a distant cousin of the Duke of Northumberland

95

who lived at, Warkworth Manse Southeast of Alnwick on the Northumberland Coast. The Proud family served the Richards for several generations. *'Ed'*, had joined the Northumberland Fusiliers at the outbreak of the war. He had a very mature head on his shoulders, and he had seen a lot of action but had not been involved in any. Corporal Proud was part of that *'Phantom Corps'* of men who embodied the qualities of the classical *'Jeeves at his master's side'* without whom the traditional British officer class were unable to function.

Eddy Proud knew how to be seen and not heard; be there but be invisible. He would have been a great asset to the enemy if ever captured. Like Jeeves, he was a mine of information, and his advice was often sought. In service, he learnt to be discrete and discerning and never breached confidences. It was strictly taboo, especially in military service, to make mention of, or identify, prior masters. In his previous tour of duty, he had been Jeeves to the CO of an Eighth Army Unit that invaded Sicily and fought on, up to Naples. They were billeted at the Grand Hotel in Sorrento after the Armistice and then transferred back to England. Corporal Proud was then assigned to what became known as the *'Task Force'* with orders to be *'Jeeves to Enzo'*, but until his new master arrived, Betty had wasted no time in putting him to use by unpacking.

Although distracted by his new environment and the job ahead, Enzo's thoughts were still not completely focused with the task in hand. He missed Angela. From the time he first met her, when she served him at the cafe in Leazes Park, he had been with her every day. Today was to be the first of many days and nights that he would spend apart from his wife. He had no idea when he would see her again and cursed the dirty trick that *'San Gennaro'* now seemed to be playing on him.

Before Enzo left Newcastle, his father-in-law, Bernardo, now manager of the Royal Station Hotel with his own office and telephone, had planned for his daughter to come to the hotel on Tuesday and Thursday evenings at seven, to be able to take any calls. Also, the family usually spent Saturday evenings playing cards at Uncle Marco and Aunty Irene's house. They too had a telephone, so he could call them there at seven in the evening. Once he got settled on the Valletta, he hoped that he too would have a telephone and could give that telephone number to Angela. It was now three o'clock, four more hours before he would be able to hear her voice.

Enzo's quarters on board the hospital ship was to be found amidships on the starboard side, on the deck below the bridge and directly beneath the ship's Captain's quarters. His suite comprised a study-cum-wardroom; adjacent sleeping quarters, eight feet by twelve feet with a porthole directly above the midpoint of his bunk; a shower closet and toilet, located next to the sleeping quarters. Furnishings were minimal and functional. In his wardroom was a desk and swivel chair and on that desk a telephone!

Enzo's eyes lit up and he turned to *'his Jeeves'* but before he could ask, his man said, "Yes Sir, it works. You can make and receive internal and external calls on that telephone while in port, only internal when at sea. External calls can only be made or received by radio telephone on the Bridge or the Captain's cabin when at sea. If you want to make an external call you need to dial nine, which will connect you to an outside line. The telephone number is on the dial."

"Am I permitted to make and receive personal telephone calls?" asked Enzo of Ed.

"One of the perks of your job, Sir," Proud explained. This

completely lifted Enzo's sagging spirits and increased his anticipation for his seven o'clock call to his love.

"Sir, do you want me to give you a tour of the ship before your meeting at sixteen-thirty with Majors Kirby, Hill and Hewitson?" enquired the Corporal.

"I came to England on this ship and know it well; we can look at it later. I would really like to see the changes made by the refit," replied Enzo as he sat down at his desk and looked at the telephone. "What meeting? And who is Major Hewitson?" he asked, refocusing his attention.

"All three Majors met yesterday and decided to hold this meeting today for proper introductions and a chat, as Major Hewitson was unable to come to the station," informed Ed.

Enzo nodded in acknowledgement and repeated "Who is Major Hewitson, Ed?"

Before he could answer, there was a rattled knock at the door to the quarters. Ed moved directly across to open it. There stood the ship's Captain who, without invitation, stepped in and over to Enzo, not giving Ed any chance to announce his arrival.

"Enzo, I thought it had to be you they had put in command. No-one better! Fantastic! Now in the British Army, well done! Welcome," announced his old friend Commander Butler.

Totally bemused and confused, Ed closed the cabin door instinctively knowing that this was a time for silence and invisibility.

Commander Butler had been Captain of the Valletta when Enzo had joined the ship in North Africa; he had wanted the then Italian Army Medic Officer to remain on board. Norman Butler's request had been refused as Enzo was at that time a prisoner of war. When ordered to Liverpool for the vessel's refit and briefed that the Valletta was to be sent to Naples on the subject mission,

Butler had resubmitted Enzo's name.

Now friends reunited, Enzo was expected with his staff to join the ship's officers at twenty-thirty hours in the Captain's Suite for dinner. With that, Norman gave Enzo a token *'man hug'* and left the room.

Breaking self-imposed silence and resuming visibility Ed enquired, "Shall I tell the Majors, sir?"

"No, I will tell them when we meet at four-thirty. Now tell me about Major Hewitson, Ed?" asked Enzo.

"He arrived just before me. An educated gent, probably Oxford or Cambridge, late twenties I would say! I understand he speaks French, Italian, Spanish and German and was on Special Ops behind the lines. Intelligence Corps, that's all I know. Oh, he's bit eccentric and likes to wind up the Matron! My apologies... I mean Major Kirby, sir!" Ed explained, only slightly embarrassed at this slip in formality with his new boss.

Enzo gave an understanding chuckle, "Suits her, Ed! Suits her! How does he wind her up?"

"He flirts with her, sir." Ed grinned.

"They will be here in about an hour you said, Ed?" Enzo queried of his batman.

"That's right, and if you excuse me, sir, I will go and get some tea ready for the meeting," confirmed Ed.

Permission granted; the Corporal left the room.

Enzo tapped the telephone one more time, got up and went to the basin for a cold wash. He looked at himself in the mirror and apologised to San Gennaro for having doubted him saying,

"Two more miracles – the blessed telephone and Norman Butler."

Chapter 15

The Honey Trap

Christopher John Hewitson was just a couple of months younger than Enzo and would be thirty in November. His background was worlds apart from his soon to become *'best mate'* and lifelong friend.

His father, James, was a career diplomat and a young consular officer in Madrid where his former actress wife, Mary, gave birth to their second child and only son Christopher. When the boy was five, the family relocated to Vienna as father took a further step up the diplomatic ladder. Young Christopher and his two sisters attended the private school where foreign diplomats educated their children. By the time he was ten, he was fluent in English, Spanish, German and being taught French at school. He was sent off to Harrow, as a boarder, when he was eleven, but spent his vacations with his parents and sisters wherever his father happened to be posted.

Paris followed the Vienna posting, and when Christopher was in his sixth form his father was appointed Head of Chancery at the British Embassy in Rome. This was a time when Il Duce was at the height of his power and in the limelight; also, about the same time as Enzo's father-in-law was getting out of the country. Of all the places his father had been posted Christopher enjoyed Rome most, taking advantage by adding Italian to his list of languages. Young Hewitson visited Florence, Turin, Milan and Venice but never ventured to the south, into the different world of the Mezzogiorno.

Of all the languages he could speak, he preferred Italian, which he spoke with the accent of Rome and too perfectly to be identified as an Italian. He would never pass as a Neapolitan with his naturally blonde wavy hair and slim build. Standing just less than six feet, he could possibly pass as one of those Italians from the north, near the Austrian border but, most likely, people on the street in Naples would take him as a German or Scandinavian.

On reaching eighteen, it had been planned that Chris would go on from Harrow to either Oxford or Cambridge, to read Law. His father had decided that his son's future would be best served by being called to the Bar. However, this plan was changed, in that young Hewitson decided that, as his father was now Head of Chancery in Dublin, he would read Law at Trinity College, in Dublin.

In his third and final year at Trinity he was admitted as a student to the Honourable Society of Gray's Inn, one of the four Inns of Court in London. After graduating from Trinity with a respectable *"second"* he was called to the Bar a few days before his twenty-second birthday, in November 1936. Through his father's contacts, his Pupillage was to be in the Chambers of Sir Lancelot Pugh KC. A set which had a wide range of work and his Pupil-Master, Selwyn Evans, exposed young Hewitson to the practise of law, warts, and all!

After he successfully completed Pupillage, he accepted an offer of a tenancy and began a fledgling practice, running around the various courts in London. One day he had been leaving Bow Street Magistrates' Court when he was approached by two very politely spoken men, too educated and well-dressed to be CID.

They invited him to join them for a late morning tea in a small cafe, off Covent Garden. Both men were in their middle thirties and introduced themselves as *'Mr Smith and Mr Jones'*, needing to talk to him on a *'very personal and private matter'*.

They found a quiet corner and *'Smith'*, being the senior, took the lead and came straight to the point. "We work for the same people as your father in MI6. He holds a very high position within our organisation and has sanctioned this approach, to ask if you would consider joining us. It goes without saying that you have all the credentials and background, but being a barrister gives more specialist depth to our work."

Without hesitation, the young man agreed, joining initially as an adviser in the legal section, subsequently progressing to an Intelligence Officer.

When war broke out, he was seconded to the Intelligence Corps, commissioned as a Captain but rarely in uniform. His languages were put to good use, and he was moved around the various neutral Embassies in Europe to help organise the release of English nationals and repatriation of wounded POWs.

Captain Hewitson's last assignment, before being posted to the Valletta's Task Force, had been in Washington DC with the Federal Bureau of Investigation (FBI). Chris had been sent to work with the *'Cousins'* as a liaison officer on a plan devised to help with the invasion and subsequent occupation of Sicily and the Mezzogiorno region of Italy.

The Americans had secretly released Lucky Luciano from Federal Prison, where he was serving a sentence following conviction of Tax Fraud. The *'Cousins'* had adopted this Chicago mobster onto their team in order to enlist the co-operation of the Sicilian Mafia, the *Cosa Nostra*; the Mafia in Calabria, the *Ndrangheta*; and the Mafia in Naples, the *Camorra*.

Post-armistice, it was envisaged that the political infrastructure of Italy would have collapsed, and a complete vacuum of power would exist. The Mafia would have total control and, if left completely to their own devices, might conflict with the occupying allied civil and military authorities.

Concerns within the British Command prompted the implementation of an alternative plan which would involve sending the Valletta to Naples. It would help set up an alternative scenario by providing medical facilities and repatriating POWs from that region, who could work from the hospital ship. Chris Hewitson was to be seconded as a Major of the Royal Ordnance Corps, to oversee and command the logistics needed to implement public health projects, as well as support the medical services needed. Major Hewitson's legend as a logistics officer had been explained to the other two Majors, Betty and Roger, at their earlier separate briefings.

All of which was unknown to Enzo, but he would be put in the picture by Chris, when all four met at sixteen-thirty hours. Hewitson would also brief all three on the covert operation that he and Enzo had also been assigned.

It had been decided by Command that Falcone and Hewitson would be the ideal duo for this job, each having exemplary backgrounds. Enzo knew Naples and the region well, being from a respected local family, he spoke and understood the local dialect and customs. Hewitson spoke Italian and, like Enzo, he had a quick analytical mind, and both could be relied upon to be decisive, discreet, cautious, and act on initiative.

The three Majors entered the small wardroom in Enzo's quarters at exactly four thirty. Corporal Ed had arrived a quarter of an hour earlier, arranged another three chairs around Enzo's desk and brought in a tray with a pot of tea and some biscuits, which he placed on a small table, a step or so away from the desk.

"Sir, this is Major Hewitson," Ed explained as the two men shook hands.

All four officers sat down together and looked to Enzo for the lead, whilst his *'Jeeves'* poured tea for the assembled quartet.

Tea served; the Corporal left the officers to their meeting. Enzo had prepared for himself a short agenda, to act as *an 'aide de memoire'* for what he had to say; he unfolded it and began, "Firstly, anything that is said in this room at these meetings remains totally confidential. Secondly, in this room and between ourselves only, we will refer to each other by our Christian names. Please call me Enzo! Thirdly, we must always be frank and as candid with each other as the circumstances will permit. As you probably know, I am an Italian and former POW, recently transferred and promoted to this rank. I am not a professional soldier but a doctor. Others have decided that I am suited for this position and not me. I assume that the same people who selected me put us all together in the belief that our talents would complement each other. More than anything else in these times, loyalty, and trust in one another is paramount. My understanding is that you were all supplied with a copy of my file, and I have seen Betty's and Roger's, but not yours Christopher."

Enzo made eye contact with Hewitson who reacted, "Please call me Chris if you like, but I prefer Hewey. It confuses the enemy!"

This totally lightened the mood and from that point on Enzo connected with *'Hewey'*, who took out from his briefcase a large *'His Brief'* and gave it to Enzo, explaining, "This contains my file and our orders. There is a copy of the order for each of us to read together at this meeting. When we have finished, they need to be returned to this envelope and given to Enzo to put in his safe."

The documents were accordingly distributed and read.

On a date yet to be determined, the Italian ex-POWs who were to be repatriated, would board the Valletta for processing, prior to the ship's departure from Liverpool on first March. These ex-POWs were specifically selected to assist in the work for which the Valletta was being sent to Naples. They included engineers, medical orderlies, and a few doctors. Twenty-four Queen Alex Nurses and thirty-six auxiliary nurses would also be sent. Apart from the specialists, the remaining ex-POWs would be a cross-section of soldiers of various ranks in the Italian Army. Enzo would have complete command through his officers.

Naples had an active black market, being supplied through allied military personnel. The level of provisions going missing was beginning to have an impact on supply lines to the front. The *Camorra* was known to be using blackmail, by setting *'honey traps'* with young women as bait, as well as cultivating greed and corruption amongst the troops.

The Valletta in Naples would be the *'Honey Pot'* to trap the *Camorra* leadership. Enzo and Hewey's roles were to be established as Officers *'open to do business'*. They would use the *Camorra* foot soldiers being returned to their *'Capos'* in Naples, to convince their leaders that the Valletta could do business with them and that it was not a regular hospital ship.

Within the ex-POWs on board the ship were those who had connections with the *Camorra* and had agreed to co-operate and work with the British Forces in identifying and contacting the *Camorra* leadership.

The orders, having been read and properly understood, were handed to Enzo, who dutifully placed them back into the folder and, in the presence of the others, locked it away in his safe.

He resumed his seat. Hewey began to explain codes, technical and other operational matters. He concluded, "The codename for this operation will be known only to us four and a selected few at Command. The codename is simple, Valletta."

All nodded in consensus.

Now six-forty. Time had flown. Enzo needed to call Angela at seven and wanted complete privacy. The meeting had come to a natural halt. They would regroup later for dinner as Norman Butler's guests.

Ed, seeing them depart, came briefly in to clear up the teacup and replace the chairs around the wardroom. He looked at Enzo. "Will that be all, sir?"

"Thank you, Ed, it will. Can you see I am not disturbed for the next hour or so? I am going to telephone my wife."

Proud acknowledged and left.

Chapter 16

A Glass of Vermouth

With a large degree of excitement and anticipation, Enzo picked up the black mouthpiece, dialled nine for an outside line, got through to the long-distance operator who then promptly connected him to the main switchboard of the Royal Station Hotel. Bernardo had primed his telephonist to expect the call and to put it through to his office. All went like clockwork as Enzo heard the deep tones of his father-in-law's voice.

"Hello son, how are you?" Bernardo asked.

"Sad to be away from you all, especially my beautiful wife!" said Enzo.

"How was your trip?" his father-in-law asked.

"Slept through it all. Papa! From Durham right through until eight in the morning," he replied.

"The drinks worked then!" Bernardo laughed. *"Gilda sends her love. Take care of yourself! I'll pass you over to Angela. I will leave you both to talk in private. Ciao!"*

Bernardo handed the telephone to his daughter.

"Ciao husband. I miss you so very much!"

Angela became increasingly tearful as she spoke.

Enzo, too emotional to speak, sent her kisses down the telephone as he tried to compose himself. He then attempted to lighten the mood.

"Some Saint Valentine's Day we had yesterday with me

having to board a train and leave you for the first time ever!"

That was the wrong thing to say, and it set her off crying again. It was soon apparent to him that anything he said would not help console her.

"If only there was some way, I could come down that telephone line to you and be there with you right now, I would!" he told his wife lovingly.

"That's impossible, Enzo! I am sorry that I am making it difficult for you. I promise that I will be strong. At least we will be able to speak by telephone two or three times a week!" Angela said between sobs.

"True. And you can always call me as I have a direct line. Let me give you the number."

At the other end of the line, his wife scribbled down the number on a hotel notepad, tore the paper off the pad. Visibly committing the number to memory, folded it and put it in her handbag.

"If I am not here when you call, a message will be taken and I will get back to you as soon as possible. Angela, next to this telephone is a photograph of us when we came out of the church, right here on my desk, which is in the room next to my bedroom."

"Enzo, it's good to know that you are safe, and it has not yet been twenty-four hours since you left. You know I love you and miss you, but it's best we keep our call short this time. I am sorry I am so upset, but it's the realisation that you are not on your way back from the RVI, but far away!"

"I understand, my darling, we will speak at the same time on Thursday. I will call you as close to this time as possible. Give my love to your parents and thank Papa again for the use of the hotel telephone. I love you."

"I love you too, Enzo. Take care, I am praying to San

Gennaro to look after you. God Bless!"

Angela blew a kiss to her absent husband and gently replaced the receiver on its stand. With her other hand she wiped away the tears with her lace handkerchief and left the room to join her father.

Enzo sat at his desk looking at the redundant telephone and reminisced to himself. The photograph on his desk, a simple snap taken by a wedding guest that he had enlarged. The camera had caught that special unguarded moment of joy and love between two people that were to spend the rest of their lives together.

There was a rap on the door. Enzo looked his watch; he had been on the telephone to Angela longer than he thought and he had to get ready for dinner.

"It's me, Hewey, can I come in?"

Enzo had to stop for a split second to remember who *'Hewey'* was.

"Of course, come in!" The intelligence major wasted no time in entering the quarters. Dressed in his formal Mess uniform he walked in with a bottle of white vermouth and two glasses.

"Now then, Colonel, you need to get yourself dressed and I will pour us both a nice aperitif," he gently admonished as he clinked the glass tumblers on the desk, proceeding to splash two good measures from the new bottle with all the skill of an experienced barman. Enzo took no persuading. Hewey seemed to know exactly what was required to deal with his CO's nostalgia.

"*Salute!* And good health to us, Enzo," Hewey toasted as both glasses met.

Enzo reciprocated the toast.

Hewey then broke into Italian with Enzo, *"As you will obviously recognise, the Italian I speak is with the accent of the north and easily distinguishable from that spoken in the south. I also have no knowledge of the Neapolitan dialect, which I understand is a bit like Welsh is to the English. It would be a great help to me, if when we are in private like this, we speak in Italian."*

Knocking back his Vermouth and moving to the bedroom to get ready, Enzo put his glass down on his desk and said, *"That is a great idea. I can teach you some Neapolitan too!"*

Enzo donned his own formal mess uniform, Hewey replenished the vacant glasses, ready for another toast before they set off to dinner.

There were eight at dinner that night in the Captain's Suite, Norman Butler's First Officer, Nick Prior. Betty in her navy-blue low-necked cocktail dress. She had brought with her Captain Patti Colvin, a dark, curly-haired career nurse in her mid-twenties. Patti also wore an elegant cocktail dress but one which would not upstage her Major. She promptly got Hewey's attention. Roger Hill too, brought his deputy, Captain Frank Potter.

Norman and Enzo sat at each end, with the ladies between the two men on either flank of the table. Norman seated his guests. Hewey made sure he sat next to Patti. A belated Christmas meal with turkey that had been stored as surplus from the crew's Yuletide festivities was enjoyed by all

The next few days came and went quickly as the team carried out their duties before the arrival of POWs. Before he knew it Thursday had arrived. Enzo made certain that nineteen-hundred hours was kept free, and he was not to be disturbed. His telephone calls to Angela would take precedence over all else.

"Angela. I have missed you so much, I ache and I..."

She stopped him in mid-sentence blurting down the

110

telephone so excitedly, *"I am coming to see you this weekend and will stay a full week with you!"*

Shocked and stunned. Had his favourite Saint done it again?

Agog he demanded, *"What do you mean, coming to see me this weekend? How?"*

"I will catch the train at the same time tomorrow as you did on Monday. I should arrive at the same time too!" Angela explained.

"How did all this happen?"

Colonel Aldridge had requested Angela come to see him at Fenham Barracks, earlier that day, and gave her a first-class travel warrant valid for seven days for her to travel to Liverpool. The warrant was valid for one week. Norman Butler had made conditions. She remained with Enzo in his quarters on board the Valletta and Enzo had to continue with normal duties during her visit.

Chapter 17

A Toast

In order to qualify as a midwife Angela had first trained as a nurse, registered with the Royal College of Nursing and then specialised in midwifery. Betty and Patti would have reached minimum competency and had experience in midwifery as part of their general nurses training and education. Operation Valletta was geared to offer a range of hospital services to the community of Naples, which included midwifery to be provided by Betty's team.

There had been another purpose in Colonel Aldridge giving Angela the week-long travel warrants to visit Enzo. He had briefed Betty to consider the possibility of Angela joining her team. Enlisting her into the Nursing Corps would be prudent not only because she was a good practising midwife but because, like her husband, she was from the targeted region, spoke the dialect and knew the area. Receptive to Aldridge's plan, Betty shared it with her deputy Patti prior to Enzo's arrival. If all went well, Colonel Aldridge did not expect Angela to be using the return portion of her travel warrant, staying on the Valletta with her husband.

Saturday could not come quickly enough for Enzo. He checked and double checked with Ed that all arrangements were in place for them both to go and pick Angela up from Liverpool's Lime Street Station. Enzo telephoned Bernardo that morning, just to make sure that she had boarded the train and that it had left on time.

Lime Street Station was less than a mile away and even though it would have taken just over ten minutes to walk, Enzo, not wanting to be late, left an hour early. Ed drove the car provided for the ship's officers' use while in port. He did not need to be told to stay with the car when they reached the station. Knowing his place, he volunteered to park the car and await the return of the couple.

Half an hour on the platform on a cold drizzly Saturday morning, seemed like half a day; even worse when the train seemed to take forever to come to a stop. Enzo's heart was pounding significantly harder when he could not see Angela as the first-class carriage went by him. Even though she was standing up in the compartment. The carriage continued past her waiting husband before it came to a halt.

Steam pressure released from the engine hissed, forming clouds which obscured visibility. Then cleared. Angela had already stepped down from the train onto the Platform. She waited nervously outside the next carriage down from where he stood, with her suitcase by her side. He recognised the outline of her body before the steam cleared and ran towards her. Nothing was said. Enzo kissed her passionately and held her body as close to him as was possible. No words could express how much they had missed each other or, indeed, how in much in love they were. That was a given.

Enzo picked up Angela's suitcase and they both headed off to the car. Corporal Ed, who was keeping a lookout for his passengers, saw them approaching. Hurriedly stubbed out the Woodbine cigarette he had been smoking and put the remaining half back into the packet, which he stuffed back into the right breast pocket of his tunic. Straightened his cap in the wing mirror, and smartly advanced to meet Lieutenant-Colonel and Mrs Falcone. Relieved Enzo of Angela's suitcase.

"I'll take that, sir. Welcome, Mrs. Falcone, Ma'am."

Norman Butler, Betty, Roger and *'Hewey'* were at the dockside to meet them. As Master of the Valletta Norman greeted them.

"Enzo, I am sure that Angela would like to freshen up or rest for a while and that you would like to spend some time together. I will arrange for a meal to be brought to your quarters."

He then turned to Ed and instructed him, "Corporal Proud, speak to Chef and let him know when the Colonel and Mrs Falcone are ready to eat."

"Yes, sir," responded Ed, standing to attention, before continuing with the suitcase to Enzo's quarters.

Before he let them go, Norman told the couple, "I have arranged for a special dinner to be held in your honour Angela. In my quarters tonight at eight-thirty sharp!"

Food was the last thing on their mind. They hungered for the warmth of each other's body, the connection that made two into one. Left undisturbed, they renewed a honeymoon which had been all too short.

Physical passion dissipated, they lay in bed side by side in each other's arms.

"Oh, Enzo," Angela sighed, *"I don't know how I am going to make it through this war without you."*

Enzo lovingly squeezed her tightly and whispered, *"I'm not sure how I will do without you either."*

He kissed her tenderly.

A sudden blast from a passing tug's navigation horn awoke the pair who had fallen into a deep slumber.

Noticing the time Angela jumped up. *"Come on, Enzo! Look at the time. You order lunch while I unpack. Then I'll go and shower and get dressed."*

Ed arrived with lunch and set it out on the wardroom table while Enzo washed.

Angela seized the opportunity to do a Gilda interrogation of *'Jeeves'*. Her husband was going to be spending more time with this Corporal than with her over the next few months, so she needed to *'suss'* him out and see what made him tick.

"Where are you from, Ed?" she asked.

"Washington, County Durham," Ed responded.

"Are you married?" Angela enquired casually.

"No, Ma'am. Still looking!" he quipped. Angela changed tack. "Ed, do you know Newcastle at all?"

The Corporal smiled. "Come there every time I can, when Newcastle United are playing at home."

Angela grinned. "You support them then?"

Ed's eyes sparkled as he explained, "My dad started taking me when I was about six. We would get up early, catch the bus into Worswick Street Bus Station and walk up through town. He would always take me for an ice cream at the cafe by the lake in Leazes Park. I have supported the *'Toon'* ever since."

Angela chuckled. "What a co-incidence, my family run that cafe and that is where my husband and I met!" Angela called to her husband to join them and recounted what she had just been told by Ed Proud. He marvelled that she had been able to get more personal details out of his Corporal in five minutes, than he had been able to do all week.

Chapter 18

Angela Aboard

The second dinner party in a week on board the Valletta was not an uncommon occurrence for its Captain, Commander Norman Butler. No real excuse was needed but Angela's visit was a good one, if he needed it. Not turkey this time; Chef had been able to dig some pork from the ship's freezer. Unlike everyone else at the table, Angela had no insight into military protocols, or the idioms used by officers in their conversations.

Enzo was engrossed with Norman, reminiscing about when he had been aboard the Valletta previously. Betty, Patti, Roger and Frank were in a four-way discussion about their work. Angela was happy to sit beside her husband and just watch and speak when spoken to. For her, it was a new world and she enjoyed just being with Enzo, taking it all in.

Whilst everyone else was eating, pausing to talk, taking another mouthful, talking more, sipping on their wine, pausing again, then more talk and more food. Hewey took the direct route of eating the food while it was fresh and hot and then talking. His philosophy was *'talk won't get cold but the food will!'* Major Hewitson had created a number of what he termed *'Hewey's Rules'* and this was one of them. It meant that he not only ate his food whilst it was at its best but, more importantly, he was usually first to finish. While everyone else continued to meander through their course, he would be able to sit back, assess their body language; listen to their conversations; join in if he wished and, in his own way, manipulate what was going on.

On evenings such as this, Hewey's attention was, covertly, centred on Patti who he had every intention of pursuing when the time was right. Tonight however, Angela Falcone had his interest, a beautiful woman, with such classical Mediterranean features, the wife of his commanding officer. He chose a moment when she paused to take a drink of white wine from her glass and spoke to Angela in Italian, *"Do you prefer white wine or red wine with pork, Signora Falcone?"*

A question more sophisticated than just the usual small talk. He thought.

"Major Hewitson. It all depends on how the pork is cooked. If it is prepared with an apple or pear sauce, then a nice white fruity wine, such as we have been served. On the other hand, if it is served with plum, cranberry or blackberry sauce, a good medium-bodied fruity red wine will complement the pork. How about you, Major, what is your preference?"

Enzo looked at Hewey as if to say *'fifteen-love to Angela'.*

And so, the Banter between the two continued. Patti joined the set and then Betty, who began to quiz Angela about her experience. Hewey took the opportunity to give his full attention to Patti.

It soon arrived time for the after-dinner Port or Brandy. Patti and Angela were the only two to take Port. Betty and the men preferred the Courvoisier.

"Let's um… make a toast!" announced Norman in voice showing a slight hint of alcoholic slur. "To the Valletta and all who serve on her. God keep us and return us home safe and sound!"

Each then made their own toast, Enzo making sure that his

would be the last, before they all retired. More drinks poured.

"I would like to make a special toast to my wife and my new family here on the Valletta."

Betty and Patti looked at each other. The Falcones were in for a big surprise. They raised their glasses and toasted Mrs Falcone.

Chapter 19

Breaking the News

Even though just recently married and with a long-term separation only days away, the couple's relationship had a maturity that did not need them to be in each other's pockets.

Enzo had to see to his duties, preparing for the arrival of the ex-POWs to be repatriated and going through their individual files with Hewey. Angela had already bonded with Betty and Patti, spending much of her time in the hospital wing of the ship with the *'girls'* as she would call them. Enzo would frown at the thought of Betty being called *'a girl'*.

That morning Betty contacted Colonel Aldridge with approval of his plan to enlist Angela into the nursing corps on the Valletta. She was going to be an ideal addition to the team.

All the ship's crew had to be inoculated against Typhoid, Smallpox and Cholera, which was scheduled to be done on that day. The POWs would arrive the following Monday and they would get their shots en route to Naples. Only half of the nurses they were expecting had arrived, leaving Betty's company depleted and understaffed. Enzo had decided that all medically qualified personnel would be made available to administer the vaccine. It would require two days to vaccinate the full complement of six hundred men and officers who made up the Valletta's crew.

Angela volunteered to administer and supervise the nurses

who were giving the Cholera shots. It had been a long time since Enzo had given any mass injections, but he rolled up his sleeves and worked with Angela. Betty and her team did the Typhoid queue and Patti's Group, the Smallpox. Roger worked with Betty and Frank with Patti. The queues had formed at ten, with an hour's break for lunch at noon, then a further break of thirty minutes at fifteen-hundred hours. The medics had given all the first batch of shots by seventeen-hundred hours on Thursday evening, and on Friday the last round was completed by fourteen-hundred hours. The medical personnel were exhausted.

Norman held his third and last dinner party of the week in the Captain's Quarters. As it was to be a special occasion, he requested of his chef a traditional English roast beef dinner with Yorkshire puddings. Chef had no beef in the ship's stores and beef was not easy to get in these times. Norman assigned Hewey the task of sourcing the beef.

"Not a problem, Skipper."

A couple of hours later he proudly produced the goods.

Enzo wisecracked to his wife in Italian.

"I think perhaps Hewey had some help from San Gennaro!"

"I understood that, Enzo!" said Hewey.

As far as Angela was concerned this was to be her *'last supper'* on this final night aboard the Valletta before returning to Newcastle the next day.

Little did she know of the offer she was about to receive. Supper complete, Hewey, rose to his feet a waving a box of cigars in one hand and a bottle of Port in the other.

"To the Bridge, Gentlemen, please! The Bridge, Norman. To the Bridge!"

Taking her cue, Betty as the most senior female officer present, announced.

"Ladies, let's us all move to the Wardroom for a quiet chat and nightcap"

Betty smiled and nodded. The five men then filed out of the mess room to the bridge, through the open door, which was gently clunked shut by the orderly, who had followed the officers out.

Entering the Wardroom, Betty and Patti ushered Angela to a pre-arranged private convenient corner with three well upholstered leather armchairs. Angela was motioned to the middle chair, Betty and Patti took those either side. Betty came straight to the point.

"Angela, there was good reason why Colonel Aldridge got you here to the Valletta. To be blunt, he wants you to join us. Your experience and qualifications speak for themselves. From our conversations about your work at the RVI you are well suited for what we have in mind."

Taken completely by surprise. "What is that?" Angela asked.

"Once we arrive in Naples, the Valletta has been tasked to provide a comprehensive medical facility and assist in the restructuring of the public health care. Even though Patti and I did some midwifery in our basic nurse training. We are not fully trained midwives. Colonel Aldridge sees you as being more than capable of filling that gap. Now we have had the opportunity to meet you, we wholeheartedly agree! So, will you join us?"

Betty intentionally put her on the spot for a reaction.

Wide eyed, Angela had taken it all in but took a few extended seconds to compose and control her thoughts. A long sip of port. She put down her glass.

"It sounds very exciting and totally unexpected."

Patti interjected, "You knowing Naples well and speaking the language are added bonuses to being so well qualified. So too, is the fact that you are married to the Officer in Charge of this operation."

Patti paused to give Angela time to think. Then added, "On a personal level, Betty and I felt an immediate connection with you. The three of us will make a great team."

"Does Enzo know anything about this proposition?" Angela asked.

"No, nothing at all! As he is in charge of this operation. He will have to give his approval," Betty said emphatically.

Angela smiled, "I will speak to Enzo. So, Betty what happens once he approves?"

"Colonel Aldridge has initiated the documentation needed to enlist you as a Captain in the Nursing Corps, subject to your consent and the approval of the team. The required paperwork is already aboard the Valletta for you to sign."

"Great, I will sign them tomorrow."

All three women clinked their glasses to *'seal the deal'*.

The Wardroom door swung open. Captain Butler and his officers entered the room, glasses and cigars half consumed in hand.

"What have you lot been conspiring?" Hewey asked with slight alcoholic slur in his voice.

"Enzo darling, I am coming with you on the Valletta to Naples!" effervesced an excited Angela.

Before an astonished Enzo and bemused Hewey had any chance to react Norman suggested a final nightcap of cognac to toast the new addition to the ship's complement.

Except for Norman Butler, Enzo had seen more action than any of the officers in his team. He may have never fired a shot, but he had been shot at, bombed and seen at first hand the carnage of battle. Under the stress of these conditions, he was able to keep his cool; organise, manage, support and encourage his staff, as well as the injured and wounded under his care.

Saturday morning, at the time Enzo had arranged to telephone his in-laws of his wife's safe departure, was when they were told of Angela's being commissioned into the Nursing Corps.

"Angela. You have done the right thing. You and Enzo should be together and look after each other. I will pass you on to your mother 'Captain Falcone'. We love you both, be safe and come back to us soon!"

Sniffing back the tears he handed the telephone to Gilda who had already been wiping her eyes with a handkerchief.

"You are a very brave girl," said her mother in a voice broken with emotion.

"We are very proud of you and respect the decision you've made. Enzo is a good man and I know he and San Gennaro will keep you safe. Please, go and see Teresa as soon as you can. Make sure they are all safe. Papa and I will pray for your safe passage and return!"

Angela emotional and in tears, handed the back to Enzo.

"Mama, we still have a few days before we leave," Enzo said trying to console his mother-in-law.

"We will call you at the hotel tomorrow, after Mass."

"Thank you, son, we love you and we can speak tomorrow."

With that, Gilda hung up.

Chapter 20

The Departure

Norman had requested that the Valletta's carpenter make alterations to Enzo's sleeping quarters to accommodate a double bunk for Angela and Enzo. It was rare but not unusual for ships captains and their officers to have their spouses aboard; the exception in this case was that husband and wife were both serving officers. Furthermore, the double occupancy freed up space elsewhere aboard.

Even if he had not planned to get up early that morning, with all the shouting, banging, clanking and engine noises going on, there was no way Enzo would have slept through that racket. He dressed himself in his battle fatigues and at the earlier invitation of Norman, joined him on the ship's bridge to watch it leave port.

Angela, for the first time in her new uniform, joined the other officers as a full roll call was taken of all crew and officers on board. Roger had been put in charge of checking all the ex-POWs were present. Betty was assigned to check and confirm a full complement of medical, nursing and supporting staff. Satisfied that all were confirmed aboard, Norman had ordered all gang planks be withdrawn and the ship's cables be released. Those aboard the Valletta who were able to come out on deck and view the departure had done so.

A very heavy clonk of iron coming from the river side of the ship vibrated the whole of that side of the Valletta as another vessel came alongside.

Over the last few days, the Chief Engineer and his team had been industriously getting everything *'shipshape and ready to roll'*. Now the time had come to start both engines for departure. Freed from its ties portside, Captain Butler gave the order.

"Slow ahead".

The Valletta inched away from the dock with the Pilot's launch ahead of it, giving three toots of its high-pitched horn as if to say.

'Follow me!'

The Valletta with three deep blasts of its own horn retorted.

'Lead the way!'

Into the outward-bound lane of the Mersey. The newly refitted Hospital Ship began picking up speed west toward the Irish Sea. The Valletta would join a convoy comprising a motley collection of two dozen or more such vessels escorted by warships of the Home Fleet.

The Germans had lost the Battle of the Atlantic but still had stray opportunist *'Wolf Packs'* of submarines harassing allied shipping when possible. US convoys of merchantmen and warships bound for the Mediterranean sailed along the north of Ireland and linked up with the convoy the Valletta joined. This massive convoy entered the Irish Sea proceeding into the Bay of Biscay then via the Gibraltar Straits into the Med.

Enzo stayed on the Bridge most of the day. Angela joined Betty and Patti who were to spend the next few days training and briefing their nursing staff. Next, they were to ensure that all had been given the required inoculations. Angela was to select those nurses and auxiliaries who had midwifery training or wished to be trained as midwives. She was to form them into a specialist section, directly under her command, for when they arrived in Naples. Nursing staff would rotate in three eight-hour shifts, zero-six-hundred hours to fourteen-hundred hours, fourteen-hundred hours to twenty-two-hundred hours and the third twenty-two-hundred hours to zero-six-hundred hours. Betty, Patti and Angela would each have charge of their own shift, when on duty they would have total command of the nursing staff. This also meant that Angela would be on night shift duty while Enzo slept.

When the Valletta eventually got out into the open Irish Sea there were ships as far as the eye could see. Smoke billowing from funnels in unison. Directed by the officer commanding the convoy's escort the Mersey flotilla took their allocated positions. As they did so they were greeted by a chorus of all sorts of ship's whistles and horns. Norman had been ordered to manoeuvre the Valletta to its designated position without the convoy having to slow down. Its position and cruising speed were to be maintained throughout the voyage. By sunset, the Valletta was neatly tucked into place. The convoy was collectively averaging between eighteen to twenty-one knots an hour. Weather permitting, it would take three to five days sailing to reach Gibraltar.

Hewey joined the rest on the bridge, as the Valletta was negotiating the Mersey estuary. Picked up a pair of binoculars, like the others, and viewed the vast armada their hospital ship was about to join. He took particular interest in the fact that the British Home Fleet had been joined by elements of the US Sixth Fleet en route to Naples. From previous joint-intelligence reports he knew that, on board one of the American Cruisers was 'Lucky Luciano'. The Notorious Chicago gangster the Americans had decided to release and deport to Naples. There, he was expected to co-ordinate the 'Mafia' gangs to work with and help the Americans in their administration. British Military Intelligence including Hewey were very sceptical of these plans. MI6 and SOE had better ideas, which were not as crude as those proposed by their *'Cousins'* from across *'the Pond'*.

Hewey began speaking to Enzo in Italian, in confidence, as they watched the merging of the ships into the Convoy.

"Tomorrow we need to get started and I will give you a full briefing. I have brought this for you",

He handed Enzo a small briefcase he had brought up to the Bridge.

"Take that back with you and read it tonight. It sets out in greater detail how we see things differently to the Yanks when it comes to restructuring and rehabilitating Naples. We want to develop our own contacts and keep an eye on Uncle Sam's Boys and what they get up to. This ship may give us the trump card with the locals at all levels."

"And here I am, thinking that I was being put in charge of a medical facility, which is complicated enough, and now you tell me I am also part of a big undercover intelligence operation."

"Not exactly true, Enzo, but you are right about it being an undercover operation. It is also a good medical facility. We intend to provide bona fide support to help rebuild the social and physical infrastructure of a city which has been the most severely bombed in Italy. Nothing can be achieved without local support. The Americans are seeking to do that through the links with Camorra in Naples and the Sicilian Cosa Nostra. As I have already told you, our approach will be different."

"Is it fully explained in here?" asked Enzo holding up the brown envelope.

"I believe that it paints a general picture for you and opens a discussion we will have between now and when we arrive. Our plan is to harness the influential Neapolitan families including

those of the underworld and gain their co-operation. They have
no idea of our intentions. You will have heard of the head of the
Camorra family, as their home is not far from where your family
lives!"

Hewey brought the conversation to an abrupt end. Norman
had called them over from the starboard side of the bridge, to join
him for supper in the galley with the rest of the retiring day-
watch.

Reverting into King's English. Hewey told Enzo, "We will
meet tomorrow morning at about ten. We can continue then!"

Chapter 21

Side Effects

Norman approached the two officers.

"Now that we have set sail, I need to have a conference with you all, to discuss rules aboard ship while at sea. Apart from my crew, Enzo, you are the only one on board who has experience at sea in this ship. Each voyage is different, and the rules must be adapted accordingly. When you were last aboard, Enzo, this was exclusively a hospital ship, now it has undergone conversion to repatriate prisoners and provide a multi-functional medical facility for when we get to our destination."

Captain Butler beckoned them into his duty room just off the bridge, where they could talk more privately.

All three sat down and were served tea by one of the ratings. Butler then took on a serious business tone and began to set out. "I want to have a meeting with our executive team tomorrow at zero-nine-hundred hours in my wardroom. Betty has already organised a three-shift system for her command, but we need to consider the rest of the personnel we have on board. We need to agree rules of conduct, a briefing timetable, organise personnel according to their expertise and skills that can be utilised during the voyage as well as for the operation. This needs to be done before Betty and her team start the next round of inoculations."

That said, the three men finished off their tea and were just about to leave when Betty knocked on the duty room door and entered. *'Other ranks'* being present Butler assumed formality.

"What is it, Major?" he asked the Chief Nurse.

"Sir, we have several down, suffering from the side effects of the typhoid shots, as well as *'seasickness'*, including my deputy Captain Colvin!"

"How many sick have we got?"

"Twenty-four as of ten minutes ago but there are likely to be more!"

"No question of turning back, Betty!"

"I understand that, sir, and this is not entirely unexpected. We have a contingency plan in place, but it means that there will have to be a certain amount of quarantine and isolation for a few days. Of course, the inoculation program will be set back until we are sure no more will present with these side effects. Details of my proposed contingencies are in here."

The Chief Nurse then placed a sheaf of papers on his table.

"For your comments and approval, sir. As you will see. With some of my staff affected I may need assistance from officers and personnel on board."

"Thank you, Major, as usual I see you have everything in hand and of course you will have whatever assistance you need."

He smiled at her. She turned and was about to leave, when Norman added in a softer tone, "Betty, what about you? Are you OK?"

"Yes, sir I am fine, thanks. I have had so many of these jabs I am immune to them all," she quipped.

"Once we get these youngsters sorted out, they will be fine too, sir. "

Norman glanced at the first couple of pages of the papers Betty had left. He promptly handed them to Enzo.

"OK, Enzo, your baby, I think. I assume you know what is

in here?"

"Of course, Norman, I will get things rolling. First thing is to identify who we have among the re-patriots with qualifications and field experience that may be of use and interview them. Betty will get on with her side of things."

"Anything I can do?" asked Hewey.

"I am sure that Betty will find you something." Enzo chuckled.

"I have never known a woman who can make tasks appear out of nowhere like she can. Even in the quietest of times."

Having been told that Patti was unwell with the symptoms. Seizing a possible opportunity to get close Patti, Hewey took it upon himself to find Betty. Preoccupied dispatching her staff in all directions. He volunteered.

"Can I be of any help, Betty?"

"Well, without medical training there is not much I can get you to do at the moment, but I will let you know."

That was not what he wanted to hear. Disappointed the downhearted Hewey went to walk away, when Betty called after him.

"You could go and see if Patti is doing all right in her quarters. I'll pop in when I can and have given her the meds she needs, but she must drink plenty of fluids. She probably feels quite sorry for herself, and a cheery word may help."

Better than he expected. He beamed and nodded.

"I can do that! I'll call into the Mess and find something as a treat."

In true Hewey style he had commandeered one of the Mess orderlies to follow him down to Patti's cabin with orange juice and ice. There she lay in bed, flushed and perspiring. Pleasantly surprised at the attention she was getting.

"Oh, Hewey, you shouldn't be here."

"Oh yes, M' lady, I can be here."

The orderly, poured her a tumbler of the juice from the jug, tonged in one large ice cube. Placed his tray on the bedside cabinet and took his leave.

"Major Betty's suggestion in fact. She wanted me to check you are OK and here I am."

"Thank you," she said quietly.

"May I?"

He asked if he was allowed to sit on the side of her bed.

She nodded. He leaned forward and brushed a stray lock of hair from her face. Concerned, he asked her, "Is there anything you need?"

Taking hold of his hand she softly answered, "No, Hewey, I will be fine in a couple of days, but when you are not too busy, I would appreciate the company. It will get a bit lonely shut up here all day!"

Squeezing her hand gently, Hewey told her, "No problem at all it will be my pleasure."

At this, Hewey reluctantly got up to leave. "Now be a good girl and drink up your juice. It is important we get you up and about as quickly as possible, you are already being missed. Get some sleep and I will be back to see you soon."

He leant over her and kissed her lightly on the forehead. Patti smiled.

Chapter 22

Executive Meeting

The executive team met at zero-nine-hundred hours, as Captain Butler had requested, in his wardroom. Betty advised that due to Patti's sickness Angela would be acting as her deputy for Patti until further notice. Then would continue as an ordinary board member.

Norman opened the meeting and required from Betty a status report.

"Another fifteen-needing quarantine, ten of whom were from the ship's crew. The contingency plan I gave you yesterday is being followed and seems to be working well."

He duly took a note for later entry into the Ship's log.

Betty continued, "I would, however, request that an announcement be made today to everyone aboard explaining that the quarantine is to protect those who have not yet been inoculated. It must be emphasised that this is not Typhus or cholera suffering but only side effects. Those who have been inoculated and showing no side effects are completely immune and can continue as normal."

"Betty, how many more do you expect will suffer these side effects?"

"No more than a couple in the next twenty-four hours as the incubation period would run out by then. I expect everyone to be recovered within three to four days thereafter, providing there are no complications."

"Thank you, Betty, keep me informed. Now let's move on. The next point I want to address is the rules aboard ship."

"Before we leave that subject, Norman" interjected Roger.". "Instead of inoculating all the Repatriates at once, we have decided to start giving the shots in minimum batches of fifty every day starting today. That should minimise any side effects and be easier to manage. A medical history is needed from everyone. After that is completed, we will be better able to identify those who may be likely to have an adverse reaction. Each will then be given their jabs."

"Sound idea," complimented Butler.

Roger continued, "We will work through them alphabetically. Betty, Frank and Angela and I, together with other medics and senior nursing staff. I am allowing thirty minutes to take the medical history and give the shots. Might take longer depending on language. This afternoon, Angela, Betty and I, will first do histories and give inoculation to those that we have identified to act as our interpreters."

Roger paused for his deputy Frank to pick up.

"Sir, I will be taking care of the logistics and administration. We want to commence the alphabetical process at zero-nine-hundred hours tomorrow morning. In order to get a clean start, we need to make an announcement over the ship's PA system explaining the process. I have taken the liberty of drafting the text in English for your approval and Angela has done the translation."

Frank handed the proposed text to Norman for his review.

Captain Butler took time and read out the text to all present, then promptly initialled it and handed it back to Frank.

"Great! Looks like that side of things are in good shape and proceeding well! Now, let's move on to the rest of my agenda. We have several hundred men aboard this ship who have not been home for a long time. Some are married, others are single. Except for Angela there are approximately eighty unmarried women on board. Such a mix can make the efficient running of this ship problematic. I am a realist and understand that it would be both absurd and not practical to introduce rules to segregate men and women on board, or to try and regulate relationships. Provided that the efficient running, management, safety of this ship, its crew or anyone on board is not put in jeopardy, there will be no restrictions. I will expect you officers to enforce any breach of military discipline. Only at the very last resort do I want to have to deal with any of those matters. Are we agreed?"

All present nodded their consent.

"In that case I need to speak with Enzo and Hewey on other matters. Thank you for your attendance. There is no need to have regular Executive meetings, I will call them only when needed."

As the group was about to exit, Norman remembered to ask. "Betty, how is Patti doing?"

"She's comfortable. It should peak within the next twenty-four hours. I expect her back on duty in about three to four days."

"Let me know when you next go visit her, and I will come with you."

The departing group left to get on with their respective tasks. Captain Butler pulled out a copy of the homework that Hewey had set for Enzo.

"Have you digested all this, Enzo?"

"Yes, I have."

"Have you two got yourselves organised?"

Both nodded in sync affirmatively.

"While I do not need to know the specifics of clandestine

ops. You must keep me generally updated for operational reasons. High Command, back in London, expects me to send daily coded reports on your work. Unless you advise me otherwise, I will send a daily message of *'Nothing to Report'*."

"We are going to start with interviewing Private De Cristofaro, when we have finished here. Enzo and I will discuss the format that the interview will take. We will brief you as and when needed, but in any event, either or both of us will give you a daily status report," Hewey explained.

"Sounds fine by me," Norman said, getting up and bringing the meeting to a close. Escorting them both out onto the main deck. He said, "By the way tell the others, my place tonight for dinner, same time."

Hewey intentionally chose a route to the wardroom that would pass by Patti's cabin. Once Norman was out of earshot he suggested to Enzo, "Let's pop in and check on Patti!"

Enzo took no persuading. As her commanding officer he had a duty to check her welfare. Perhaps, an even bigger duty, to help Hewey in his courtship of Captain Colvin. Enzo knocked on Patti's cabin door and was surprised when his wife answered.

Kissing Angela gently on the cheek.

"We were passing and thought we would check in on the patient."

Having heard the arrival of Hewey and Enzo, robed in her ankle length heavy towelling dressing gown tightly fastened around her waist with its sash. Her thick army socks acted as slippers, clutching a steaming hot mug of camomile tea Angela had prepared. Patti came in from her bedroom and sat down in the living area of her quarters. Both men went over to where she sat and kissed her on the cheek, as if she were a sick younger sister.

Hewey pulled up a chair next to her.

"How are you feeling?"

"Not a hundred percent. But I should be through this thing in the next day or two. Nice of you both to pop in."

Angela had assumed the role of Patti's private nurse, housekeeper and secretary. She asked, "Would either of you like some tea or coffee?"

Enzo answered his wife with a mischievous smile.

"Can I have the same as your *'mistress'* please?"

"Make that two," chipped in Hewey.

"Angela was filling me in on what happened at this morning's meeting. You two had a separate brief with Norman about the intelligence side."

"Just in general terms, nothing specific yet. When we leave here, Enzo and I are going to prepare our agenda for interviewing our first of the repatriates, Private Emilio de Cristofaro, who we suspect has contact with the Neapolitan *Camorra*."

"The *Camorra*!" piped up Angela, "That lot in Naples or those in Castellamare, Hewey?"

Appearing to be far more knowledgeable than any of them on the subject.

"What do you mean?"

Angela gave them both their camomile tea, sat down with her mug and began to educate all three.

"For what it is worth, the *Camorristi* from the City used to take the *'Ferragosto'* annual holiday at Castellamare not far from where we lived in Torre del Greco. Eventually they ended up buying property in both places and began controlling the docks and everything south to Calabria including Salerno. They became independent from their city *'brothers'* but are inseparable."

"How do you know about this?" asked an increasingly

interested Hewey.

"Unlike my husband's family, who lived in another world, everyone else knows about the *Camorristi*. They were just there! A fact of life, nothing got done without their say so. They got a percentage of everything, and still do! From what I understand, the Valletta will get nothing done in Naples unless they are involved."

Angela stopped and took a drink of her tea.

Even though he was from a privileged family and knew nothing about the *Camorra*, in his youth, Enzo had heard about underworld activities in Naples. However, it had been through the various newspaper articles which headlined the activities of the *Mafia* in the United States, and specifically New York City, which had educated him on how this criminal organisation functioned and had its roots in Italy.

The group chatted for a while. Seeing that Patti was becoming visibly more fatigued, Angela with her eyes cued the visitors. Both placed their empty mugs on the table and moved to leave.

"Well, Captain Colvin, as your Commanding Officer I am ordering you back to your sick bed!"

Chapter 23

Lucky Luciano

Of course, Enzo had heard of *'Lucky Luciano'*. He wondered how, as a Sicilian-American, he could be expected to have influence on any of the 'Camorra'. It dated back to the eighteenth century, deeply entrenched in the whole cross-section of the Naples and Campania region. They did not, and would not, tolerate interference from anyone. Especially from a high-profile American thug the *'Cousins'* were planning to use. Most likely he was going to get himself killed. Naples was completely under the control of the *Camorra*. Nothing would get done without their involvement and co-operation. With no obvious Head or overt organisational structure, it made it even more difficult for the Allies to identify a Leader with whom to have dialogue and negotiate. The main *'Capos'* of the clans kept a very low p profile, fronting themselves as shopkeepers, stallholders, retirees and local businessman. Locals all knew their respective *'Capos'* but also knew to keep quiet.

British Military Intelligence had rejected proposals put forward by the United States Naval Intelligence promoting the use of Luciano to gain the co-operation of the Sicilian Mafia. As far as they were concerned, he would be a *'dead man walking'* the minute he set foot in Naples. He would be more use to them in Sicily. The Brits would try to make separate contact with the *Camorra*. Hewey had been tasked to do just that with Enzo.

Reports made by field interrogators of Italian prisoners soon after capture, were subsequently used to categorise and classify prisoners. A trawl was made of these reports to pick out those POWs who were from Naples. They would then be further interviewed while aboard the Valletta to ascertain any connections with the Camorra. Some men were genuinely ignorant; others said they knew nothing, but clearly did. Nobody admitted being a *Camorristi* or knowing one. What did become apparent in these follow up interrogations was that there existed various levels of influence that the *Camorra* had. It went high up. These influential people never got their hands dirty.

Hewey had conducted an in-depth analysis of all the field reports, statements and interrogation summaries and concluded that there was one POW of interest. Without advising his superiors of his suspicions he made sure that he was included in the POWs transferred to the Valletta for repatriation to Naples. Enzo and then Norman Butler were the only two he shared this information with when he gave them his confidential dossier to read.

Emilio De Cristofaro, known to all as *'Leo'*, was a gentlemen's tailor by trade. Interrogation revealed that his family had been tailors to the *'Savino' Camorra* clan. For generations his family had suited the Savino family. Through this connection, the *'De Cristofaro Brothers, Bespoke Tailors'*, had encountered the *'Vomero Camorra Clan'*. The report went on to describe the Vomero district as "a hilly and urbanised area in the centre of Naples, inhabited by the wealthy middle classes". Leo explained that his uncle and father were the tailors of other *Camorra* clans; The Arenella Clan, to the north, Soccavo and Fourigrotta Clans to the west, Chiaia clan to the south, Montecalvario Clan to the east, and the Avvocata Clan in the Northeast. Until conscripted into the army, Leo worked with his father Antonio and Uncle Nicola. Their tailor's shop was opposite the Vesuvian Railway Terminus in Naples. Leo was expected to carry on the tailoring business when he returned after the War.

As far as Hewey was concerned Leo could become the main conduit to the Camorra. Once he had read through the brief Hewey had provided Enzo came to the same conclusion. This potential British asset could be the key for dialogue and co-operation with the *Camorra*. Their job was to convince Leo to work with them in implementing Operation Valletta.

Early next morning both officers took their seats in the wardroom. Leo was to be interviewed in his own language. Normally, Hewey would request the guard on duty leave when intelligence matters were the subject of any meeting or interview. Fortunately, the guard neither spoke nor understood Italian. So could stay and be their *'go for'*. Enzo had done the homework Hewey had set for him the previous night and was well prepped. For obvious reasons it had been previously agreed all conversation about the case would be in Italian.

"Enzo, forget all that crap about Lucky Luciano. The Americans are not releasing him, so he was not on that Cruiser I showed you yesterday. As far as we know, they have dropped all plans they had about trying to work with the 'Camorra' in Naples. So, we do not have to worry about the Cousins fucking things up, which they are inclined to do! I have asked 'Jeeves' to fetch us tea and toast in about ten minutes. Private De Cristofaro will be here for interview shortly. Gives you and me time to have a quick cuppa and chat about the format we use."

"Hewey, how do you want to do this? Formally or informal?"

"Not as an interrogation, more conversational. We need to

know in detail what he knows about the Clans, and the families to whom they have allegiance. He needs to be comfortable with us. It needs to be explained from the outset that the purpose of this meeting, and other meetings with him, is to see how best the Valletta can serve the needs of the people in Naples. We must play it very much by ear. It does not matter who leads the questioning. Today will be just an in-depth exploratory conversation to establish the head of topics we will need to explore further."

Ed knocked and entered with his tea tray and warm toast for the officers and placed it on the desk.

"Will that be all, sir?"

"In just under half an hour we have asked a Private De Cristofaro to come and see us. When he arrives, let us know. He will probably be here with us for the rest of the day."

Enzo instructed his Corporal, who gave a nod of acknowledgement, then left the room.

Hewey took up where he had left off.

"Enzo, your local knowledge and speaking the same dialect should relax him. We are not trying to trip him up. Our understanding is that the 'Camorra' pedal and cultivate influence on the highest level, using the 'favours' and 'respect' principles of old. Each of the clans have their respective foot soldiers and enforcers allowed to run their respective rackets with a degree of impunity under the protection of the traditional rules and connections. This an old, well-lubricated, invisible, deniable symbiotic relationship, which has worked well, since before Garibaldi.

"It's an alternative 'black' or 'under the counter' economy and society which, like the Sicilian Mafia, has kept the social structure intact regardless of war or political change. Unlike the Sicilian 'Cosa Nostra', they have kept under the radar and

blended in with the average Giuseppe."

"But what I cannot understand, Hewey, I knew nothing about these families until I read it in this report."

"Well, Enzo, they are either very good at keeping their heads down, or you have led a very sheltered life!"

Chapter 24

The Tailor's Son

Befor Enzo had a chance to reply, voices were heard outside. *'Leo'*, in very broken English. Trying to coach the NCO how to pronounce his name. Ed opened the door after a loud short knock and escorted his charge directly in front of the two seated officers.

"Private... er... Di Christof... ferro, sir," the corporal announced. Turning to the young Private, called him to attention, ordered the removal of his crumpled Italian army-issued cap, slanted on his head, like only a Neapolitan could wear. The anxious soldier stood to a very uncomfortable attention, saluted. Ed like clockwork gave a mechanical sharp salute and marched out.

Leo had no idea why he was there, by now familiar with rank insignia, he could see that they were both British Officers, one a Lieutenant-Colonel and the other a Major. This was the first time he had been so close to British Officers of that rank. Leo's command of English was, at best, the broken pidgin-English he had picked up while a POW. He understood Italian from the north but spoke only the classic dialect of Naples. Leo had no idea that these two senior officers were about to conduct an interview in his mother tongue.

Leo stood a short while silent in confused stunned shock when Enzo introduced himself and Hewey in his Neapolitan.

"How is it that you speak Neapolitan so well, Colonel?"

Lieutenant-Colonel Vincenzo Falcone invited Leo to sit down. Hewey, in fluent Italian then proceeded to give the Private a five-minute explanation as to how Enzo came to be serving in the British Army. Followed by a short introduction of himself.

"Colonel, can you explain to me why you want to speak to me? Have I done something wrong?"

Hewey began. *"As you know this hospital ship is bound for Naples. It will remain in port to provide additional medical facilities after the repatriation of the former POWs, who will be returned to their various units. About half come from Naples, and they will be based with the Valletta, to help with the hospital and public health facilities we propose to give. Colonel Falcone oversees this mission, for which we need to enlist your help and co-operation."*

"But what can I do, sir? I am just a Private and my only experience is working as a tailor for my father and uncle in our family tailoring business!"

The Major continued. *"It is not what you know, Leo, but who you know. We know that nothing gets done in Naples without the co-operation of the Camorra. We need to meet with them to explain the nature of the Valletta's work. Our Intelligence tells us that your father and uncle have, among their clients, the members of at least seven of the main Camorra clans. Also, that they are personal tailors to Don Benito Savino, a prominent and outwardly legitimate businessman, who we know lives in a large villa opposite the station at Bella Vista. Savino produces and sells industrial and marine paints. He owns substantial properties in the city, vineyards, olive groves and tomato fields. The seven Camorra clans who use your family tailors have been under Don Benito's family protection for generations. The De Cristofaro brother's tailor shop is the only link between the Don and these*

145

clans. We have assumed that this is just co-incidence, but would like you to explain the connection?"

The concerned look on Leo's face prompted Enzo to interpose. *"We are not accusing anyone of having committed any crime, nor do we want to suggest anything wrong. In all probability we may both be able to help each other. From what I understand, Don Benito and his kind have access to many people, organisations and institutions as well as hospitals. If that is so, we can utilise his good offices and enhance his standing by having him serve on the Valletta Hospital Management Board. However, before that can be considered, the matters we are asking you about, the Savino family and the clans, need to be satisfactorily resolved."*

"Understood, Colonel."

Enzo paused to let Hewey resume. He signalled to Enzo to continue the conversation.

"Now will you explain the connection?"

Leo sat quietly in thought digesting what he had just been told. He nodded and began.

"First, there is nothing criminal going on. It all started with my grandfather's father. He was tailor to the Savino family way back in the last century. Businessmen, merchants and the wealthy were subject to being attacked and robbed. Don Salvatore Savino decided that he would start carrying a concealed gun. He came to my ancestor and together designed a suit, overcoat and other men's outfits, which had hidden gun pouches. Ever since then, we have been known for tailoring men's suits and outfits for the concealment of guns. We can tailor an overcoat to hide a shot gun or machine gun. I started work with my father and uncle when I was twelve. Several weeks before Christmas, my father and uncle would get all their account books ready. Then one day before the end of the year, the Camorristi would arrive with one

of their bosses. I would be sent away for the rest of the day and when I came back the next day, all the books were gone.

"Not until about five years later, when I was seventeen, was I allowed to stay. As I had guessed, the Camorristi took away the books. Traditionally my father and uncle would make a new complete outfit, gratis for the current capo of each of the seven clans. In return, they were assured business from all its members, who followed their capos and ordered suits, which they did not get for free, but at a good discount. For that favour, the books were taken, and any monies owed to my father and uncle were collected with interest and paid to my family. So, by the end of the year, nothing was owed to them.

"I do not know if Don Benito is aware of this or not. Chances are that he does know, through family history, but he never came to the shop. Either my father or uncle would do the business of measuring and fitting him at his home. I now have been taught how to make concealed pouches... We started to get custom from the Italian military."

Leo saw that both officers had gone quiet. Deep in thought. With arms outstretched he asked them both. "Have I said something wrong, Colonel?"

"No, not at all! Fascinating, Leo, you could not have made up something like that!"

"I totally agree with you on that!" added Hewey.

"This seems a good time for us to take a break for lunch, we can resume in an hour!" Enzo decided.

Leo stood up, saluted both officers and left.

Chapter 25

Camorra

Lunch over, the trio resumed where they had left off.

"So, the only contact you had with the clans was when they came to get measured for suits, trousers, coats and so on?" Hewey asked.

"Correct, Major"

"Did you know them by name?" enquired the Major.

"Just about anybody in business knows the names of the different clans, but the members adopt the name of the clan as their surname and will even use a different Christian name. For example, Don Luigi Soccavo is Capo of the Soccavo clan, but everybody knows, that is not his surname. Nobody can be sure that Luigi is his real Christian name. Likewise, if someone introduces themselves, as say, Pino Vomero that tells you that he is one of the 'Vomero Clan' and you should call him by that name. You find out more as you go up the food-chain. I found all this out from listening to my father and uncle, as well as what you pick up... and what any Neapolitan living in the city knows."

"Was Don Luigi one of the shop's clients?" Hewey probed.

"Of course, yes! He was one of the Capos who got his suits and outfits done gratis by my father and uncle each Christmas."

"Did your father and uncle know his real name and do you?"

"No, Major, I was never told his real name, but they both

knew his real name and that of the other Capos, including the identity of the Black Widows. They all seem to give my father and uncle a lot of respect, but I never knew why and still don't."

"Black Widows? I have never heard of them. Who are they?" asked Enzo.

"Well, Colonel they are not always widows! It is just a title they are given. Comes from when the widows of dead Capos took over the Clan. Some Black Widows are Capos in their own right, like Donna Assunta of Fragola. Others have that name when they are the wives of Capo that either wield the real power or deputise for their husbands."

"And through the tailor's shop your father and uncle knew all these people?" Hewey followed up.

"Certainly, Major, but not only Camorristi; police chiefs, mayors, military and even members of the Royal Family were all clients. We had so much work that we sub-contracted out a lot to other tailors, but my father and uncle would tailor personally for the special clients. Sometimes I wondered how things ever got done, there was so much coming and going. Uncle Nicola and my father always seemed to be having to go out, to take fittings, or show samples of cloth. For such a small family business we seemed to have developed a very good clientele and we were well respected," Leo explained with a sense of pride in his voice.

"Did you get to know any of these Capos socially?"

"Well, not really except some years ago, when I was about thirteen, I remember Don Luigi came and stayed a few weeks at our house in Bella Vista, and then a few weeks with Uncle Nicola down in the Piazza. Ever since then Don Luigi has always seemed more grateful. Years later, Uncle Nicola told me that the police were looking to arrest Don Luigi for some murder and that he had to lay low until his lawyers could get the charge dropped.

That was considered a very big favour by Don Luigi, and that was not lost on the other clans. Apart from that, things went on as usual. Before I got conscripted, my father and uncle were going to gradually start introducing me around as their successor."

Hewey sensed that there was more to this 'Private' than he first thought. He got the impression that the Private Leo might be playing things down a little too much. Careful not to let on Hewey scribbled down a few more notes.

"Tell us about your relationship with the Savino family, Leo," Enzo requested.

"We all live in Bella Vista, Colonel. Don Benito has his Villa opposite the station. My parents, me, my older sister and two younger brothers, live on the first floor of a building my mother's family owned on Via Caportano, about a ten-minute walk downhill from the station. Uncle Nicola and his family live in a villa off the Piazza that was built and owned by my paternal grandparents. That's about two minutes further on. Uncle Nicola met me and my father every morning outside our Palazzo at about seven thirty and we would all walk up to the station. It had become a tradition that we would go over to Don Benito's for a caffe latte. His wife, Donna Carmen, would always join us. She forbade any talk of business in her presence. From the patio where we took our latte, we could see the train approach. Some days Don Benito would get the train with us, but not very often. We would occasionally meet as families at holidays like New Year. In the summer my siblings and I, our cousins and Don Savino's kids, would go to the Savino vacation villa on the beachfront at Torre del Greco. 'Ferragosto' was another holiday we would spend together."

"Sounds to me as if you were almost family," interjected

Enzo.

"Yes, I suppose you are right, Colonel. Paolo, Don Benito's eldest, is the same age as me. We played a lot together as kids; went to the same school and hung out together. He finished school then went to university. I came into the family business. Like me, when he gets qualified, he too will go into the family business. Paolo would travel into the University on the train with us in the mornings sometimes, when he had lectures to attend. Paolo is studying Economics and Business Studies; his father wanted him to do Law, but he had no interest. We both joined the army the same day; because he was a graduate, they made him a second lieutenant. As a simple tailor, they made me a Private. When Don Benito heard that! He told my father that he could easily get me commissioned."

"How would he do that?" Hewey asked.

"Obviously through his connections, Major."

"Tell us more about your relationship with Paolo?" Hewey continued.

"It is fair to say I spent more time with him than my younger brothers. We are close," Leo admitted.

"When did you last see him?" asked Enzo.

"Until we boarded this ship, I had not seen him since we were both posted to different regiments, the week after we joined up," Leo said.

A pregnant pause! The two Officers replayed in their heads what they thought they heard Leo say, *'Until we boarded this ship.'*

Hewey just had to clarify.

"Are you saying that Paolo Savino is aboard this ship?"

Leo replied with an emphatic, *"Yes!"*

Another elongated silence and puzzled look between Enzo

and Hewey, who reached for the ship's manifest from one of the folders he had with him. Rummaged through the papers. Leo's intervention made Hewey's intended search redundant.

"He is listed as Lieutenant Paolo Sacco. I don't know why his name has been changed, but he came aboard with another officer, Lieutenant Fabio Corso."

Listed, in a separate file. These were two repatriates that had been POWs with the Americans. Last-minute additions to the Valletta, by special request of the US Sixth Fleet Command. Enzo and Hewey were on the same wavelength and had a pretty good idea what the *'Cousins'* might be up to. Leo saw the officers' brains *'clicking'* over something but had no clue what, so he just sat back and waited.

"Did he recognise you? Have you spoken?" Asked Colonel Falcone.

"Yes, to both. He introduced me to Lieutenant Corso. I am sure that he is an American-Italian posing as an Italian officer. His parents must be from Naples as he speaks with our accent and knows some of the dialect. Paolo looked uncomfortable and said that they both needed to talk to me before we arrived in Naples, when he would explain everything. The 'American' made a point of telling me where he was from in Naples so as to impress me. He was full of crap. I knew it, and so did a very embarrassed Paolo."

"Do they know that we are interviewing you? Have you met with them again as Paolo requested?" Hewey asked earnestly.

"No, to both, Major!"

A different Leo began to surface. Not the easy-going, uncomplicated young tailor from a long dynasty of tailors, but that of an astute operator. With a realisation of what might be on

152

offer by the British, Leo was looking to get as much out of this interrogating duo as they were seeking to get from him. Staying a Private had so far kept him under the radar. It now dawned on him that these two officers had the better of him. They were privy to something which he knew nothing about. Paolo must have changed his name for good reason. The *'American'* was pretending to be an Italian Officer and these two British officers did not know why. He saw and seized the moment of opportunity that had presented itself. Leo also wanted answers from the Officers. They obviously needed something that they thought he could give. This poker game had to stop! All the cards needed to be put on the table.

Leo was silent. Deep in thought considering all that had been said. A break was called. Ed escorted Leo up a deck to a waiting area away from anyone else. The NCO and his charge both lit a cigarette. Leo was preoccupied with his thoughts staring out to sea. Enzo and Hewey had remained behind.

"Not at all what I expected, Enzo. We must act. The tailor's shop is the nexus of everything. Everybody has been looking at the Savino family and the like, when all the time they are just a front. The Camorra clans are the troops and enforcers. We have probably just spent the best part of the day with the heir apparent of the De Cristofaro Camorra dynasty. Our focus has been to, in some way, contact Don Benito, thinking he was the 'Capo' but all along everyone has been fooled by these tailors!"

"The Cousins may have ditched the Luciano Plan because of what they may have learnt from Paolo Savino. Discovered that Leo was on board the Valletta, which would account for their last-minute additions before we left. We also have to assume that Corso is Paolo's minder, probably OSS or Naval Intelligence."

"I agree, Enzo, but too subtle for the OSS. They are a bunch

153

of cowboys. *Naval Intelligence must be behind this. They were the ones that came up with the Luciano plan. The Sixth Fleet is having a lot of problems in Naples with the Camorra. Just trying to keep operational in the Bay is proving very difficult, tying up troops, delaying preparations, and supplies being stolen. Preparing for a final push north, troops being assembled in and around Naples, it is essential that there is a common purpose to re-establish an order that will continue, even after the war is won. To do that, we must tap into the local power bases. We need to get Leo as part of our team before he is contaminated and plucked away by the cousins. The best way that I can see is to put our whole case to Leo."*

Chapter 26

Metamorphosis

The metamorphosis from the plain conscripted Italian tailor private to the heir apparent of some considerable clout in the Neapolitan underworld, which had started before the break, was complete by the time the last of the meetings got underway.

Before Enzo and Hewey now, stood an astute young man who was beginning to fully appreciate that he had something that these two British Officers needed, probably the same thing as the Americans. He came back and sat down feeling that he had a good hand to play; this time he opened the conversation.

"Gentlemen, what is it you want from me and my family? Or can, I guess? The same as the Americans... namely control of Naples... and if we can deliver that, what can you offer us in return?"

This new, confident, direct approach from Leo was unexpected by both Enzo and Hewey who, although a bit surprised, acted unfazed. It was a welcome development because they could be candid with each other. Leo felt that he had done enough talking. Now it was up to the Officers to explain. That was not lost on Hewey, he reached for his briefcase and took out more documents, all written in Italian, which had been prepared to show to the leaders of the *Camorra* once contact had been made in Naples. He passed them over to Leo. Enzo took out his copy.

"This is the blueprint that we have, initially for post – armistice, then post-war Naples. None of this can either proceed, or be achieved, if there are corruption, crime and inter-clan territorial wars going on. It is accepted that the Camorra are part of the social infrastructure in the city of Naples and in the Campania Region of Italy. In that context The British Government feels that an 'accommodation' should be explored. At least for the duration of the war and perhaps beyond, depending on how it all works out," Hewey explained.

"What about the Americans, Major?"

"Leo, I imagine that they could be looking for the same as we Brits, but probably wanting Luciano and his people to take over!"

"What, with those stupid half breed American-Sicilians who dare to call themselves 'Cosa Nostra'! They do not even know the real meaning of the word 'Mafia. A bunch of semi-literate thugs: they would never be welcome in Naples! So, what is it you are offering Major?"

"That depends what agreements we can come to when we get to Naples. This Hospital Ship will serve as our HQ. Everything will operate through the Valletta. As a facility to the people of Naples, what we have available and on offer, will be channelled where it is most needed. Your people are best placed to identify those needs and targets,"

"How do we do that then Major?"

"Trust and respect on both sides; that is how it works with your setup, and we are happy to go along with that, Leo!"

With that the meeting came to a natural conclusion. In principle a total consensus between all three. Nothing that the American *'plant'* may say or do would change Leo's commitment. Exceptionally, Hewey leaned over and whispered something to Enzo in English which Leo did not understand. Acting upon this short sotto voce dialogue, Lieutenant-Colonel Falcone, as senior officer present, took from his briefcase a folder, removed the contents and spread them on the desk in front of Leo. It was immediately apparent that these were formal military documents written in Italian.

"Subject to confirmation from the Allied Command, you are to be given the rank of Major in the Italian Tenth Army. That will give you the authority you need to become part of this group. You are to be immediately segregated from the other repatriates."

"Colonel, and just how are you going to do that without drawing attention?"

"That cannot be avoided, but as you have heard, all those on board are to receive inoculations. Today shots are being given to personnel from the Italian repats that have been identified as being able to assist. Tomorrow the alphabetical process will begin. All will be told that you have been given your shots today. It will be announced over the PA that you and others are being quarantined as a precaution to a possible adverse reaction to the injections. We have arranged with our Corporal to prepare quarters for you next to his cabin. In that way you will be able to be kept separate and work with us on this operation. Do you have any objection?"

"No thank you, Colonel. I understand."

On previous instruction, Corporal Ed knocked and entered and announced.

"Captain Falcone."

Jeeves held open the door as Angela came into the interview room, carrying a surgical tray containing phials of the three anti-serums, syringes and antiseptic swabs.

"Private De Cristofaro, this is Captain Angela Falcone,

Queen Alexandra's Nursing Corps and my wife, who is originally from Torre del Greco. She will give you your shots now."

"It's a great pleasure."

Stunned, Leo as he held out his hand. Angela shook the Private's hand, then asked him to roll up his sleeve. Without hesitation he complied.

"When was the last time you had any inoculation?" she enquired.

"Never, before now. Ma'am."

Leo sheepishly rolled up his sleeve offering his upper arm for the first of the three injections. He went very quiet as Angela prepared the second.

"How do you feel?" she asked him.

"Fine, no problem, go ahead, let's get it over with."

With the third and last of the shots Leo went pale and fainted in a heap at her feet. Jeeves and Hewey carried Leo to his new quarters and placed him on the bunk. Enzo and Angela followed and remained with him until revived.

"No need to be embarrassed or apologise, your reaction was perfectly normal. As you have never had any inoculation before, this was a shock to your system. Rest up now and we will check in on you later," Angela instructed.

Chapter 27

Breakaway

Leo's fainting meant that he needed to stay in bed in isolation and be kept under observation for a few days. This presented Enzo and Hewey with perfect timing for the two to plan their next move. Interview Paolo Savino and the *'American'* Fabio Corso. Norman was subsequently briefed. A coded report was then sent to London.

Next morning, rough seas hampered the convoy's progress across the Bay of Biscay. The after effects of the mass inoculations and rampant sea sickness left few well enough to properly function. Enzo, Norman, his crew and a few of the Italian repats had *'sea legs'*. Everything that had been planned for that day and the next two days at sea had to be abandoned.

Sturdy enough to cope with these angry seas and storms, the Valletta was getting tossed around and battered. As a hospital ship it had on board medical supplies and equipment which were needed even though it was built to withstand the punishment being meted out. Norman took the decision to seek permission to break away from this convoy to seek shelter in the Neutral Portuguese Port of Oporto. Permission granted, meant that the Valletta would be stuck in port until allowed to tag onto the next passing convoy en route through the *'Straits'*. That would not be for another two weeks. Captain Butler ordered the announcement made. Diverted from the convoy, the Valletta steamed full ahead to calmer waters, eventually docking as the sun set in the serenity of Oporto harbour.

Complete rest for twenty-four hours for all on board was ordered. No-one was allowed ashore until clearance was given by the Portuguese authorities. Skeleton crew duties, comprising a bare minimum of men keeping the ship's essential operations functioning while in port. Captain Butler, his Executive officer with an armed escort of two, welcomed aboard the Harbourmaster, the Mayor, and Naval officer representing the Portuguese Naval Command. After the anticipated formalities were complete, the visitors were entertained in the wardroom where the ship's and other officers had gathered.

By the second day all were fully recovered and rested. Enzo and his medical executive team, including a fully recovered Patti, met and decided that the alphabetic system of selection was to be abandoned. Now that they expected to be in port for at least the next ten days, they would push ahead with a mass inoculation immediately. Any side effect would have dissipated before they were put back to sea. Norman took the opportunity to refuel and restock.

Fully recovered, Leo was given the news that his promotion to Major had been authorised. Enzo and Hewey had arranged for an Italian military attaché to the Embassy in Lisbon to formally do the honours of presenting him with an officer's sword, new uniform and insignia. The tailor's son was way beyond being impressed. Nevertheless, he had to remain *'quarantined'* until after Savino and Corso had been interviewed. Based upon the coded report sent by Norman orders from London approved the proposed actions recommended which included keeping Leo segregated. Enzo and Hewey directed that they were to continue with their present course of action, Leo was to be kept segregated from Savino and Corso. Typically, Norman suggested a private *'officers only'* promotion dinner party in honour of the new Italian Major.

Norman saw absolutely no point in putting back out to sea, until everyone on board the Valletta was fully fit. That meant all the inoculations had to have been completed and those who would suffer from the side effects fully recovered. Anyone who did not recover or had other complications would be allowed to continue the journey only as far as Gibraltar. There they would be transferred to one of the shore-based military hospitals. Naples was the epicentre of an aggressive typhoid epidemic. Butler needed everyone fully fit, ready and able to be fully operational. The Valletta would remain in Oporto until that time. Portuguese authorities granted permission for the stay and allowed the ship's crew and passengers to come ashore but had to remain within the city boundaries of Oporto.

Before the war, Norman Butler had been in the Merchant Navy. He started as a cabin boy on a steamer based in Southampton, tramping cargo around the Mediterranean ports. Butler worked his way up through the *'Mates'* Tickets and had a *'Master's Ticket'* five years before the war began. He was single, now thirty-eight, with no plans to change that status.

Butler had lost count of the number of times he had taken this route stopping to refuel at Oporto. It was on one of those earlier trips that he met Maria Verde. Her parents ran a small hotel with a restaurant overlooking the harbour. Maria and Norman had become lovers. Every time his ship took this frequent journey, he stopped off for a few days to be with Maria. Not having seen each other since the commencement of hostilities, he organised things aboard to leave Bill Smart, his Executive Officer, in charge of the

Valletta for a few days.

'The Fisherman's Rest' hotel, owned by Maria's family, was a few hundred yards up the cobbled street, clearly visible from where the Valletta was tethered. He planned to stay with Maria until departure. Leo's promotion dinner party was to be at the *'Fisherman's'*. A few years younger than Norman and a couple of inches shorter, unlike the classical Latin women, Maria had a mass of thick curly blond hair. Her limited English had been picked up by osmosis and she spoke it in a way that charmed any listener. The morning after his first night ashore, Norman proudly walked his love down the cobbled street. Boarding the Valletta. he introduced Mari to his officer contingent, now congregated in the wardroom awaiting his daily briefing. Norman announced, "Party tonight to honour Major De Cristofaro's promotion. Twenty-hundred hours. Just up the road at the Fisherman's Rest. Only one thing on the menu. Fish and Chips! Civvies please; no uniforms!"

Patti was back to her old self and resumed her responsibilities from Angela. Leo too, had fully recovered. He had never been the guest of honour at a dinner, nor ever eaten Fish and Chips. Betty took it upon herself to organise the *'dinner party squad'* to meet on the shore end of the gang plank. Eight of them in all slowly meandered up the cobble way. Maria's mother welcomed them and led them to a private room which overlooked the harbour. A long old oak rectangular table occupied most of the fenestrated bay of the main dining area. The place of honour at the head was for the newly promoted Major Emilio De Cristofaro.

Everyone relaxed and spoke in whatever language suited them. Betty sat to the right of Leo. Enzo was to his left. Angela next down the line from her husband. With Hewey next to Betty and as close to Patti as he could get. The new Italian Major did his best with what little English he could speak. Betty warmed to Leo so much she acted as matriarchal elder sister toward him.

Party over, the squad ambled their way down hill back to the Valletta. Mr and Mrs Falcone, Hewey and Patti arm in arm chuckling at the sight of Leo ahead, linked to his newly found big sister's arm, deep in a one-armed gesticulated conversation, which only they understood.

It was well after midnight when they all re-boarded the ship. Patti took Hewey back to her cabin. That night in Oporto they became lovers.

Chapter 28

Cuckoos in the Nest

Unbeknown to Captain Butler, the convoy from which he had broken away to seek shelter was to be the last of its kind to the Mediterranean. Plans had been secretly implemented to prepare for the Normandy landings, scheduled to take place later that June. German forces were now defending on the Russian front and retreating from the allied attack through the *'soft underbelly'* of the Italian peninsula. This was now a land war, all German naval aggression at sea having virtually ceased. Shipping that was routed to the Med via Biscay no longer needed to travel in protected convoys; air cover was deemed to be sufficient.

The Valletta had been docked in Oporto for four days when Norman received this information from London. As part of new orders, he was to set sail for Gibraltar no later than 11th March, three days away, or he would lose his refuelling berth. The Valletta would proceed alone with regular air cover. These orders were shared first with his officers and an edited text was read out over the ship's PA system later. All personnel and crew were to be aboard at midnight on 10th March, ready for departure on the first high tide the following morning. Norman, like everyone else, made the best of the remaining time ashore.

Instructions had also been received by Captain Butler for Enzo and Hewey. Discussions had taken place with the Cousins about Fabio Corso and Paolo Savino, which, when referring to them, HQ thereafter began to refer to the two as *the 'Cuckoos in the Nest'*. Enzo and Hewey were instructed to arrange a meeting with the Cuckoos and the newly promoted Leo. The Cousins had now been fully briefed about Operation Valletta and had requested that the Cuckoos join the team under Enzo's command, to assist with logistics and any other operational duties. In addition, Lieutenant Corso would act as the Valletta's group liaison officer with US Naval Intelligence attached to the US Sixth Fleet anchored in the Bay of Naples.

Based upon these new orders from London, Norman Butler had Enzo convene a meeting that afternoon of all the Operation Valletta personnel including the Cuckoos. Savino and Corso were summoned to the wardroom, Captain Butler asked that Angela act as interpreter for both Leo and Paolo. He took the *'American'* aside, discreetly told him he could continue using his cover as the Italian Army Lieutenant Fabio Corso. But immediately drop the sham of speaking and understanding only Italian. Corso, taken aback, swallowed hard and answered with a Brooklyn twang.

"Yes, sir, Captain!"

Norman invited both men to sit down at the table with the rest of the Operation Valletta team and made the introductions. Norman left Leo until last. The look of shock on Paolo and Fabio's faces when he introduced the former private as Major Emilio De Cristofaro was apparent to everyone. He then handed Corso the orders from his US superiors which assigned him to Operation Valletta.

"Please read this as confirmation of what I have just told you. Initial it, time it and date it and hand it to Major Hewitson for his records. Although I am in command of this ship, Lieutenant-Colonel Enzo Falcone is now your Commanding Officer."

Corso read the order, penned as instructed, then handed it back to Norman with a. "Thank you, sir."

Norman quickly eyeballed the document and handed it to Hewey for his records and stood up.

"I have a ship to run and get ready for departure. It is not necessary for me to be involved in the Valletta's Group operational matters."

He then left the meeting.

At Falcone's request Hewey started off proceedings explaining Leo's stellar promotion from Private to Major. Next, he covered the object and set out the proposed deployment of Operation Valletta. Before handing back to Enzo he said, "One final thing, the code for this operation will be *'OV'* or *'Oscar Victor'*. For short, simply 'Oscar'!"

Some days earlier, Enzo, Norman and Hewey had met to discuss and finalise the various roles and assignments to be distributed to each officer in *'OV'*. As commanding officer, it was his task to announce the respective roles and duties assigned.

Corso and Savino would now form an Italian speaking logistics and planning sub-group, to implement operational targets. That sub-group would report to the full executive and comprise himself, Hewey, Angela, Leo, Paolo and Fabio.

Betty and the other three of the Valletta team had already been given their assignments in Liverpool, before they had set sail and had been requested to come to the meeting for informational reasons. The rest of the meeting did not concern the Medical Officers and would be conducted in Italian. Angela's presence as an interpreter was no longer required. She joined her colleagues and left.

In the days that followed, the two Cuckoos and Leo integrated well with the team. Fabio Corso became the main translator and interpreter for the team when having to deal with the repats. Leo did not need to wear his new uniform to command respect from the Naps. Instead he continued to hold court in his well-worn comfortable Private issue. Savino requested and was granted permission by Captain Butler to access the ship's PA system to make broadcasts in Italian. Soon Savino became the 'unofficial' communications officer spending most of his time on the PA, broadcasting.

By the time the Valletta had been forced to dock in Oporto, it had become apparent that with all the personnel on board space was extremely restricted. Medical and nursing staff had nowhere to have meetings. They were having to make do with moving beds in one of the wards and curtaining off that section to meet. Or otherwise book a time for the wardroom. Ad Hoc or emergency meetings were almost impossible. Practical and improvisational as ever, Betty came up with an idea. One of the rescue launches cradled over side the ship could be brought onto the surgical deck close to the entrance to that ward. Some box steps for access could be made by the ship's carpenter. With a few minor modifications, removal and re-storage of the fifty life belts, this launch could serve as a makeshift common room, office and meeting place for all the medics and nurses.

Norman heard Betty out. At her request, he then went with her to inspect both the subject launch and the intended locus where it was to be placed. Greeted by the fellow conspirators, Butler contemplated the proposal which in normal circumstances would never be entertained. He pondered a while. War changes everything. Improvisation was to be supported and encouraged. Betty's proposal would serve to improve the comfort of essential staff who could then be better prepared for any eventuality.

"Approved! Great idea, Betty."

Chapter 29

Last Supper

Now that both Cuckoos were part of the Valletta group, Norman declared that there would be one last Fish and Chip supper at the *'Fishermans'* on the eve of the ship's resumption of voyage.

Betty again took charge, but on this occasion, she had the escort of two Italian officers and an American. Fabio had not really had much contact with Betty until he had become part of the operational team. This cuckoo was a career officer in US Naval Intelligence who had been given his current legend as Lieutenant Fabio Corso. His real identity was available to both Enzo and Hewey, but for operational reasons, they did not want to complicate matters by having it divulged to them until needed. Unlike Leo and Paolo who enjoyed Betty's company and attention, Fabio who was their interpreter, felt uncomfortable with the sisterly attention she gave to the two Naps. Fabio, as interpreter, was more of a conduit than a participant in their conversations, so by the time they all sat down to eat that last night, Betty and Fabio had talked a lot but said nothing to each other.

That was realised in an awkward silence between them when Leo and Paolo got into their own private conversation; neither Betty nor Fabio knew where to look or what to say. Eye contact with each other was impossible to avoid and when it happened, they gave each other embarrassing smiles. Simultaneously, they both decided to break the silence and speak which caused them both much amusement.

"Sorry, you first," insisted Fabio, deferring to Betty.

"I saw from your medical history that you and Paolo had already been given the jabs before you joined the ship at Liverpool?" she asked.

"As you now know, we were fully prepped for this trip by my people which included getting all the shots. I was not sure how I was going to explain all that and keep up our cover story. Luckily it turned out the way it did," answered Fabio.

Betty told him, "If you had said nothing and had the injections again, it is likely that you would both have suffered severe side effects, which would have blown your cover anyhow."

"Obviously, it was not factored into the frame at the time we got the shots. It had us both worried when the announcement was made over the PA. Fortunately, it all worked out as it did," he commented.

Betty and Fabio were suddenly very comfortable with each other now that the ice was broken.

"Have you picked up much Italian since coming aboard?" Fabio asked.

"Well, it's hard not to, but I understand more than I speak. My hope is that by the time this war is over I will be fluent," Betty answered.

This bonding dialogue between Betty and Fabio continued for the rest of the meal. Eventually, it was time to leave. Norman was to spend this last night with his love at the hotel and join the ship the following morning for departure on the afternoon's high tide. The rest made their way back to the Valletta. Patti and Angela, chatting and arm in arm, led the way. Hewey and Enzo

169

followed behind, taking in the scenery and stars but saying very little. Roger and Frank were dissecting some mundane public health rules and Leo and Paolo were locked in an animated discussion about where the best pizzerias were in Naples. Betty, having accepted Fabio's offer to walk her back, linked arms, and they were last in the group making its way down the cobbles to the shore.

"Tempus Fugit, when you are having a good time. That's about the only Latin I can remember from my school days. Even then I have probably got it wrong," commented Betty to Fabio. They were the last to negotiate the gang plank.

"It was a great night for me too! The first of many I hope." Fabio smiled.

By now the others had gone to their respective quarters and they suddenly became aware of being alone. The American took a responsive Betty in his arms and they kissed. It felt right for both and in time they would be lovers. On this last night in Oporto, Betty gave Fabio one more kiss goodnight that would forever stay in his memory.

Chapter 30

Back at Sea

It was a hive of activity the following morning aboard the Valletta to prepare for departure on the early afternoon tide. Captain Butler was back on board by seven a.m. His ship had to be in top condition as this next leg of the journey would be solo, no convoy and no Royal Navy. Patrolling RAF Sunderland Coastal Command would be watching out for any danger from a greatly depleted enemy naval force. Norman's plan was to travel full speed ahead for the *'Straits'*, which he would expect to reach within forty-eight hours weather permitting. By fourteen-hundred hours The Valletta was making its way out along the River Douro estuary to the open Atlantic and south to the Rock. Unlike when they left the escorted convoy, almost a week earlier, there was not a ship in sight. It looked as if the Valletta had the whole North Atlantic to itself. The weather forecast was good for the rest of the week and the sea was relatively calm. In these conditions at a full speed of eighteen knots, and with a good wind behind him, Captain Butler would make his destination with about twenty-four hours to spare.

On the surface it seemed little had changed between Betty and Fabio. Such contact that they had with each other before the last night ashore was always very cordial and professional. They were both people who were naturally very discreet, especially about their personal lives. Other than the group who had gone ashore for the Fish and Chip supper, Norman was the only one who knew anything about the *'thing'* which now existed between the Chief Nurse and the American.

Based on current estimates, the Valletta would take two days after leaving Gibraltar to reach Malta, then after two days it would leave for Naples. Norman expected to be in the Bay of Naples on seventeenth March, Saint Patrick's Day. With this time frame in mind, Enzo and Hewey organised and held the first meeting of what became known as the *'Vesuvius section'* of Operation Valletta. This comprised Enzo, Hewey, Angela, Leo, Fabio and Paolo. Proceedings were conducted in Italian and its role was to prepare plans in which the Valletta *'Honey Pot'* could be best used to foster the participation and loyalty of the Camorra Clans. Leo proposed that as soon as they reached Naples, he would first speak with his uncles and through them set up a meeting with the clans Capos.

It was early evening of twelfth March that the Valletta moored in Gibraltar where Butler would take up his final supplies and refuel for the next leg of the trip to Malta. Enzo and Hewey had been summoned to the Allied HQ on *'the Rock'* for a de-briefing as to progress with Operation Valletta and the dialogue with the Camorra repats. They had been requested to bring Fabio, Leo and Paolo with them to participate in a final briefing from High Command. That meeting included a two-star US Marine General, Bill Ward, his staff officer, an Italian Brigadier General, his staff officer, a Royal Navy Rear Admiral, his flag officer and Lieutenant General Simcox from Military Intelligence, who chaired the briefing.

The progress that had been made by the Valletta Group was acknowledged by the Command Officers. General Simcox re-iterated to Leo and Paolo that their continued co-operation with the armed forces once landed in Naples was essential and that the

Valletta was to be the focus of collaboration. As the meeting dispersed, the Italian General requested to see Paolo and Leo separately and beckoned both along the corridor. Enzo, Hewey and Fabio moved a discreet distance to the opposite end. The General then proceeded to admonish both men before dismissing Paolo who joined the others. Leo sheepishly followed the General Ward, and his Staff officer out of the building. Paolo explained to the other three, *"The General was not happy about our appearance. He said neither of us knew how to wear a uniform properly and called us both a disgrace and an embarrassment. He was even angrier with Leo, now a Major, turning up in a private's uniform. He got really pissed off with him when he found out that he had made no attempt to get a new uniform. If it was not for the importance of this operation, he would have us both up on charges. I was dismissed, but Leo was ordered to go with the Staff officer to get his new uniform."*

All four left and made their way back to the Valletta. Enzo and Hewey reported back to Norman, who had been busy with ship's business in preparation for departure the next day. Butler announced that he would hold a *'working'* dinner party that evening at the usual time. In that way everyone could have a good meal and full briefing. His view was that once they left Gibraltar there would be very little time to meet socially as before. He expected Fabio, Paolo and Leo to be in attendance. Betty, Roger and the others had already been told of his plan. Norman walked Enzo and Hewey out of his room onto the bridge, just in time to see a very smart Italian Major walking towards the Valletta. All three could not resist jeering and applauding Leo as he came aboard, alerting everyone else to follow suit with 'wolf whistles' and laughter, especially from the Italians on board.

Unknown to Norman and the officer group he had at his working dinner that night, because of events which were about to unfold, the Valletta would never make it to Malta. Although it was a *'working dinner'*, it was in fact much like all the others, except that Norman had each of those present give an update.

Captain Butler commented that when the Valletta left Liverpool, the Falcones were the only obvious couple but by the time he had to dock at Oporto, Patti and Hewey had made it two. Now they were in Gibraltar there were three couples; he looked at Paolo, Leo, Frank and Roger and asked, "Who will be the next pair?"

This brought great laughter all around the dinner table. Without needing any translation, even Leo and Paolo had understood the humour and appreciated the joke. Dinner ended earlier than usual, as there was to be an early start that next morning. As they all dispersed to their respective quarters, they were oblivious to Fabio discreetly going with Betty to her cabin to spend the night.

The Valletta was about four hours out from port, en route to Malta, when Captain Butler received orders, direct from Naval High Command in London, to immediately change course and head directly to Naples. The information in the telegram could only be shown to the Senior Officers. The crew and repatriates were to be told that the change was for logistical reasons; this would avoid any panic or undermining of morale. The main text of the message was read out by Butler to the Officers called to his wardroom.

"On thirteen March 1944, the conelet on Mount Vesuvius partially collapsed forming a depression of about twenty metres in depth. Volcanic activity and seismic movement is increasing which indicates the likelihood of an imminent eruption, the extent and impact of which cannot be determined at this time. Areas from Torre del Greco to San Giorgio a Cremano, Pompeii, San Sebastiano, Massa and Fosso Della Vetrana are anticipated to be in the direct line of any lava flow from the pending eruption. Evacuation of civilians and military personnel from these areas will meet with great difficulty due to infrastructure damage. There is currently an epidemic of Typhus in Naples, which has caused parts of the city and surrounding areas to be closed. This will further restrict any rescue or evacuation operation. Further orders will follow."

Enzo's first thought was of his parents and their home in San Giorgio a Cremano. His in-laws came from Torre del Greco, where his wife's elder sister, Teresa, still lived. Bella Vista, where Leo and Paolo's families resided, was closer to the volcano than San Giorgio a Cremano. There was no way of contacting anyone to give warning, nor any idea of what they would face when they arrived, probably on 16 March. Nothing could be done until they docked in Naples.

Enzo and the newly formed 'Vesuvius Committee' set to work. Major Hewitson had no emotional or personal involvement in the pending eruption and its subsequent consequences. As an Intelligence officer he was more objective and recognised an opportunity to take advantage of these events to enlist the co-operation of the *Camorra* and the *Families* through Leo and Paolo's being part of the *'Vesuvius Committee'*. Intelligence sources became more aware of the increasing value of what the Valletta was bringing to the Gulf of Naples, proportional to the escalating crisis being exacerbated by the volcanic eruptions. Hewey picked the right moment to explain this analysis to Enzo and they began to plot how this may be implemented to gain maximum benefit for their operation.

Chapter 31

Further Orders

The radio telegraph, which ordered the Valletta to change course and head directly to Naples, had also intimated to Captain Butler that High Command in London were now reconsidering their original plans in the light of the unpredictable natural events. Within hours further orders from Allied High Command were received. *Marked 'Restricted. Need to Know Only'*. Having quickly read the content, Norman summoned his inner cabinet of officers and read to them the communiqué:

"Allied Forces are assembling north of Mount Vesuvius with supplies and equipment in preparation for the final push north to Rome. German forces are dug in and holding out at Monte Cassino. The focus of the Allied attack.

"Casualties from that battle to be treated initially at field hospitals, set up near troop assembly point, close to Capodichino airport. The Valletta to receive the more serious casualties for treatment. Lieutenant-Colonel Falcone will command and administrate all medical and surgical facilities. Daily escalation in the volcanic activity of Mount Vesuvius is causing serious concerns regarding an imminent eruption. Movement of ground forces is being hampered by civilians evacuating the more vulnerable areas. US Marine Major-General Bill Ward is now Officer in Command of allied troops. The typhus epidemic continues to spread unabated."

The captain looked around at the stunned group of officers slowly digesting the import of the communique they had just heard.

"Colonel, looks like you and your lot would have had your work cut out in the next few months, even without the bloody volcano erupting!"

"Nobody could have made any contingencies for an eruption. We have no idea what to expect! What if it is like what happened when Pompeii was wiped out?" he replied.

Captain Butler, concerned at what they were to be sailing into, spoke up again "Tomorrow, is St. Patrick's Day, we will have sight of the Italian coast and begin our approach to the Bay of Naples from the south; we need now to consider the repatriates and the others on board. They have been able to get limited information from the radio. It would be wrong to say nothing and just arrive in the Bay of Naples with Vesuvius erupting, or about to erupt. I do not want panic on board this ship, or a mad rush to get ashore when we dock. These are problems to be addressed and solved by us, now. We need a realistic and workable plan."

Betty agreed and suggested that everyone aboard should be told as soon as possible, however, there had to be consensus as to the form of words to be used. Following some discussion, it was agreed that Norman should arrange to muster all the repatriates in the ship's main galley, where Enzo would address them. Enzo had already assumed that this was his responsibility. Hewey was delegated to make the same announcement and explanation in English. A short but accurate status report was prepared and agreed. This became the script. Further updating announcements would follow. Enzo spoke first.

"We have been advised that Mount Vesuvius has become extremely active, and an eruption is imminently possible. To

make matters worse, there is an epidemic of typhus throughout the Naples region. At our present rate of progress, we expect to be in the Bay later tonight or in the early hours of tomorrow morning."

Enzo then read out a translated excerpt from the full report received from Allied High Command:

"*'Eleven-hundred hours Saturday, March, seventeenth. Be advised that huge red streams of lava have been seen flowing down the sides of Mount Vesuvius, combined with moderate earth tremors that shook buildings and broke windows. The estimates of the magma discharge rate suggest a shift to the more explosive character. An eruption is inevitable.' Combined with the current typhus outbreak, the situation is cause for concern. Our current orders remain unchanged in that we are to land, set up and man field hospitals to support the community of Naples and all allied military personnel. That is all the information we currently have.*"

Enzo felt that he had to meet with all the Italians on board. At the end of his address, he called upon all his compatriots to muster outside the ship's chapel. There they could all assemble and deal with concerns arising from his announcement. Hewey, Angela and the three Italian officers, Paolo, Fabio and Leo would be in attendance.

Pockets and groups formed into loud, animated emotional debates, complaints, cursing of saints, choice swearing and exclamations of *'I knew it!'*, *'didn't I tell you we are all cursed'*.

The chorus of voices went on in their individual groups. Declarations of doom; others blaming the *'Stupid Il Duce'*.

It was all Hitler's fault, and progressed to being both Hitler and Mussolini's fault. They had both planned it by dropping bombs down into the crater, or they had set explosives… so they mused.

No, it had to be the Americans, they did not care where they dropped the bombs. And so, it went on!

In disbelief, Hewey turned to Enzo and the others. *"Normal people would be worried and upset about what they have just been told. These guys just seem to use it as a free for all, to start arguing among themselves... And we are in charge of this lot!"*

Accepting that this was the reaction they expected from Naps, his colleagues in unison just shrugged their shoulders in knowing acquiescence.

When one of the assembled shouted out to Enzo. The cackle went silent.

"Colonel! What would happen if the ship was unable to dock because of the eruption?"

This set off another round of frenzied cursing, blaming and speculation.

Enzo waited for a convenient lull in the cacophony.

"As soon as anything else is known we will make an announcement over the loudspeaker."

There then followed a barrage of questions which after a genuine attempt to respond to as many as they were able it became completely unmanageable. Leo turned to Hewey.

"If these were British, American or even German troops assembled, it would be a simple exercise to bring the room to attention; then either leave or dismiss them all. But it does not work that way with the Naps. You would be completely ignored; they would just continue arguing and complaining amongst themselves."

Unnoticed, the group of officers walked out.

Chapter 32

Preparations

In addition to the outbreak of Typhus there was also an epidemic of lice. Much of the city was cordoned off, isolating the residents. All those living within had to be sprayed with pesticides to kill off the lice that were carrying the Typhus bug. Those who needed access to these zones were also sprayed as they entered and left. Water supply, electricity generators and anything else that worked had been blown up by the retreating Germans. The conditions that this created had been the genesis of the plague of lice and Typhus which now gripped Naples. To make matters even worse, as part of their rear-guard action, the Germans had laid hundreds of delayed mines in public buildings and places. When they detonated hundreds were killed and injured leading to spontaneous panic.

All Allied military operations in the Naples Command Zone were suspended. The Valletta had received orders to dock alongside the US Sixth Fleet and disembark all but essential medical staff needed to administer and operate the hospital ship, and crew. Personnel under the command of Enzo were to be sent to man existing field hospitals and form ambulance / rescue squads. Field hospitals were to be immediately made available to the civilian administration, to cope with expected casualties from the impending eruption. Once the Valletta had disembarked all its passengers, as per the direction, it was to lie out of range of

Mount Vesuvius. Captain Butler had to sail the Valletta to the Island of Ischia about thirty kilometres north of Naples. That harbour would become the ship's base until further orders.

Enzo and his officers had to start implementing plans for the deployment of the Italian repatriates to support and assist the civilian population that would be affected by the eruption. The Valletta would continue to be the HQ of the operation but would remain offshore, unless called upon to evacuate serious casualties. A fleet of forty trucks and ambulances that had been used in the Salerno landings were now available for Enzo's command.

The Vesuvius Committee decided to divide Naples up into the various Camorristi Clan turfs, which in any event, were almost identical to the municipal boundaries within the region. This blueprint, setting out the various clans, was based upon the information provided by Leo and Paolo as well as what was collated from Nap soldiers. As the Commanding Officer, Lieutenant-Colonel Falcone would be expected to stay onboard the Valletta, which was Operational Headquarters. Due to this emergency he was needed in the field, Roger would deputise in his absence.

Continued deterioration of the public health, social structure and administration of the Naples and Campania region had to be reversed and needed to be brought under control. Establishing these links with the local officials and Camorra Clans had become more urgent and important. Operation Valletta had been designated to cover the area south of Naples from San Giorgio a Cremano to Torre del Greco. This division included the district of Portici in which was the village of Bella Vista where the Falcone, De Cristofaro and Savino families lived.

Captain Butler received further updates from Allied HQ.

Predictions were being given that the areas to be most impacted by the eruptions were Portici and Torre del Greco. Both locations within the zone for which Enzo was responsible and many families of the Italian soldiers lived. Raw information given directly to the troops was likely to cause panic. This was a scenario that as Master of the Valletta, Butler, could not contemplate. He turned to Enzo for counsel and advice.

"Norman, those of us who have been brought up and live at the foot of Vesuvius, especially in Portici and Torre del Greco, know the dangers of being in the direct line of lava flow, should the volcano erupt. It is not something we like. Always a possibility. This new update will do no more than confirm what they have already come to expect. No need to say anything. Just leave it."

"That's one hell of a relief, Enzo. I leave it all up to you."

Approximately seventy nautical miles south of the Gulf of Naples, marked in the sky above it with thick dense dark, clouds emanating from the ruptured cone of the volcano, the whole of Vesuvius was completely blocked out and as the Valletta got closer a smell of sulphur began to contaminate the air. First light cautiously navigating to harbour, Mount Vesuvius came into view in the distance. Columns of fire spasmodically and indiscriminately shooting thousands of feet into the air, lighting up the countryside for miles. The entire top of the volcano was a towering inferno. Masses of lava spewed into the atmosphere solidifying as it poured down on the terraced scorched terrain below. A black crawling monster landslide of burning solidifying lava crushing, destroying and consuming all that was in its path. Each propulsion of the eruption sent shock-waves which moved out to sea, which could be felt aboard the Valletta.

Sight of the erupting Vesuvius was the genesis of a focused

resolve, absent in the Italian Army when they had surrendered to the Allies in North Africa, but now bubbling over. Regardless of the dangers, these troops had to get ashore to rescue their families. This was not going to be another Pompeii!

Chapter 33

Eruptions

Escalation of volcanic activity, the ensuing disruption to a fragmented battle-torn city and plagued citizens, made transport and communications in and around Naples almost impossible. The extent of the eruptions was more easily assessed from the sea than on the ground amid the volcanic hinterland. Naval Command ordered Captain Butler to send hourly reports until further notice. Rescue parties were to be organised from the repatriates aboard to be headed by Lieutenant-Colonel Falcone. Vesuvius was in full flow and showed no signs of remitting. Pavement and road surfaces were being rocked with each eruption. Red hot larval rocks of all shapes and sizes continued to be propelled thousands of feet into the air, and came crashing down to the ground. Molten white-hot flow moved downhill, towards areas packed with small villages.

Formation of Rescue Parties aboard the Valletta before it docked in the Port of Naples became a priority. Each group would have a bilingual British officer to translate. Angela was not expected to be asked but, in any event, volunteered. The original plan to initiate contact with the Capos of the Camorra Clans was shelved as the rescue was to take precedence. However, through Leo and his contacts with the Camorra network, they were the best source of intelligence as to what was happening on the ground. From this information a more precise rescue plan to extricate civilians was devised to focus on locations in imminent danger. One of the main lava flows was heading steadily towards Torre del Greco where Angela's sister, Teresa, lived with her family and other kin.

Anxiety increased as the Valletta moved closer to the shore. Sources on the ground relayed updates that a potential catastrophe was in the making. Liaising with the US Sixth Fleet, Fabio had been able to secure a convoy of nine *'Deuce'* half-ton triple-axle trucks originally designated for the final push north to Rome. That attack, having been made impossible by the eruptions, was now postponed. Hundreds of vehicles were released to be used for humanitarian and rescue purposes. Four ambulances were under the command of Betty with Angela acting as her deputy and interpreter. Fabio was to oversee the non-medical rescue personnel, and the collection of injured and wounded. These fully equipped ambulances would be at the rear of the convoy. Evacuee casualties would be put in the last of the ambulances which when full would return to the designated zone at dockside adjacent to the Valletta. They would then be triaged, treated, documented and registered. Serious cases would be ferried to the Valletta now docked in Ischia. Patti stayed on board to oversee this work. As each ambulance was relieved of its charge, it would immediately return to the convoy.

The leading five trucks of the rescue convoy carried twenty rescue troops each including an NCO. At specified locations they would be deployed to assist local rescue forces as directed by the local commander. Make camp and remain in situ until further orders. Walking injured would be triaged and made ready for evacuation when the convoy returned. More serious cases would be placed in the ambulance to transport casualties back to the port. Packed with evacuees, trucks returned to the port, where they were all marshalled off. Fed from makeshift canteens and kitchens that line the harbour wall. After preliminary assessment, the masses were directed to makeshift dormitories improvised in the few dockside warehouses still intact. Refuelling complete, the trucks were reloaded with equipment, supplies and more troops to reinforce or replace those already in the field. This shuttle with changing shifts was kept in operation twenty-four hours. With each trip more trucks, ambulances and heavy plant machinery joined the rescue convoy. No-one had any idea how long Vesuvius would continue to vent its fury nor the frequency, magnitude or nature of its eruptions. The city itself appeared safe from the larval flow, but its old structure was very vulnerable to tremors and quakes.

Lieutenant-Colonel Falcone led the convoy in a donated US Marine four-seater jeep driven by his corporal. Each of the trucks could carry twenty seated and ten standing but more than twice as many would end up being crammed into the vehicles on their return. He sat in the back of the Jeep with Major Hewitson. Leo, in his new major's uniform, rode shotgun. Paolo and Fabio were behind in the cab of the convoy's lead *'Deuce'* half tonner. Its full complement of concerned eager repatriated Italian soldiers, returning to their decimated homeland for the first time since the commencement of hostilities. Their driver was one of the Nap repats local to the area particularly keen to reach his village. He kept them entertained as he cursed and swore in his dialect at the violent volcano, interposed with praying to the *'Holy Mother Maria'* and one of her subordinates *'San Gennaro'* patron saints of Naples.

The road south to Portici, running parallel to the curvature of the Bay, was adjudged the safest route to take in order to get as close to Torre del Greco as possible. Now three in the morning, conditions were deteriorating by the hour. Lava flow began to stream towards the sea. Prospects of reaching even Portici were diminishing fast. Torre del Greco was now only reachable from the sea and the south. San Giorgio a Cremano would be the first stop. Bella Vista next, both of great family importance to the Valletta officers. However, there were other more immediate priorities as the anger of Vesuvius persisted as they approached Portici. Troops stationed at the local garrison had been urgently deployed to free the only accessible road to the town of Torre del Greco now blocked with volcanic debris. Halted by order of the local military commander, Enzo released those men aboard the convoy who had family in that area to join the local forces working to remove the volcanic debris from the road. Unable to proceed, the convoy was re-routed to head uphill to the Railway Station at Bella Vista, pick up evacuees, then to back track north along the Vesuviana Railway returning to Naples.

This detour routed the rescue convoy past the home of Leo's Uncle Nicola and his parents, past the Savino's villa opposite the station, and north to the next village of San Giorgio a Cremano where Falcone's family home was located. Enzo had no idea if his parents had survived, nor if they knew he was alive or dead. All contact had been lost after the surrender in North Africa. The pungent smell of sulphur was everywhere. When the sudden thunder of another apparent eruption roared, the convoy was instantly abandoned by passengers and crew. Scattering to the relative safety of the open field and ash covered vineyards. Only when it turned out to be a distant thunderstorm did the convoy resume its trek.

Pulling into Piazza San Angello, a stunned crowd had gathered awaiting the arrival of the rescue convoy for evacuation. An emotionally charged reunion ensued with rescuers and the rescued who appeared to be all interrelated to each other, hugging, kissing, and embracing each other. Leo De Cristofaro's family was absent. Paolo was told that his father *'Don Savino'* was not among the Piazza evacuees. First, the De Cristofaro's now badly damaged, ash covered family villa. A tearful, emotional and much relieved Uncle Nicola, his aunt and cousin Rita came in response to Leo's shaking of the main gates and calls. Crying with joy and relief they all hugged. Clutching an outsize light tan leather suitcase each, Leo and Paolo escorted them to the convoy in the Piazza where they were quickly shuffled into the back of the first truck.

News travelled fast about the rescue convoy and the route it was taking back towards the city, along the road parallel to the Vesuvian track. The Valletta Rescue Convoy, now about a quarter of a mile long, had been joined by other cars, vans, trucks; packed bicycles, overloaded Vespas, carts pulled, by mules, horses, buffaloes and anything else on wheels that people could muster to flee to safety. Progress was slow and it was late morning as it arrived at the Port.

Chapter 34

Rescue Convoy

To the ridicule of family and friends, Paolo Savino's father *'Don Benito'* always kept at least one car and a truck at the Villa for fear that one day Vesuvius would erupt. His prudence had paid off! Once he heard warnings of eruption the family Fiat 2.8 litre saloon-car was packed with everything they could get in. Any space in his company truck was packed with evacuating neighbours and their belongings. Orders from the local command had advised that all evacuating vehicles join the end of the redirected Rescue convoy returning to the Port of Naples. Concerned that the convoy may be further diverted and not reach Bella Vista, he and *'Donna Savino'* decided not to wait but had left earlier that day and joined the back of the line. By the time it reached Bella Vista many more evacuating vehicles attached themselves to the convoy.

Crawling along at ten to fifteen miles an hour on the road which runs parallel to the Vesuvian Railway track, Paolo brought the convoy to a halt outside his family villa opposite Bella Vista railway station. He jumped out of his leading truck excitedly and anxiously to get his parents, only to find the iron gates locked, all the window shutters were down and secured. Seeing Paolo upset, Enzo and Hewey went over to comfort him.

Word had gone down the line to Don Benito that officers from the convoy were trying to get into his villa. Confused and concerned he quickly made his way to where they were calling to them as he approached. At first, he could not be heard, but then Paolo recognised his father's voice turned and ran towards him. The whole convoy watched as father and son tearfully embraced. Donna Savino had got out of the car to see what was going on and became so emotional that she fainted. Revived by those around her and joined by her son and husband she thanked every saint she could think of, especially San Gennaro and the holy mother Mary. Her son had been returned to her safely *'the greatest miracle of all!'*

Next station and stop were to be San Giorgio a Cremano, Enzo's home village. He did not know if his parents would be at home or at the station rendezvous. Just like what happened to Paolo, the villa was all locked up, secured and empty. Gone too was his father's wine red *'Fiat Topolino'* car.

One of the villagers told him that his parents had left in their *'Topolino'* the day before for their apartment in Naples.

Another rumble and burst from Vesuvius as Lieutenant-Colonel Falcone spoke on the radio telephone the darkness of the night and headlight beams from the vehicles behind silhouetted him. Betty and Angela were now back at the port with the ambulances which would be returning without them. Recent collapsing of buildings in Naples and forced further evacuation to the relative safety of the Ports. Both were now required to stay at the port, assist, organise and support the needs of the new influx of evacuees from the city. Enzo, Hewey and Leo were breaking away from the convoy and returning to supervise the clearing of the road from Portici to Torre del Greco. On reaching 'Torre', organise the evacuation of residents back to the Port Central Unit. Savino and Corso would take over command of the Rescue Convoy and continue along the Vesuvian route as designated. Enzo quickly convened a conference with the others and gave them their orders.

Most of the contingent that had originally left in the Valletta Rescue Convoy, had been unloaded earlier to work on removing the volcanic debris that blocked the only remaining access road to 'Torre' from Portici. The latest eruption redirected larval flow away from the road, pushing the amorphous monster landslide in the opposite direction. Now manifest was a window of opportunity to gain access to the coastal town and rescue the trapped. Rescuers needed to move fast as the next blow of the volcano could make 'Torre' another Pompeii. By the time they arrived the first evacuees were being rushed into waiting trucks that had recently arrived direct from the US Sixth Fleet manned by American personnel few of whom spoke or understood Italian. Announcements were being made over handheld loudspeakers in broken Italian. Leo immediately took over. Since most of the men in situ were those from the Valletta, Enzo and Hewey resumed command, directing the evacuation of several hundreds of people that had been trapped. Most of the Town's population had left as soon as the first warning had been given a few days earlier.

Dawn that morning, scientists that had been monitoring the volcanic activity determined that it was subsiding. Mount Vesuvius had reshaped itself so that any existing or subsequent larval flow or ensuing landslide would be into the fields full of olive trees, grape and tomato vines. Away from the inhabited areas. Consistent with this prediction the dense volcanic clouds that blacked the sky and cloaked the sun began to dissipate. The last of the 'Torre' evacuees were all safely out of harm's way heading back to Port.

What only Enzo and Hewey were privy to, was that the De

Cristofaro and Savino families were now to be considered British Intelligence *'Assets'*. These Assets would help in getting the co-operation needed from the Camorristi Clans. Don Benito Savino had been located and was safely on his way in the Valletta Rescue Convoy to the Port. Leo's father and uncle who were considered the more important of the two *'Assets'* had yet to be located. Effective governance and organisation needed the respective *'Capos"* involvement without them little could be achieved. Don Mimmi, and his brother Don Nicola, were keys and catalysts to secure that essential dialogue. Locating the De Cristofaro family was now the priority.

Leo had been told through his contacts that his parents, uncle, aunt and family were in Pozzuoli, several miles west of Naples away from Vesuvius. For family reasons, not connected with the eruptions, the Clan had decided to move into their summer villas. Only the volcanic clouds and dust impacted towns and villages that far from Vesuvius, most of which including Pozzuoli, had become safe havens.

"Next stop. Pozzuoli!" Enzo ordered.

Chapter 35

Pozzuoli

Situated just over fifty kilometres northwest of the angry volcano the town of Pozzuoli is far enough away to be a haven from the lava flow and landslides of the eruptions. Nevertheless, it was well within the radius of the volcanic dust which fell to ground with each burst of Vesuvius. From Roman times the town was a favoured coastal resort for the more affluent of the province and has the Flavian Amphitheatre at its centre which is considered the third largest in Italy. Despite heavy bombardment the structure survived relatively unharmed.

Back in the late twenties Don Marco, a local Capo had decided to move to New York to join the rest of his family who had emigrated some years earlier. He owned a small farm which comprised several acres of prime land between the Amphitheatre and beach. Don Marco and his family lived in the main residence which sat back from the beach overlooking the bay almost directly opposite Vesuvius. A private beach was bisected by a concrete landing, a boathouse which had been modified with freshwater showers and changing facilities. To the rear of the residence was a good view of the Amphitheatre and the hills beyond. Entirely self-sufficient, the farm comprised grape and tomato vines, vegetable plots, olive and citrus groves, as well as a variety of livestock.

Over several generations two families living in tied properties tenanted the land. In addition to tending to the farm they also produced olive oil, wine, and cheese they sold at the local market, with all other produce from the land and livestock. A third of profit from sale of the produce at market was to be paid to the Landlord, also a regular supply of wine, olive and free supply of whatever produce required. For generations this had been the arrangement, which had proved to be both workable and acceptable to all parties. As the 'Padrone' of the farm and its tenants Don Marco would only sell to the De Cristofaro brothers if they if they agreed to perpetuate and continue this concord. The deal was done, Don Marco and his family packed up what they needed, then left.

From late June until after the feast of San Gennaro on 19 September two De Cristofaro brothers and their families were in residence. With all the destruction, street fighting with the retreating German troops, occupation by the allies, the typhus epidemic and now the lice plague. The brothers acted wisely by not leaving Pozzuoli that previous September and staying put at the farm. In the city the tailor's shop had been badly damaged by bombing and the adjoining streets full of debris made accessibility to the premises impossible. Even though the produce had been sequestrated by both occupying forces the De Cristofaro, their tenants and residents of Pozzuoli were better off than the disease ridden Populous of the City and its outskirts.

It was approaching noon when the four from the Valletta in the borrowed Jeep pulled up outside the De Cristofaro Pozzuoli residence. Leo instructed the others to stay in the vehicle until he signalled them to come in. He wanted to make a surprise entrance. The smell of cooking from the kitchen was picked up by them as soon as they had stopped. As he crept around the side of the Villa to the back, Leo heard the voice of his mother and aunt as they oversaw their old maid who owned the kitchen.

"The water is about to boil. How much pasta do we need to put in?"

Leo heard his mother ask, just as he walked into the kitchen.

"Enough for another four Mama!"

As if on cue, the three women turned around and screamed with joy so loud that the menfolk came running in to see what had happened. The prodigal son was back! Tears, hugs, kisses and pinches of his cheeks came from all directions. Only the boiling over of the water in the pasta pot extinguishing the gas flames rescued him from the emotional attack. His mother linked Leo's arm. There was no way she would let him go and ordered her husband out to invite those waiting in the Jeep in for lunch.

In all the excitement neither Don Mimmi nor his brother Nicola, had missed the fact that Leo wore an Italian Army officer's uniform. When he had left, he was just a conscripted Private. Any explanation could wait until later. Compliant with his wife's orders he went out to the parked Jeep to the three who, unlike Leo, were dressed in British Army uniforms. Two Officers and a Corporal. English was not a language that the tailor spoke other than what he had picked up from the cinema, and recent Allied occupation. Instinctive Neapolitan sign language supplemented with such pidgin-English he could muster, he beckoned them to follow him.

Enzo, Hewey and the driver, joined Don Mimmi. They followed him into the residence.

"Thank you, for your kind invitation Don Mimmi."

"I don't understand. You speak Italian well."

"Let me explain. I am Lieutenant-Colonel Vincenzo Falcone, this is Major Hewitson. Our driver Giovanni, like me, is from Napoli. Originally, we both joined the Italian Army, captured in North Africa then sent to England. When Italy surrendered, we joined the British Army to help in the invasion. Major Hewitson is English but is fluent in Italian."

Chapter 36

Explanations

Despite prevailing wartime conditions, and the now dissipating seismic and volcanic eruptions, Leo's family were able to give their guests a lunch which even before the war was Neapolitan cooking and hospitality at its best. The first of five courses put on the table about half past one with the last eaten around three o'clock. A much-needed siesta followed in the spare rooms offered to the guests by Don Mimmi. Leo crashed out in his own bedroom.

Enzo could easily have slept much longer; half-awake he looked at his watch which showed seventeen thirty-five hours. Self-discipline and professionalism compelled him to get up and splash cold water on his face. Now more alert, he woke Hewey and the driver.

"We have work to do."

During the meal Leo held court, telling his story of how he was now a major in the Italian Army, Enzo then the other two gave a more abridged account of themselves. But there was more to tell. More to talk about. Things to discuss. Operation Valletta, the real reason they were there. Later, after the siesta over an *'espresso'* all would be explained Hewey had volunteered.

Refreshed and comfortable, served with their coffee by the women, the men were left in the large comfortable sitting room. Don Nicola was first to speak, *"So Major please explain what two hard working tailors can do to help the British Army?"*

Leo interrupted his uncle, *"Zio, they know all about the Camorra, our connections and the roles you and Papa have. So, there is no point in pretending!"*

Acquiescent, his uncle nodded, looked at his attentive brother equally comfortable with what he had just heard from his son, and gestured Hewey to explain. Given the floor the British Intelligence Major set out his stall and explained, *"We can do all that, Major. But there will have to be tolerance and respect from both sides. You people will eventually leave, and life will go on as before here in our part of Italy as it always has even with the Germans and now your forces in 'occupation'. As you already know the Camorra and its Clans are part of our heritage which is tolerated and accepted by all Neapolitans otherwise, they could not exist. Now how do you propose to proceed?"*

Enzo took over, *"Don Mimmi, on our way here in the Valletta from England, Leo was fully briefed. He was given the rank of Major in the Italian Army to accord him the status and access needed for military co-operation. Leo will be my liaison officer with direct access to the Medical and Surgical Facilities of the Valletta. This is a fully equipped Hospital Ship, now docked at the Port of Ischia and will also act as our Headquarters. We also have a shore base at the Port of Naples. Leo can go into more detail with you."*

Both brothers turned to each other with a look of consensus; they got up from their seats followed by the rest, then shook on the deal.

"Now what! Colonel?" asked Zio Nicola.

"Leo stays here with you to set things up. Pozzuoli is closer to Ischia than to the Port of Naples and is away from the chaos, confusion, people and traffic movements. If you agree, we can use this residence for logistics and communications, US Marine Captain Corso, and Lieutenant Savino (who you know) will be assigned to work from here with Leo. I will also assign a small

section of eight Italian soldiers (all from this region) as support."

Leo put his arms around his father and uncle, both taken by surprise with what they had just heard. He spoke for them all, *"We agree. Let's get started!"*

As Enzo and Hewey were driven away from the De Cristofaro residence, the Sun was just setting over the horizon to the west of the bay. Blackness from the receding volcanic activity of Mount Vesuvius now mingled with the advancing darkness of the night.

Once Leo got started, the communications room aboard the Valletta became a hub of activity. From Pozzuoli, Leo co-ordinated the onshore operations and logistics. He proved to be a natural. Having gained the confidence and co-operation of the Capos of the *Camorra* clans he was able to maximise the use of all the available resources. Local Capos liked the idea of having the apparent legitimacy they got from being part of Operation Valletta. Leo made sure that these heads of the Neapolitan underworld became increasingly dependent upon him and what he could provide. Cultivating them for the long term would benefit not only himself but the objectives of British Intelligence. Leo was able to access all public health, medical and surgical resources and facilities provided by the British Military via the Valletta in Ischia and the shore base in the Port of Naples. The US Navy was able to fulfil materialistic needs such as jeeps, trucks and motorcycles with a supply line of fuel all via the conduit that Leo established.

Chapter 37

Teresa

Norman Butler had been ordered that once he had disembarked the Rescue Team and the Convoy had departed, the Valletta would be escorted to the Port on the Island of Ischia. For reasons of safety not only from the continuous bombardment of Vesuvius but also to prevent it becoming the focus of any attack or invasion by the evacuees. One of the two redundant armed landing craft assigned to the Valletta rescue operation would escort them. These two Landing craft would then be tasked to ferry casualties to and from the portside at Naples to the Valletta in Ischia.

When re-routed to the Bay of Naples, Butler had checked out the Porto d' Ischia, as a possible harbour for such an eventuality. A circular volcanic crater with an entrance to seaward. It gave a good defensive position from any potential attack, and was well protected from the weather. Unspoilt and unlike most islands, it was self-sufficient. Clouds of sulphur generated from the continued volcanic eruptions, continued to darken the skies of the bay. Everyone and everything in the Naples area had been or were being doused in DDT to combat the Typhus epidemic and destroy the infestation of lice. Ischia was a complete haven from what was happening on the mainland. In this relative tranquillity the Valletta was able to better function as both a hospital ship and communications centre directing shore operations.

Angela had volunteered to go with the first rescue convoy, in the hope to be able to contact and rescue her sister Teresa and family who lived in Torre del Greco. When the town became completely encircled and blocked off, then the rescue convoy turned back she became extremely worried. Upon her return to the port, Angela immediately contacted Leo, in Pozzuoli, and sought his help. Within hours Leo had tracked her down. Heavily pregnant Teresa and family had been evacuated by one of the Italian Civil Rescue Teams to the Portici Barracks. A local garrison had been converted for temporary use to house the evacuees from Torre del Greco. Leo ordered the officer in charge of the barracks to have Teresa and her family brought to the Valletta shore base.

Teresa had been married for some years to Fillipo Bianco and was last known to have a daughter, Simone, now nearly six, and a son, Sebastiano aged three. Vetted and disinfected, the family had been allocated a section of one of the smaller dormitories in the barracks. Cupping bowls of well needed hot minestrone they had joined the other evacuees encircled around a central wood stove all sharing their various experiences.

A sergeant and two soldiers entered the place.

"Will Fillipo and Teresa Bianco please show themselves?"

Instinctively, Fillipo complied and stood up. The NCO approached.

"You, your wife and children are required to come with me?"

Too stunned to even ask why or what for. they obliged. Fillipo carrying Sebastiano followed by Teresa holding Simone's hand. What little belongings they had were collected by the two soldiers. The Bianco family were escorted to the Commandant's office.

Preempting Fillipo, Teresa asked the Commandant, *"Why have my family and I been brought to your office, sir? What have we done?"*

The Italian officer, tired from the war, worn down by the eruptions and illness all around him, further irritated by pieces of paper giving onerous unhelpful and inconvenient orders, contemptuously, picked up the latest such sheet from his desk and read out loud:

"To the Officer in charge:

Please ascertain the whereabouts of Teresa and Fillipo Bianco and their family, assumed to have been evacuated by the Italian Army rescue units based at Portici.

Once this family has been located, arrange for their immediate transportation to the Port of Naples and advise me accordingly.

Major Emilio De Cristofaro,

Operation Valletta."

Shocked. Teresa and Fillipo examined the document handed to them. Dumbfounded and without any explanation they handed it back to the Commandant.

"What's this all about, sir? Why can we not just stay here until we can get back to our village?" Fillipo asked.

"Signore Bianco, I have spoken to Major De Cristofaro. He has explained to me that he is acting under the direct orders of his Commanding Officer who is a British Army Colonel. He insists that you must now be sent directly to the Port."

"But we want to stay here with our friends and neighbours!" pleaded Teresa.

"I am very sorry, Signora, but it is out of my hands. I cannot ignore the orders of a British Colonel. There is nothing that I can do. Transport is on its way to take you to the Port. I am sure that you have nothing to worry about!"

Chapter 38

Labour

Predictably, the combination of the stress of not knowing why the family had been ordered moved and the journey from Portici Barracks to the Port of Naples, brought about the onset of labour. Teresa's nausea and, in pain with her contractions now becoming more prolonged and severe, held on as long as she could. Her birth waters broke just as she was being helped by medics from the back of the truck. Fillipo took charge of the children and followed his wife who was being taken to the medical emergency unit. Betty, who had no idea that this woman in labour was Angela's sister, took charge. She directed that Teresa be taken to the operating theatre, then Filippo and the children were ushered to a waiting area. Betty after a cursory examination decided that a midwife's expertise was needed, she left Teresa who was attended by other nurses and went to get Angela.

Exhausted, Angela had fallen asleep wrapped in an army blanket in one of the vacated ambulances.

Betty gently touching her shoulder woke her.

"Angela, are you feeling OK?"

"Fine, thanks."

"Good, we have an emergency. I need your help," Betty announced.

"What? A patient?" Angela quizzed.

"She's having a bit of a rough time, possibly with pre-eclampsia."

Fully awake and alert, Angela quickly walked back with Betty to the theatre. Without any sign of recognition Angela glanced at the delirious patient, she briefly introduced herself as the *'Duty midwife'*. Teresa, concentrating on dealing with the pain of the contractions, willing the birth to be over and comforted by nurses, did not care who it was. Her sweat pouring into her eyes gave only vague outlines of anyone more than a few inches away. Angela focused on the pertinent part of Teresa's anatomy. She made a quick assessment.

"This baby has to come quickly and by the sounds of it, it is too late for a C section. Both mother and baby could be at risk."

Satisfied that the baby was not in distress, working quickly and skilfully, with the next contraction, Angela delivered her nephew. He announced his arrival in the usual way with a healthy gurgling cry. Betty took the new-born and carried out the necessary checks before handing him to his anxious but relieved mother. Angela in professional mode completed her work, went over to the sink washed up and came to check mother and baby. Propped up in the bed with her son on the breast Teresa screamed, starling everyone.

"Angela it's you!"

Instinctively the sibling bond brought a flood of emotion as both sisters embraced and held each other. No longer another new-born, Angela, tearful with the joy of the moment, kissed her nephew as she hugged her sister. Betty brought in Fillipo and the children to see their baby brother, she too burst into tears of joy as the reunion expanded. Despite the exhaustion of a difficult labour Teresa was reinvigorated, she surrendered their son to Fillipo pulled her sister towards her and sobbed.

"Teresa, I had you all brought here when I found out where you were. I was so worried about you all. I had no idea that you were pregnant. Mama and Papa will be so pleased that we are

now together."

Betty interrupted the reunion and through Angela asked if the parents had decided on a name for their new son.

"We agreed, Matteo!" Fillipo proudly announced.

Angela turned to her brother-in-law. *"Teresa needs to rest now. Once Matteo has taken enough, we will give her medication which will make her sleep. You and the children will stay with me and Enzo."*

Angela made sure that they all said goodnight to Teresa before they left with her. Nurses then moved mother and infant out of the theatre to her allocated bed on the ward. Matteo was laid in the cot alongside.

Simone had hold of her aunt's hand as they exited. Sebastian held onto his father's jacket which trailed under his arm.

"Where are you going to take us to, Angela?"

"To the Valletta. It is a British Royal Navy Hospital Ship anchored in the Port at Ischia. It is our base and Headquarters. Enzo is commanding officer of this rescue mission. We are housed on board in our private cabin. Teresa will be transferred to a bed aboard the Valletta tomorrow. You will come with me tonight and stay as long as needed."

"Will Enzo be there?"

"No. Enzo led the rescue convoy I was with those that were ordered back here, he had to break away with others and travel to Pozzuoli. Not sure when he will be back. But expect him to return to the Valletta when done."

Chapter 39

Minor Tremor

Before, during and after eruptions from Vesuvius, there were always varying degrees of tremors or minor earthquakes. Even when dormant the irritated bowels of the earth would unpredictably generate seismic movement collapsing structures of all nature and types. Crevasses and potholes would open in the roads creating havoc with any traffic. Various predictions from the volcanologists tasked with monitoring seismic activity were indicating that eruptions were receding due to decreasing pressure. However, declining pressure was increasing the number of 'minor tremors' until they too disappeared. For operational purposes authorities including the Allied forces were given updates twice a day supplemented with further reports as required.

A lingering scent of sulphur and ash in the air spoiled what would otherwise have been a beautiful spring evening drive back to the port along the coast road from Pozzuoli. Giovanni sang as he drove, his two passengers speaking little, taking in the view as the Jeep progressed. For that time, traffic was moderate, consisting of more Jeeps and military vehicles with a motley of ranks and nationalities travelling in both directions. Giovanni kept at least three truck lengths back from the six-wheeler ahead of him. To the rear, and far too close for comfort, was another Jeep with two US Marine Sergeants with two local women in the back, heading for a night out. On the other side of the road, a fully manned tank leading two other Shermans, part of a small convoy, chugged its way back to base.

In absolute agony with an indescribable pain in his right thigh, blurred vision and sounds of women screaming, men moaning, smell of diesel engines revving, Enzo found himself regaining consciousness. He was hanging from the upturned Jeep with the front passenger seat jammed into his right leg. The engine was still running and the front wheels were spinning. Giovanni, head partially ripped from his spine, lay dead next to him. His driver's blood had squirted into Enzo's face and eyes. Hewey, bleeding from his head with his left arm hanging limp, was directing rescuers carefully recovering Enzo from the tangled mess.

Extracted from what looked like a major battle scene or bombardment, neither Enzo nor Hewey knew what had happened as they sat propped up against the stationary tank being given shots of morphine to kill pain by a US medic. A massive deep crater had swallowed up everything in a radius a couple of metres from where the tank now stood. The two US Marine Sergeants and Giovanni were dead. Except for the two Valletta officers, everyone else had escaped with minor injuries. The tank commander, a US Army Captain, oversaw the first aid being given to Enzo and Hewey at the roadside. From the insignia on their uniforms, he was able to identify their unit and had contacted the Valletta shore base. He told them that Leo was closest and, on his way, so too was an ambulance from the port base with Roger and a very anxious Patti.

"What the hell happened?" Hewey asked.

"A 'Minor Tremor', they call it, sir!"

In shock, dazed, fragile, distracted by the dull pain and the growing impact of the morphine shot, Enzo stayed quiet and listened.

"When the Tremor ripped open the road it came to a stop, a couple of feet in front of the leading tank. Your Jeep disappeared into the crater. The Jeep behind you was thrown in the air and landed on top of yours. Both women passengers were thrown clear into the hole. Apart from some cuts, bruises and shock they're OK. At first, we thought that, like your driver, the other Jeep had also killed you both when it landed on top. Somehow the main impact was to the front of both Jeeps missing you but knocked you both out."

Incredulously both Enzo and Hewey looked at each other in disbelief as to what they had been told had happened. They were fortunate, but their driver Giovanni, having fought in North Africa, captured, then as prisoner of war shipped to England survived to return to Naples as part of Operation Valletta, was now dead. Killed in his own backyard He had been looking forward to being reunited with his family later in the week. Now they would have to bury him.

Until the scientists were satisfied that the danger had passed, and all seismic activity had ceased they would not give the 'all clear'. Without waiting for that to happen, Roger dispatched two ambulances to the locus, with supporting medics. The journey took longer than usual because of the damage the 'minor tremor' had wreaked on the route. Leo arrived at the scene just as the ambulances pulled up. Horrified at the sight of what he saw at the scene, he broke down and wept when he saw Giovanni's mangled corpse being loaded into the back of a truck. A short time earlier they had all been enjoying a meal together. Had he not stayed at Pozzuoli he could also have been killed or badly injured by the 'minor tremor'. Leo, still in uniform, took command of the situation controlling the locals who had gathered. As the senior Italian officer, onlookers and Italian military personnel looked to him for direction and leadership. Medics from the Ambulances focused on the injured first, the dead to be removed by the ad hoc rescue team of locals and soldiers who had been in the other vehicles. Leo took charge of a small group to remove Giovanni's body, they laid it on a stretcher and respectfully covered it with a patchwork quilt brought out by a tearful woman before he was put in the truck. From nowhere a priest appeared, joined by all those within earshot, he recited a prayer over Giovanni's body, leaned over him and with a sign of the cross blessed him in Latin. Leo arrived at the scene just as the ambulances pulled up. Horrified at the sight of what he saw at the scene, he broke down and wept when he saw Giovanni's mangled corpse being loaded into the back of a truck.

Shock, severe pain and a good dose of morphine had Enzo unconscious. A compound fracture of his right thigh needed to be carefully immobilised with splints. The broken tibia and fibula of the other leg presented a greater problem as they had come through the flesh and could become infected. Protruding bones had to be gently and carefully rejoined then manipulated back into position. His wound was sutured and dressed, followed by an injection of antibiotics, before he could be stretchered back to the ambulance with a third medic holding the intravenous Saline drip.

Hewey looked on from the back of the open ambulance as Enzo was being treated several yards away. He was quickly diagnosed as having a dislocated shoulder probably caused when Hewey landed after being catapulted from the jeep into the crater. That was promptly snapped into place by one of the more senior medics, who then put the major's left arm in a sling and strapped it securely across his chest. A second medic saw to the cuts and abrasions. He was given a cigarette, lit for him by one of the nurses. She sat him down just inside the rear open doors. Hewey, drawing in on his cigarette tried to understand what had happened, shook his head and cursed.

"A minor tremor!"

Chapter 40

Recovery

Angela was aboard the landing craft with her brother-in-law Fillipo and the two children being ferried to Ischia when the Minor Tremor struck. Its effect in the bay was to disrupt the calm sea and generate moderate wave activity rocking the vessel for several minutes. Roger decided not to pass on any information to Angela about the Jeep incident, until Enzo and Hewey had returned in the ambulances. He and Betty would then carry out their own assessment and act as needed. It was close to midnight when the ambulances were returned. Now conscious, Enzo's injuries were further examined by the duty surgeon who determined to operate that night. No detailed explanation was required by Enzo, he knew that to properly reset the fractures, repair muscle damage etc. to prevent any long-term disability, immediate surgery was needed. It was too late at night to alert Angela, Enzo instructed that she could be told later in the morning.

Unbeknown to Enzo he was being trolleyed into the same operating room in which his sister-in-law, a few hours earlier, had given birth. Surgery complete and with both legs in plaster cast he was transferred to the 'General Ward' to await transportation to the Valletta. This was a non-segregated ward and as per Betty's direction his bed was moved next to Teresa. She was in a deep sleep recovering from the exhausting labours of giving birth. Her brother-in-law was in the induced state of unconsciousness from the general anaesthetic. Both oblivious of each other and the logic of Betty's strategic positioning. Efficient and practical as ever she would call Angela and give a status report as to Teresa and Enzo. Angela was also told to await the transfer of her husband and sister to the Valletta which would be in a couple of days.

Teresa was first to awake as baby Matteo needed to be fed. Once settled in his mother's arms, Betty, through one of the Italian nurses, explained to Teresa that the man in the next bed with his elevated legs in plaster was the Commanding Officer Lieutenant-Colonel Falcone. At first, Teresa did not understand the relevance of this information or, indeed, why he had been put next to her. Then it suddenly dawned, and she asked, *"Enzo Falcone? My brother-in -law? Angela's husband!"*

Betty did not need any translation, Teresa's reaction said it all. Betty beamed and nodded in confirmation.

Shocked at the state of Enzo with both legs plastered and winched up, various dressings on grazes and small lacerations from the crash; he lay in the adjacent bed with a saline drip maintaining hydration. Teresa said, *"What happened to him? Is he going to be alright?"*

Before she got any response, Matteo bellowed a cry which got everyone's instant attention and woke up his fractured uncle from his deep induced sleep.

Totally confused, dazed and feeling a bit nauseous from the cocktail of drugs and anaesthesia he had been given, Enzo grappled in his mind as to where he was and the excruciating cry of what he imagined to be that of a baby. Too focused on the baby, Teresa, Betty and the nurse had not realised that Enzo was now conscious. Initially startled by the cry which had awoken him, he lay back on the raised pillows gradually taking in his surroundings. He looked up at his hoisted legs and reflected as the fresh memory of what had happened replayed in his head.

How was Hewey? he wondered to himself.

Enzo knew with the injuries that he had, it would take many months before he could be up and about again. Concerns about his command, his immobility, and suppressed pain of his fractures, made him oblivious of the siren of cries coming from his newly born nephew behind the segregating curtain of the adjacent bed to his left. Suddenly, all went still. Matteo, now content with his nourishment, had fallen asleep. The nurse assigned to the care of Teresa and baby, took the infant from his mother and transferred him back to the makeshift nursery of which he was sole occupant.

Betty joined the surgeon, Jim Newman, in his morning rounds and his first port of call was Enzo.

"You know the prognosis, Enzo. It is all going to take time. You and Hewey were very lucky not to have been killed. Fortunately, no nerves were severed in either break, the bones should knit together well, and the muscle damage heals with time. No weight to be put on either leg for at least two weeks subject to further examination. Danger of postoperative blood clotting having dissipated; your legs can now be released from the pulleys. I am going to keep you on analgesics and blood thinners for now."

He turned to Betty and said, "Best if you can get him to the Valletta as soon as possible where we can get him properly X-rayed. I will check on him later in the week when I am back on board."

Newman added to his notes on the clipboard which he rehung on the footrail of the bed.

"Thanks, Jim, I hope that Betty can arrange the transfer later today."

Jim shook Enzo's hand and wished him well, took his leave and continued his rounds. Betty stayed and positioned herself between Enzo's bed and that of Teresa which was still curtained off. Her mischievous look and demeanour provoked Enzo to ask, "What is it, Betty? Why do you have that look on your face?"

Without a word in response, she drew back the curtain like a magician revealing his trick.

"Enzo, meet your sister-in -law Teresa. The baby you heard crying was your newly born nephew, Matteo. You should get to know each other. I have made arrangements for you both to be ferried to the Valletta later this afternoon."

Chapter 41

Another Reunion

Patti had been the first to receive the call for ambulances to be sent to the scene of the accident. She was also the first to establish the identity of those involved and was very relieved to hear Hewey's voice on the radio from the ambulance at the scene. Patti took control from shore base and had everything arranged when the ambulances returned. While the others focused on Enzo, she attended to Hewey. Their overt bond had continued to flourish and everyone recognised it, applauding the fact it never interfered with their professionalism. The once committed bachelor now had Patti who cared for and loved him. As a walking wounded with his dislocation reset Patti could see the glazed look of shock in Hewey's eyes. She hugged him and walked him to a quiet side room used by the medics for their breaks. She sat him down in an old armchair next to which was the tea urn steaming with stewed tea. Patti saw the look of horror in Hewey's eyes as she moved towards the stainless-steel cylinder, mug in hand.

"Not that poison! What about that bottle of Strega you lot keep locked in the cupboard for medicinal use only? I would prefer a mug of that please."

Patti took the cue. Opened the cupboard and poured about a double measure of the liquor into the mug and handed it to Hewey. She sat on the arm of the armchair and gently kissed him on the temple as he took the first sip. Exhausted, he fell fast asleep without finishing his drink. Patti took the mug from him, covered him with a blanket, and then went to get on with checking the others.

Whilst Enzo was in surgery and Hewey fast asleep, Betty, Roger and Patti conferred as to what was to be the next step. The structure of command for Operation Valletta was that if Enzo was not able to command, Hewey would deputise while Betty would continue in charge of the clinic with Roger overseeing the logistics. It was obvious that because of the injuries to both Enzo and Hewey they would be incapacitated and unable to carry out their duties. Whilst Hewey's injuries were far less serious and less debilitating than Enzo's he would not be fully fit for a couple of weeks. In Enzo's case his injuries would take many months to heal. All three agreed, Hewey's injuries would prevent him getting around but did not impact on his ability to make decisions and take command. Once he has recovered from shock and rested, he should assume command. Roger would prepare a full report to be sent to Allied HQ.

Facilities at the Shore Base in Naples plus the prevailing volcanic environment did not make it suitable for either Enzo, Teresa, or Matteo to stay any longer than was clinically necessary. Ischia being situated to the northwest of the Bay of Naples with the prevailing winds blowing from the north pushing the contaminated air south and out to sea meant the island was less polluted. Self-sufficient for centuries, Ischia could cope. On board the Valletta docked in the island port it was another world, fully sheltered and functional. Patti made plans for all those being transported from the Shore Base to be moved on the early evening shuttle.

Angela had resumed her normal duty aboard the Valletta and that day she was overseeing the reception of transported patients from the Shore Base to bed allocation. Betty decided it would be at that morning radio briefing that she would explain to Angela the events that had led to Enzo's injuries and following surgery. In this way she would be kept busy preparing for the intake of all the transported patients and not just her husband, sister and newly born nephew. The latter two would not be put on wards but join Filippo and the children in the Falcone's quarters. The Admiral's Suite, previously known as the Royal Suite in the former days of the Valletta, was preserved for visiting Admirals and other dignitaries. Norman ordered this suite opened and made available for Enzo and Angela, one of the rooms to be fully equipped with a proper hospital bed and necessary accessories. He personally supervised the positioning of Enzo's bed so that he could face out and get full view of the Port and bay beyond.

As a precaution and to avoid any involuntary movement of the fractured legs Enzo was sedated and unconscious throughout the trip from the shore to the Valletta. He had been told about his impending move earlier that morning and had consented to the medication but did not expect it to knock him out. Carried aboard the landing craft on a stretcher followed by Hewey and Patti, Enzo looked as if he had just come off a battlefield. Teresa was rattling close behind in a wheelchair being pushed by one of the crew onto the ramp. Matteo was carefully carried by his nurse who was also returning to start her tour of duty on the Valletta.

When Enzo woke, he was alone, and had no idea of what time it was. He guessed that as it was still daylight it had to be around mid-afternoon. Rather than announce his consciousness by calling for attention he preferred to lie looking out through the large porthole, take in the view and listen to the hub of activity aboard. From experience he knew that someone would be regularly checking in on him and it was not long before Angela appeared.

"You're awake! I have been so very worried about you. I only found out what had happened just before you were to be ferried here."

She went over to his bed and, carefully avoiding his two plaster casts, kissed and hugged her husband. Reunited they held each other close.

"Angela, there was no point telling you as it had got so late. There was nothing that you could have done other than get stressed out, upset and probably not slept all night. Well, now I am here with you and we will be on the Valletta together for some time until I'm fully recovered."

Hewey came in followed by Patti and Norman after a brief courtesy knock on the cabin door. His arm still in a sling, Enzo reached out to Hewey's free arm, took his hand and pulled his Number Two over towards him for a brief fraternal embrace.

"It was a close thing! Hewey! If that Jeep had landed on top of us, we would not be here to tell the tale. Just as well we were being looked after by… "

Hewey anticipating what Enzo was about to say, interrupted, "Don't you start on about San Gennaro and his miracles. If this happened on his watch, he should have stopped it ever happening. Poor Giovanni and the other two men would still be alive"

"You are right. But we should still be thankful we are still alive. Now, we need to talk about what happens next, make decisions and get focused on Operation Valletta. There is still a lot to be done!"

"No way! You need to rest and recover first!" Angela insisted, backed up by everyone else in the room.

"Enzo, Operation Valletta, continues to run well based upon

the plans we set out before we made dock here in Ischia. Hewey and you need to just let things take their course. Roger, Betty, Patti and I are quite capable of making sure things run smoothly while you and Hewey recover. In a few days we can revisit the situation. So just relax both of you. We can manage."

Norman's Captain's logic said it all and set the scene.

"He is right, the more you are rested the quicker you will recover!"

Patti volunteered in support.

Chapter 42

Relocation

Always alert to an opportunity and never one to stand still for very long, Fillipo realised that it would be some time before they would be able to get back home to Torre del Greco, so he decided to stay in Ischia. Being accommodated aboard the Valletta was always going to be a short-term solution. He wanted to move onto land as soon as he could. When they had been evacuated, he and Teresa had brought with them all the cash they had and such valuables as they could carry. They also brought with them the deeds to their house and property which could not only be used as proof of ownership but also as collateral. Now Teresa was recovering well from the birth, regaining her strength and able to cope, they both decided to find a suitable residence to rent near the port. Before contemplating moving out of the Valletta, Fillipo had secured a job with the ship's Catering and Supply Officer to source supplies for them from the island and help run the catering staff. In a Jeep with a driver, twice a week, Fillipo would go with his list of requirements, source them, and return with the supplies. On the other days he would work a twelve-hour shift in the kitchen from 'seven to seven'. Sundays he would have free.

Many of the holiday villas owned by Italians from the north and Germans had been left unoccupied. Now that the Germans were on the run and would end up being defeated, Fillipo figured that he would seek out vacant property owned by Germans and move in with his family. By searching the municipal land registry, Fillipo found one such property which overlooked the port with a good sight of the Valletta and view of the Bay of Naples. A medium-sized seven-roomed villa plus a sizeable bathroom and a large ground floor kitchen which opened out onto a well-stocked but much neglected vegetable, fruit and herb garden, it also boasted of a flat open terraced roof with wrap-around balcony on the first floor. Four substantial bedrooms, lounge, dining room and family rooms. The German owners were a retired couple who had bought the villa in 1929 as a holiday home, travelling from Hamburg each year in early May to Ischia, returning to Germany in late September. Allied bombing had killed them. Now vacant, neglected and with uncertain ownership, Fillipo staked his claim by paying all the outstanding taxes to the municipality which acted as a lien on the property until Fillipo could purchase it after the war.

The place had not been occupied for some time, so Teresa and Fillipo set about opening the shutters and blinds and removing all the dust covers. They were pleasantly surprised at how well preserved and maintained the interior with its furnishings were. Everything they needed, bed linen, crockery, cutlery etc., was there. A full day's work cleaning and airing the place out was all that was required for them to move in. By the end of that week, Teresa, Fillipo and the children had settled into their new home. It had a perfect view of the volcano and its eruption, which had brought the family to Ischia, so they called it 'Villa Vesuvio'.

Enzo, confined to his bed, was kept well informed of all developments and had frequent visitors. The frustration of not being able to get around was to some extent alleviated by keeping himself occupied with decisions and the respective paperwork. Hewey, as Enzo's deputy, did all the legwork and trips to the shore base. In fact, not much had changed in the organisational and command functions of Operation Valletta as Commander

Enzo was still capable of making the decisions needed. Meetings were held in his room and, as his fractures slowly healed, he could move around on crutches and, when possible, a wheelchair. Often restless, Enzo took every opportunity to get around the Valletta with his limited mobility. Angela gave as much attention to her husband as time and he would permit. While Enzo appreciated the attention that he received, he insisted that things proceeded as they should if he were not incapacitated by his injuries. During the day, Hewey spent more time with Enzo than anyone else, not just because he was second in command, but because he too had been injured and was not considered fully fit for duty. There were frequent contacts with Leo in Pozzuoli, who by now had charge of all offshore operations. Fabio Corso was Liaison Officer with Major-General Bill Ward, now Allied Forces Commander for the Port of Naples, and Paolo fitted in where needed. The medical team was well organised and efficient. Except for the first two weeks of Enzo's *'hospitalisation'*, he was able to continue with his weekly meetings aboard the Valletta with his officers.

Having originally ordered The Valletta to the Port of Ischia as a temporary measure because of the erupting Vesuvius, it was now recognised by Bill Ward and Allied Command that its location isolated it from the various problems such as the Typhus epidemic and lice infestation prevalent in Naples. The Valletta was becoming self-sufficient and able to maximise treatment of both military and civilian wounded and sick. General Ward decided that until further notice the Valletta would stay docked in Ischia. Further, landing craft were to be made available to ferry personnel, sick and wounded to and from the hospital ship from its Shore Base in the Port. Necessary alterations to the Valletta to accommodate more beds and operating theatres were also ordered. Because of these new works, Enzo and Angela moved in with Teresa and Fillipo. Hewey, Patti, Roger and Betty were all billeted in the Hotel San Marco located on the harbour access road and in walking distance from the hospital ship. Norman as Captain remained resident on the Valletta. Local craftsmen and labourers were contracted to do the conversion work. The Italian Coast Guard offices, close to where the hospital ship was berthed, were also expanded to facilitate the needs of Operation Valletta. A communications room was to be set up and offices for Enzo and his team were all to be completed by the end of the month.

Easter had come and gone on the island and the celebration very much subdued because of war and angry Vesuvius. By now Enzo's condition had improved, the original plaster casts hand been removed, both legs X-rayed to check progress of the healing fractures, and new splints applied and enclosed in much smaller plaster casts allowing him greater mobility. Prognosis was good. Another month at this rate of healing and he would be cast free. This would be put in his report to Allied Command. Coincidentally, Bill Ward had decided to include a visit to the Valletta on his current round of inspections. He could see for himself how well Enzo and Hewey had recovered from their injuries, view the work now completed on the Valletta, and check out the new facilities in the Coast Guard Block.

Norman had been warned of the General's visit, he knew he would arrive early in the morning and return to Naples that evening. Bill Ward would first inspect the Valletta and the work done, then check out the Coast Guard Block and finally meet with Norman, Enzo and their teams for a working lunch at the Hotel San Marco.

Chapter 43

Inspection: New Orders

A day before the proposed inspection, the US Marine General's aide de camp arrived with a minor invasion of cooks, guards, clerks and other ranks with supplies and provisions, which meant the complete occupation of the Hotel San Marco. That following morning Bill Ward arrived with his entourage of US Marines, a token British Brigadier, his staff officer and an Italian General with his supporting cast. They disembarked from the ferrying landing craft which had tied up alongside the Valletta. Norman Butler in full dress Naval uniform and Enzo propping himself up with crutches also in full uniform saluted the General as he was piped aboard the hospital ship. Not being very mobile, Enzo sat out on deck in the morning sun while the General and his contingent were taken around the ship.

Formal inspection complete, Bill Ward sent one of his staff officers to escort Enzo to the Captain's Wardroom to attend a confidential meeting. Present and seated around the table were the General, Norman, Hewey, the British Brigadier and the Italian General; the staff officers stood behind their principals. Enzo was ushered in and seated next to Hewey. General Ward got straight to the point.

"What I am about to say does not go beyond this room and has the highest secrecy classification. Soon the bombardment of Monte Cassino will force the Germans to abandon the old monastery and continue their retreat out of Italy. There will also be a western front launched from across the English Channel and preparations are well in advance. Less allied troops will be required here in Italy as now the Italian Army can take over. This will release allied troops to return to England to prepare for the new offensive. Certain Allied Forces personnel, equipment and assets will be required to remain in situ to assist in the normalisation and restructuring needed in Naples and the Campania region. On 1st May, Captain Butler, Major Hewitson, Major Roger Hill, Major Betty Kirby and Captain Patti Colvin will report to the Allied Air Base at Capodichino to be flown back to London. Lieutenant-Colonel Falcone will be promoted to full colonel as of now and is appointed Allied Military Governor of Ischia, his wife, Captain Angela Falcone, will be promoted to Major and assume Major Kirby's role. US Marine Lieutenant Corso will be promoted to Captain and remain here in Naples and continue to act as liaison officer to the US Sixth Fleet and Governor Falcone. Italian Command will be in contact with Savino and DeCristofaro."

A stunned silence descended as the impact of Bill Ward's address was digested. Norman Butler was first to speak.

"What about The Valletta, General?"

"She stays and will continue to be a hospital ship but more focused on the local needs. Troops will be moving north, wounded and injured will be treated locally or flown to England."

The General looked at his watch.

"It's now twelve-twenty-five hours, let's all head off to the San Marco for lunch. I am expected back in Naples at seventeen-thirty hours. We can talk about the details more personally over lunch."

Bill Ward got up and headed out with his group. Norman,

Hewey and Enzo stayed seated at the table.

"Don't know about you two but I need a stiff drink!" Hewey said as soon as the Wardroom door clanged shut.

Norman needed no prompting, he went straight to his drinks cupboard and poured three large navy brandies for themselves.

"Today is the eleventh! That is just under three weeks before we must leave! We need to make the best of it, *'Governor'*!"

Hewey teased Enzo who, still in shock, took a large sip of the brandy and gave a concerned smile.

"To the Valletta!" said Hewey and as Norman raised his glass all three in unison clinked their glasses and toasted, "To the Valletta!"

Chapter 44

Beginning of the End

Italy had surrendered on 8th September 1943, Mussolini was ousted on 25th July that same year, by the time of Vesuvius erupting in March 1944, the Allies were in full control of the south of Italy. The Germans continued to hold out at Monte Cassino, buying as much time as they could, while retreating from their defeat in Russia. Invasion by the soft belly of Europe through Italy had not been fully expected. Capitulation by Italy made matters worse. Hitler came to the rescue of Mussolini who attempted to set up a separate fascist government in the north of Italy. It was inevitable that the Germans were facing defeat. By the time that the Valletta was harboured in the Port of Ischia the war was over in the *'Mezzogiorno'* region of Italy. Fighting at Monte Cassino would go on for several weeks but the injured and wounded would be treated closer to the battlefield. Since the Valletta was ordered to Ischia its function was to support the rescue operations as result of the eruptions. More importantly it had been decided that the Valletta would now serve as a British asset to administrate the Island of Ischia, where the Royal Navy was based but completely independent to the Valletta. The US was to administer Capri.

Civilian governance of Ischia was by way of an elected Mayor and Councillors. Gaetano di Fiore, the incumbent mayor (*Sindaco*), who had been in office when the Germans were in occupation was now subject to British control. Nevertheless, it was the Camorra that ruled. Black market, corruption and crime persisted. Mayor di Fiore was no more than a token puppet for the Capos now resident on the island. Brigadier Soames had explained to Enzo at the working lunch that, before the Valletta had been diverted to Ischia, Gaetano had been summoned to appear before Allied Command. Munitions and supplies to the Royal Navy base were being stolen and then sold on the Black Market. This was beginning to adversely impact the military supply chain. Like the Germans before, anyone caught stealing could be summarily executed by firing squad. Local produce, supplies, food, other provisions and medical supplies intended for the general population could only be distributed through Camorra outlets. This situation needed to change. A British Military Governor to administrate the island was to be appointed, the mayor and elected officials would act as his advisers. Local laws when needed would be supplemented by martial rules and regulations and imposed by the Military Governor. Once the Valletta had docked in Ischia and completed its rescue mission Enzo was to be formally appointed. However, the accident with the Jeep as well as other non-related operational considerations had postponed his promotion and appointment. Mayor di Fiore was not told the name of the appointee at the meeting.

Pending his transfer back to England at the end of the month, Brigadier Soames had given Hewey the task of helping Enzo set up his administration. Given the problems that Enzo was to face, the help of both Leo and Paolo was essential. Unlike Hewey, they would be staying, and it was important that they worked with Enzo. Both the De Cristofaro and Savino families were well known and highly respected so their participation as part of the Military Governor's administration was to be invaluable to Enzo.

With his usual organisational efficiency, Hewey set up a meeting at Ischia's Municipal Chambers with Mayor Gaetano di Fiore, elected counsellors, local Capos passing themselves off as *'businessmen'*, and Leo and Paolo. Hewey in his best educated Italian accent had explained to the mayor that the British Military Commander had ordered the meeting. Angela was in attendance not only as the wife of the Military Governor but in her capacity as a newly promoted major in the Queen Alexandra's Royal Army Nursing Corps. Enzo, Angela, and Hewey were in British uniform. Paolo and Leo dressed in their Italian army uniforms were present with Fabio Corso as US liaison officer. The meeting had been stage managed by Hewey so that he would act as *'master of ceremonies'*, once all those invited were present, he would introduce the British Military Governor and his wife. Enzo would take the mayor's seat and Angela would sit next to him. Gaetano would sit in front of the Capos who generally populated the Chamber. The mayor and the others had assumed that Hewey would be acting as an interpreter for the new Governor, an assumption that was not discouraged by Hewey. Gaetano, having checked that all those required to attend were present, nodded confirmation to Hewey who then announced, in Italian, *"Colonel Falcone the new Military Governor of Ischia and his wife Major Angela Falcone."*

Hewey opened the door, they both swiftly moved to their allocated seats. In unison all present then sat down. It took all Hewey's will power for him to hide his excited anticipation of the reaction of the Ischians when Enzo spoke in fluent Italian.

"I was born Vincenzo Gennaro Falcone, in San Giorgio a Cremano, the only son of Il Cavaliere Domenico Falcone and his wife Adelina. We spent our summers at our villa here in Ischia. I studied medicine at the University of Florence, qualified as a

doctor, then returned to do my practice in San Giorgio before going to London to specialise in Anaesthesia. To avoid being conscripted I volunteered and was commissioned as 'Medical Captain' in Aqui Division of the Royal Italian Army. My wife Angela is a qualified and experienced midwife also from this region. Her elder sister, Teresa, brother-in-law and their children have just been evacuated from Torre del Greco to this island. I became a Prisoner of War in North Africa then was transported to England. When Italy surrendered, I was offered a commission in the British Army and transferred north to Newcastle where I met my wife. I was put in charge of Operation Valletta which brings me here. I am now a Colonel in the British Royal Army Medical Corps and have been appointed Military Governor of Ischia. To help me properly administrate Ischia I have the authority of the Allied Command in occupation, which includes the Royal Italian Army. My wife will oversee and manage all medical matters with direct control over the Valletta, which will act as Ischia's General Hospital. Major De Cristofaro and Captain Savino are from 'well known' local families and have been tasked to help 'normalise' life on the island. US Marine Captain Fabio Corso who is also of Italian parentage will be the American Liaison. Once I am fully recovered from these leg fractures, I expect to be much more mobile and get around the Island. As Governor I look forward to your full co-operation."

The New Military Governor's speech was completely unexpected and took Mayor di Fiore by surprise as well as everyone else. Gaetano di Fiore had recently hosted Enzo's parents at a recent municipal reception. They had never made any mention to him of their son other than that he was taken prisoner in North Africa and they believed he had been transported back to England.

As soon as Enzo had delivered his address, all were invited to mix and partake of the refreshments provided. Mayor Gaetano took the opportunity to move towards Enzo. who Angela was helping take a more comfortable seat in the chamber. He just had to ask a question to which he was certain he knew the answer.

"Colonel, do your parents know that you are here?"

"No! Are they here in the villa?"

Enzo's eyes lit up with excitement.

"Of course! Where else would they be? They came not long after you went off with your regiment. They still think you are a prisoner in England. Why have you not contacted them?"

"When I realised that they were not at San Giorgio I suspected that they may have come here. I had intended to go and check after my return from the Rescue convoy. On our way back I was injured in the accident which kept me on board for a while. Now I am recovering and able to get about. Tomorrow, I will have my driver take Angela and myself there. Please don't tell them! I want to surprise them! They don't even know I am married!"

Mayor di Fiore put a finger to his lips.

"Not a word Colonel I promise!"

Gaetano took his leave and moved toward the various agitated and gesticulating groups of his Counsellors and Capos all in deep conversation about what they had heard. Not knowing what to expect, if they needed to know from the mayor, if they were going to continue with their various schemes.

"Gentlemen, all my dealings have been with his deputy. Like you I met him today for the first time. I know his parents. They have that villa that overlooks the San Francesco beach. Cavaliere Falcone and his wife think that he is being held as a Prisoner of War in England. They don't even know he is here!"

Don Peppino, self-appointed spokesperson for the anxious

and aggrieved Capos, complained.

"The De Cristofaro and Savino boys, now officers in the Army working with the Governor to help 'normalise'! What the hell does that mean? They must both have the blessing of their families. We don't want to upset them! Gaetano."

"Well, Don Peppino, looks like the British have done their research. You have no choice but co-operate."

Inwardly laughing to himself Di Fiore turned away to speak with the huddle of his counsellors, he left the unhappy and disgruntled lot to stew.

Chapter 45

The Request

Adelina and Mimmi Falcone were not happy that their only son had volunteered to join the Army albeit as a Medic. They understood that it was the best alternative to being conscripted which in any event was inevitable that Enzo would get the call-up. His leaving was a great concern, something they had to adapt to but could never get used to. At first, he was able to have leave and visit but soon he was sent abroad to undisclosed locations. Post was heavily censored, more infrequent until it ceased completely. Lack of contact from her son in a time of great peril would reduce both herself and Mimmi into tears of utter desperation. Together with many other parents on all sides, their anxiety led to them falling into bouts of depression. After many months without any word, Adelina would have days when she would just cry unconsolably all day. Mimmi decided that he had to act and see what he could find out. Through the Vatican, contact was made with the Red Cross who were able to confirm that Enzo was alive and well. He was taken as a Prisoner of War by the British in North Africa. Transported by hospital ship to England. He was in a Prisoner of War camp in the north of England attending to the sick and wounded Italian Prisoners. This welcome news lifted the spirits of both the Cavaliere and his wife who considered themselves much more fortunate than many other parents that had lost sons in combat. By way of thanksgiving, Cavaliere Mimmi and his wife paid for a special mass to be said for all those who had loved ones fighting in the Italian Armed Forces. The couple also made a financial contribution to the local parish fund supporting families in need.

The first year of the war the Cavaliere and his wife decided to move away from San Giorgio; their grounds and vines were managed by their tenants.

Moving to the apartment in Piazza Mercato was not an option. The City and Port of Naples was a hub of violence, crime and had become a very inhospitable place. Ischia was the obvious retreat of choice. When they were due to leave for the annual visit to their villa on the island all was packed for the Falcones to transplant themselves for the duration of the war. However long that would be. Ischia was sufficiently far away from all that was taking place in and around Naples that life there just seemed to carry on as normal. The Germans came and went and now it was the turn of the British with the Americans to come. In many ways it seemed like any tourist season but this time the visitors were in uniform, armed, giving orders and on occasion dangerous. Now that the British were in occupation, Enzo's parents thought that there may be some prospect of getting news about the whereabouts of their son and current status since Italy's surrender. They intended to ask the mayor if he would make an inquiry on their behalf.

Most Wednesdays, Cavaliere Falcone and his wife visited the weekly market in Ischia di Castro, in the area of Viterbo, in the city centre. On this visit they had both decided to call in at the municipal buildings and put their request to the Mayor Gaetano. As they approached the building, British military vehicles pulled up outside the main entrance. Three British officers, two male and one female officers, exited a chauffeured Army staff car. Close behind were two Italian Army Officers

233

sitting in the back of a US marine Jeep with a US Marine Officer in the front passenger seat being driven by a corporal. Mayor Gaetano with his entourage emerged from within the building to greet and escort the visitors inside. The Senior British Officer was on crutches and being helped by the others.

"Must be the new Military Governor come to meet the mayor. Wonder what he's like?" Adelina Falcone asked her husband.

"No idea. But he seems to have something wrong with his legs."

"Mimmi, shall we go wait inside and see if the mayor will let us speak briefly to the Governor about Enzo?"

"Can't do any harm. They can only say no. I expect that they will be in there for a while. So, let's go get the shopping then we can go and wait inside for them to come out," Mimmi answered, as they resumed their casual *'arm in arm'* stroll towards the market. Adelina double checked that she had bought everything she needed on her list, while Mimmi, hands behind his back, looked on.

"All done! Now let's go see what we can find out about our son."

She linked her husband's arm and they both set off to catch the mayor and governor.

They walked up the steps to enter the main stainless-steel-framed double plate glass doors with the colourfully embossed crest of the Island of Ischia. A uniformed doorman enquired about their business which they explained.

"Please, Cavaliere Falcone, follow me. They are all in the Council Chamber having a meeting."

He set them down on the padded well upholstered seats, in the waiting area, outside the Chamber.

"I am not sure how long they are going to take, but as soon as they break or end, I will tell the mayor of your request."

"Thank you," the Falcones replied in unison.

The doorman nodded respectfully and resumed his station at the main entrance.

Directly above the doors at either side of the Chamber were two lights, one red and the other green. Both red lights on meant the Chamber was in session. Part of the doorman's role was to ensure no unauthorised person entered on the red light. The Falcones sat for more than an hour patiently waiting for the green light to come on. When it did, the doorman with his Neapolitan sign language indicated to the Cavaliere and his wife that he was going to enter the Chamber to pass on their request to the mayor.

Deep in conversation with his colleagues the mayor was distracted by the doorman's approach.

"Sir, Cavaliere Falcone and his wife are outside. They say that they need to speak to the British Governor about the whereabouts of their son who is a Prisoner of War in England."

Mayor Gaetano beamed a smile at the doorman.

"Please, tell them to wait and I will be out with the Governor shortly."

As instructed the doorman left to deliver his message.

Gaetano put down his drink and moved swiftly to Enzo on the other side of the Chamber.

"Governor, I have a surprise for you. Will you and your wife, please come with me?"

Chapter 46

The Mayor's Surprise

Hands behind his back, Cavaliere Falcone wandered over to the notice board on the opposite side of the entrance hall to eyeball the municipal announcements. Adelina sat, handbag in her lap and shopping basket to the side of the chair, as they both awaited the return of the doorman with news. The Chamber door swung open held by the doorman for Mayor Gaetano to exit who was followed by Enzo on his crutches and Angela.

"Donna Falcone, I have a fantastic surprise for you..."

Adelina had suddenly stood up, made immediate eye contact with her son, instantly recognised Enzo, and called out, *"My son!"* Then he fainted.

Angela instinctively pushed forward to her mother-in-law's aid. The mayor and doorman helped lift Enzo's mother back into her seat while Angela loosened Donna Falcone's clothing. Oblivious as to what had caused his wife to collapse, Mimmi feared that she had suffered a heart attack, so he rushed to her side. He took her hand not realising that Enzo stood directly behind him and said, *"Please, God, do not let her die!"*

Enzo put his arm around his father. *"Papa, I think that it is my fault. She fainted when she saw me."*

The sound of her son's voice brought Adelina around. No, it had not been a phantom of her imagination. It really was her son that she saw coming towards her on crutches behind Mayor

Gaetano. Freeing himself from his parent's tearful embrace, Enzo discarded his crutches and sat himself down next to his mother. Wiping away the tears, she composed herself, keeping a tight grip of Enzo's hand she kept on kissing it stroking his cheek with the other.

"My son, my son! Thank you for bringing him back to us. Mimmi, we got him back! Thank you, San Gennaro."

Cavaliere Falcone was just as emotional as his wife but tried to maintain some self-control. Angela took his arm.

"I am Enzo's wife," she declared.

There was a pregnant pause as Enzo's parents looked at each other to absorb what they had just been told. They looked at Enzo who reached out and took Angela's hand. *"Mama and Papa, this is your daughter-in-law, my wife Angela, her family are from Torre del Greco."*

Without letting go of her son's hand, Adelina got up, pulled Angela towards her, burst into tears and hugged her.

An emotional spectator to this Falcone lachrymose reunion opera, the mayor and the entourage backed off and allowed them space. Hewey and the others emerged from the Chamber to the scene. Picking the right moment, Hewey tactfully intervened, pointing in the direction of the Chamber, he suggested that they all go back inside including Enzo's parents and resume the interrupted buffet reception. Clinging to both her son's and daughter-in-law's arms she followed Mayor Gaetano back into the Chamber. Cavaliere followed close behind in deep conversation with Hewey.

"You speak excellent Italian, Major! My compliments. How do you know my son?"

"Cavaliere, thank you. My father was a diplomat and was posted to Rome for several years where I went to school. I met

Enzo when transferred to the Valletta as his Deputy and Intelligence Officer before we sailed from Liverpool. Enzo, Angela and I have become very close ever since."

"Why is Enzo a British Officer? How did he get injured?"

"Cavaliere, it's a long story about why he is a British Officer. I think it best you ask him and have him give you the full story. Both Enzo and I were being driven back to the port from Pozzuoli, when there was a minor tremor which threw our Jeep off the road. Our driver was killed. Enzo received fractures to both legs and other injuries. We were lucky not to get killed."

"What about you, Major?"

"I was very lucky. Dislocated shoulder, various other minor injuries and concussion. But please, Cavaliere I would be honoured if you and Donna Falcone called me 'Hewey'. Enzo needs a few more weeks before the breaks fully heal."

Mimmi nodded as he and Hewey entered the Chamber and joined the re-constituted group.

Once everything had settled down and got back to as they were before the mayor's surprise, Gaetano clinked his glass to call to order, he had some important announcements to make.

"I will be brief. As you now all know. Until further notice, Colonel Vincenzo Falcone has been appointed the British Military Governor of our beautiful island. He will be in this building, and I look forward to working with him. As elected mayor I will continue to carry out my office over civilian matters with elected councillors. During his tenure Governor Falcone can be assured of our full co-operation in all matters!"

Not expecting to have to make a speech Enzo had been hijacked into make a reply.

"Thank you, Mayor Gaetano. Ischia is a place my family and I spent our summer months. It is sad that it took a war, the

eruption of Vesuvius and the Valletta to bring me back to this place I love. But here I am back."

Spontaneous applause broke out interrupting Enzo's flow. He paused, became emotional, then concluded.

"The war will be soon over. We need to repair and prepare for whatever comes next!"

Cavaliere Falcone, in his enigmatic paternal voice, told Enzo, *"Today you and Angela will come home with me and Mama."*

Still holding on to her daughter-in-law's arm she wiped away her tears and endorsed her husband's words. *"Your father is right. There is no excuse, and you know there is plenty of room!"*

Hewey seized the moment before either Enzo or Angela had the chance to say anything.

"It will be done. Take your parents with you in your car up to the Villa. Your driver can then return to the Valletta. I will go back and organise your things ready for when the car gets back to collect and bring to you."

Neither Enzo nor Angela protested.

Chapter 47

The Governor's Residence

'Villa Falcone' was well known to all the locals, its prominent position high up overlooking the San Fransisco beach. Il Cavaliere and his wife were very well respected in the community. Ownership and residence of the villa carried with it clout and assumed authority which Enzo's parents never sought to presume. The Bishop of Ischia was a frequent visitor to the Villa, in keeping with the Papal knighthood, Cavaliere Falcone and his family he allocated VIP seating in all the island's churches. Inevitably, when the Germans came to occupy Ischia, they had originally considered sequestering the Villa for their own use. Acting on the advice of the bishop, Cavaliere Falcone took the initiative and invited the Bishop and the German Commanding Officer to lunch at *'Villa Falcone'*. The bishop had met then Captain Karl von Prout, now Colonel before the war when he was a young priest at the Vatican. He described the German Colonel as a professional soldier, of the traditional Prussian officer class, a devout Roman Catholic, a loyal German and definitely *'not a Nazi!'*. Karl von Prout had been a military attaché to the Vatican and attended the church where the bishop was first posted after being ordained. He spoke Italian with a heavy Teutonic accent, it became more diluted and incomprehensible with red wine. The topic of commandeering *'Villa Falcone'* to serve as the colonel's residence was never

discussed. He found quarters nearer to the Port and on occasion paid a visit to the Cavaliere.

Moving into Villa Falcone with his parents was ideal for Mayor Gaetano, the villa was big enough to be used as a formal residence. Enzo could conduct gubernatorial administration from there without the need of having to take an office in the municipal building. Before being elected mayor, Gaetano had never been inside 'Villa Falcone'. Out of respect to the new incumbent, Cavaliere Falcone invited the newly elected mayor and his wife to lunch. After the meal Gaetano and his wife were first given a tour of the house, then the grounds, introduced to staff and a slow walk back to the villa. A liquor and espresso on their return. That first visit to the Falcone home was the only time Gaetano had been around the whole villa. He had stamped the layout in his memory from which he was able to picture how it could work at the 'Governor's Residence'.

Hewey, as Enzo's deputy, had organised things so that Enzo and Angela were not required to leave the 'Residence' for some days. Hewey could deal with all the mundane day to day matters connected with Operation Valletta. This gave Enzo and Angela time to settle into living in the villa and an opportunity to explain the missing years to his parents. Liaising with the Valletta's communications officer, Enzo arranged for calls to be made to Angela's parents. This would be done when Enzo and Angela brought his parents to show them around the Valletta. Teresa, Filippe and their children were the first invited guests to the Governor's Residence and would become frequent visitors as part of the now extended Falcone family. In a very short space of time 'Villa Falcone' had transformed from an echoing almost empty house to an active family home. Angela and Teresa spent as much time together as they could caring for Matteo while

'*Mammina Adelina*' fussed over Teresa's other two who called her '*Nonna Adelina*'.

After discussion with Norman and Hewey, Enzo decided that '*Villa Falcone*' would become the formal Governor's residence and office. Its hilltop prominence gave it much better transmission and reception radio communication capabilities than the masts on the Valletta at sea level. The ship's communication officer arranged to set up a radio room on the roof terrace of the villa and organised operators from the Valletta to work a shift system to man the station. Direct contact was maintained with the Valletta communications room which was now the auxiliary. Everything was up and running within forty-eight hours of concept. Field portable telephone equipment was set up on a desk adjacent to Enzo's in the main ground floor reception room now dedicated to his office. This had become Angela's desk who had now assumed the role of secretary and '*gatekeeper*' to the governor.

Much had happened in a very short space of time. Vesuvius was now settling down. Montecasino was on the verge of being taken from the Germans and Enzo was British Military Governor of Ischia. Back in Newcastle, the last news Bernardo and Gilda Di Carlo had of their two daughters was that because of the eruptions, a heavily pregnant Teresa, together with her husband Fillipo and two children had fled Torre del Greco. Angela and Enzo had set sail aboard the Valletta from Liverpool to somewhere in the Mediterranean. Using one of his few privileges of rank, Enzo arranged for contact to be made with his in-laws back in Newcastle and requested they come to the Radio room at Fenham Barracks. He would then bring all the family together at the villa for a conference call set for Sunday evening when all were gathered after lunch.

At the pre-arranged time of five p.m. *'Ischia time'* all were gathered at the villa for the call. Bernardo and Gilda had made their way to Fenham Barracks to arrive half an hour early and reported to the duty officer. He took them to a small conference room equipped with a loudspeaker, from which the attending radio operator would initiate the call to Italy at the agreed time slot. Promptly, at five p.m. the telephone rang at the villa. Enzo answered in English.

"Yes, this is Colonel Falcone. We are all present and correct I can also confirm that this call is on loudspeaker."

"Thank you, sir. We too are on 'speaker. There is an allocated time slot of thirty minutes for this call. I will now bring Mr and Mrs Di Carlo to the mic. I will remain present throughout."

At both ends of the call there was excited anticipation. Everyone spoke at once, loudest were Angela and Teresa. Enzo interrupted and took control, each would have an opportunity to speak, but first he wanted to introduce his parents which he did. Mid-stream through this emotional telephonic family reunion call, the duty radio operator from the villa roof top radio control centre opened the door to the room waving a piece of paper and beckoned Enzo to come over to him. The others were too involved in the call to pay any attention to Enzo heading over to the door.

"What is it?" asked Enzo.

"Sir, I have just received a coded communication from the MOD in London marked *'TOP SECRET'*. It is addressed to you, Major Hewitson and Commander Butler. It requires immediate attention with a response by midnight today!"

"What does it say?"

"Don't know, sir, it is in code. Major Hewitson is the Intelligence Officer, and he will be the only one with the code,

Colonel!"

"Contact them both and explain what has happened. Request them to come for a meeting here with me at nineteen-thirty hours. See that Major Hewitson gets a copy of the message to decipher before the meeting!"

"Very well, sir!"

Chapter 48

Top Secret

Hewey and Patti were relaxing on the upper deck of the Valletta's stern and taking in the early May sunshine after a substantial lunch at a nearby Trattoria. As they were making plans for their flight back to England at the end of the month, Norman appeared.

"Sorry to ruin your well-deserved rest, Hewey, but I need to speak to you privately."

Hewey got up out of his deck chair, kissed Patti on the forehead, then followed Norman to his quarters. On the way Norman explained.

"MOD business. TOP SECRET. |You need to decipher a message we have just received from the Admiralty in London, then we need to go and meet with Enzo at the villa. London needs a response by midnight."

"Understood! I need to get my deciphers. Go ahead, I'll be with you in a couple of minutes."

The coded message was in a sealed envelope, delivered by motorcycle messenger to the Valletta for Hewey to decipher.

Norman and Hewey sat side by side at the table normally used for meeting and conferences in the captain's quarters. To Norman's eyes the message made up of about a dozen short lines of incomprehensible jumbled letters, numbers and random punctuation. As an intelligence officer Hewey had been trained in code; at first reading he got the basic gist of the communication.

"Norman it's about the Western Front and the Valletta being reassigned. New Orders to leave as soon as possible but not more than seven days. Proceed to Gibraltar and further orders as to your destination will be given at sea. The Valletta, under your command, will depart with Betty, Patti, and Roger. I am to fly back as soon as the Valletta has left port. Enzo is to continue as Military Governor. Angela is to oversee the transfer of sick and wounded from the Valletta to local hospitals and remain in situ until further notice!"

"Hewey, get the message fully decoded I will then call Enzo, give him a brief summary and set up a meeting for tomorrow morning around eleven here on the Valletta instead of going to the villa as Enzo requested."

The family call between the Di Carlos and Falcones had been emotional, and the thirty minutes seemed to fly by. As they made their way back home from Fenham Barracks, Bernardo, and Gilda both felt a sense of relief and contentment. Their two daughters and families were safe and well. The war needed to be over soon so they could visit Ischia and be reunited.

"It won't be too long now, Gilda."

"I hope so. Bernardo, I miss them so much!"

Meanwhile, back at Villa Falcone the conference call had ended, similar sentiments were being discussed. Just as Teresa and Fillipo were leaving, Enzo was called to the telephone.

"Enzo, Hewey has decoded the message, it will be with you shortly by messenger. Cannot say much on this line, but the Valletta is needed elsewhere. Unless you have anything to the contrary, I am setting up a meeting down here tomorrow morning at eleven-hundred hours in the Wardroom."

"Understood, no objection. I'll read the message when it

arrives. Angela and I will be there."

As expected, there was a full turn out in the Wardroom that following morning. Paolo, Fabio, and Leo came across on the first morning ferry from the port. Norman helped Enzo shuffle in with his walking sticks while Hewey handed out an edited version of the message in both Italian and English.

"Take a minute or two to read the memo you've just been given by Hewey," Enzo invited.

He then asked if there were any questions or comments.

"Now I don't need to worry about having to pack!" Betty volunteered.

"The Valletta has been my home and I did not want to leave. As far as I'm concerned, I go where the Valletta goes!" Roger declared.

Except for Patti, there appeared to be an overall acceptance by all of the new orders. Patti on the other hand was visibly upset. Hewey who stood beside her tried to give comfort but that only made matters worse and she broke into tears. Betty and Angela took over.

Hewey began to explain, "We were looking forward to flying back to London together and planned on getting a special marriage licence so we could be married before the next posting. Now, because of these new orders, that is not going to happen!"

Norman interrupted and declared, "That is easily fixed!"

Everyone's attention focused on the Master of the Valletta and what he was about to say.

"By the lawful authority vested in me as Captain of His Majesty's Hospital Ship the Valletta, docked in foreign waters in time of war, I can wed you both here and now. I am satisfied that you are both adults of sound mind in active military service and there are witnesses here present. Indeed, one of the witnesses is the Military Governor who is also your Commanding Officer, his consent is all that is required for you both to marry!"

Norman paused.

Enzo interposed, "In my capacity as Military Governor and their Commanding Officer I have no objection and give consent to the marriage of Major Christopher Hewitson to Captain Patti Colvin!"

But nobody had bothered to check with the couple if that's what they wanted to do.

Chapter 49

A Change of Course

Shell-shocked, Patti and Hewey looked into each other's eyes. Then suddenly the tears of disappointment, which had just abated, were now tears of joy. Cheers and applause broke out as Norman took his leave to fetch the Ship Master's Manual and a copy of the King's Regulations from his room.

What had started up as a briefing to announce the new orders from the Admiralty, had transformed into a marriage ceremony. Overcome by what had transpired, Patti and Hewey acquiesced to the evolving events being marshalled by Betty and Angela. Pending Norman's return, the conference table was moved back to give standing room for the ceremony.

Betty became the self-appointed wedding organiser.

"OK. Angela, you will be Patti's *'Maid of Honour'*. Enzo, you will be *'Best Man'*. Roger, will you give Patti *'away'* please?"

Roger, with a huge smile on his face, looked at Patti and with a small bow of the head said, "It will be my pleasure."

"Thank you, Roger," Betty continued, "Leo, Paolo and Fabio you will be our ready-made congregation, while I will assist Norman. Angela can help Patti prepare herself."

The Bride and Groom had it all done for them at no cost, no need for any licence, no planning and minimal fuss. As they all awaited Norman's return, Betty realised she had taken charge without involving the bride and groom, so she posed the question.

"Are there any objections to what has been organised?"

Hewey, with his arm around his intended, voiced, "Of course not, it's amazing! Truth be told we're both still in shock. This whole thing was not something we had ever possibly contemplated!"

Now more composed, Patti, leaning further into Hewey with delight written all over her face, explained, "I've read and heard about people being married on cruise ships and the like by the ship's captain but never, in my wildest dreams, did I expect it to be happening to me!"

Time was passing. Roger was getting concerned that Norman was taking longer than expected so went and stood lookout at the door.

"At last! Here he comes and he has got the mayor with him!" Roger announced with a tone of excitement as he turned to face everyone.

Norman had been delayed because he had decided to stop by the galley to arrange champagne and glasses to be brought up to the Wardroom. When he had emerged from the galley, Mayor Gaetano had just stepped aboard for the arranged noon visit to discuss arrangements for the proposed Valletta's farewell party. The Master of the ship seized the opportunity to co-opt Gaetano to help officiate.

Norman, the mayor and two stewards, one carrying a tray of glasses the other two bottles of champagne, entered the room. While the Mayor was greeted by everyone, the stewards set down their wares. The atmosphere was electric with anticipation. Then in walked Patti and Angela, having taken the opportunity to slip out in Norman's absence and prepare for Patti's up and coming nuptials. Her tear-stained face having been washed in cold water and her make-up freshly applied, Angela had even managed to conjure up a small posy of flowers for Patti to hold. The bride was radiant. The Mayor, acknowledging Angela, went over to Patti and kissed her on both cheeks, holding her hands in his, he told her he was so very happy to be there to share such a happy occasion. Patti was overjoyed.

Finally, everyone shuffled into the various positions that Betty had allocated.

"Proceedings will go ahead without a rehearsal."

Betty said, as she manoeuvred and directed all, then suddenly she realised they had no rings!

Once satisfied everyone was in their place, she flanked Norman on the bride's side while Mayor Gaetano faced Hewey.

Suddenly Betty had a concerning thought and leant over to Norman and whispered in his ear, "We have forgotten about the rings!"

Norman turned to Betty and in a comforting tone said, "Don't worry we'll improvise."

All eyes were now focused on Norman to begin the proceedings. However, he hesitated and looked towards the door. Norman waited. Everyone began to look at each other and then at Norman trying to work out why he was not starting the ceremony. Then, when he realised, he could not hold up the proceedings any longer, there was a knock on the door.

"Enter," Norman said in a loud voice as he looked to the door.

In came one of the ship's engineering crew, wiping his blackened greased hands the best he could on the overalls he was wearing, he handed a shoe-box size wooden container full of assorted rings, washers, nuts, bushes, and clips to his captain.

251

"This is all we could find in the workshop, sir. Hope you can find ones that will fit!"

The engineer took his leave and left.

Norman then turned to Hewey and Patti and explained, "On my way to pick up the *'regs'* I had to pass the workshop. So, it struck me that they kept copper washers, bushes and rings in there for plumbing jobs. I asked the chief to send me a selection to use as temporary wedding rings."

Norman then turned to Betty and handed her the box. She foraged around in the box until she had selected some that were likely to fit Patti and Hewey. She gave them to Angela for her to try on the intended bride. Mayor Gaetano passed Betty's choice for Hewey.

Once they found the near perfect fit rings the ceremony began.

The King's Regulations required that the Ship's Master commence and end the ceremony by announcing his name in full, rank and name of the ship, with all the dignity and pomp he could muster.

By noon it was all done except the paperwork which both Norman and Enzo would later complete. Mayor Gaetano's original plan had been postponed due to the wedding. Whilst post-ceremony drinks were in progress, the mayor sent one of his staff off to the Hotel San Marco to book tables for the ad hoc wedding party lunch.

Until the paperwork came through Patti would continue to be known by her maiden name 'Colvin' and that would take some time. In any event it was more convenient to leave things that way. She and Hewey were now lawfully husband and wife, but in a few days, current orders meant that they would soon be parted. Hewey was to be flown out on the day the Valletta left port. The time they had together was limited and, in war time, very precious due to its unpredictable nature. The impromptu reception gave the newlyweds a few joyous hours amongst loyal friends in the cocoon of the Hotel San Marco, a time oasis of life when the world was at peace.

Chapter 50

Persons of Interest

Procida, four square kilometres in area, is the smallest of the three inhabited islands in the Gulf of Naples and about nine kilometres from Ischia. It was part of the jurisdiction of the British Military Governor (BMG). The island, like Ischia, was self-sufficient through fishing, small holdings, vines, and citrus groves. It housed a large prison built in the seventeenth century. A small garrison of Royal Marines and naval personnel occupied the island which, like Ischia, was self-governing under the BMG supervision. In peacetime, Procida was a popular honeymoon destination for Italians. Enzo in his capacity as BMG was required to make monthly visits to Procida, but his legs had not recovered enough for him to risk taking the twenty-minute ferry to the island. Instead, he sent Hewey, his deputy and new wife Patti in his place. As Hewey was on *'Official Business'* a suite at Procida's only hotel *'The Savoia'* was booked for three nights. Whilst there he had to meet with local elected officials, inspect the garrison, police, and visit the prison, all of which could be achieved in a day visit. This *'duty'* Hewey had been delegated to perform for the BMG was Enzo's wedding gift. Forty-eight hours after Patti and Hewey returned from Procida the Valletta was to set sail and the honeymooners would be separated.

When it was Enzo's turn to make his short speech to the nuptial gathering at lunch, he made the announcement, "As the

BMG of Ischia and Procida, I hereby deputise Major Christopher Hewitson and his wife to travel this evening on the last ferry to Procida to act on my behalf."

Enzo resumed his seat, to the applause. Patti, tearful again, got out of her seat came over, and hugged him.

At eleven the next morning, Mayor Gaetano returned to the Valletta for the meeting which had been postponed due to the surprise nuptials. He, Enzo and Norman were to finalise the arrangements for departure that following Monday including the transfer of all wounded and sick to shore facilities on the island or transported back to the Port of Naples. Norman's orders were that the Valletta was to set sail with all beds vacated. A sanitation and sterilisation team would need to be recruited locally. They would be required to work on the hospital ship, en route to Gibraltar. Mayor Gaetano proffered that there were several repatriated ex POWs who had travelled back to Ischia on the Valletta, now willing to serve as crew or any other capacity. The mayor reached into his briefcase, took out a list of their names, and put it on the table before Enzo and Norman.

"They are all single between twenty-three and thirty-five. Volunteer anti-fascist pre-war serving professional military, air-force, and navy men. Thirty-four in all. They can be ready to leave within twenty-four hours."

"Can you have them all report to the Valletta tomorrow morning at ten-hundred hours?" Enzo ordered.

After some minor discourse about the departure celebrations, the meeting was concluded, and the mayor left.

Norman and Enzo then took the time to peruse in more detail the list provided by Gaetano.

"Not sure about this list, Enzo. Gaetano means well, but we need to have a look at them first. Then, when Hewey gets back, day after tomorrow we will have him check them all out before we make our final decision!"

"Makes sense but, to save time and before he returns, we should submit the list to London and Allied HQ in Naples," Enzo proffered.

Norman agreed, took the list to be copied and sent out to the mainland on the next ferry for urgent delivery by messenger. He also had the list ciphered and sent by Morse Code to the Admiralty in London.

"The next ferry out of here will be at fourteen-hundred hours. It should be at HQ by around sixteen-hundred. So, we're not likely to get any response until when Hewey is due back," Norman concluded.

"In that case I will head back to the Villa for lunch," Enzo responded.

Norman walked him to his official car, where the driver relieved the BMG of his two walking sticks and helped Enzo into the back seat.

Cavaliere Falcone and his wife had arranged a private family lunch for just the four of them back at the villa. For once everybody was free that afternoon and nothing had been planned. Enzo's parents would have another chance to spend time with their son and hear about the missing years. This would be the first real opportunity for her in-laws to casually interrogate Angela. Both Enzo and Angela knew full well the real motive for the *'pranzo privato in famiglia'* Over the five-course traditional meal served with wine, they answered everything asked of them as fully as they could.

Normally, after such a long lunch an afternoon siesta was in order and this occasion was no exception. *'Pranzo'* had ended at around four-twenty and they all retired to their bedrooms, which were shuttered against the heat. When they woke at about half past six, espresso coffees were served with pastries on the balcony. If it were not for Enzo's injuries all would have walked down to the beach and back. His parents and Angela needed very little encouragement from Enzo to go without him due to his limited mobility. He stayed behind, watching their progress from the balcony in the early evening sun and warm sea breeze, sipping *Amaretto* from a brandy glass. Peacefully contemplating as little as he possibly could, he was interrupted by the ringing of the telephone which had been put on a small table next to where he sat. It rang a couple of times loudly before he picked up the handset.

"Enzo?" General Bill Ward barked down the line in his unmistakable American tones and, without waiting for any response or confirmation from Enzo, he continued, "Got that list you and Norman sent! Understand that all of them on the list are reporting to the Valletta tomorrow morning at eleven-hundred hours. I will be coming over with my team for eight-hundred hours. I have already told Norman."

"Is there some kind of problem, General?" Enzo enquired.

"Not really. The list of names you provided include several *'persons of interest'* which we will discuss when we meet tomorrow morning."

Chapter 51

Intelligence

Enzo and Norman were in the Wardroom that morning by seven. Neither had any real idea why Bill Ward was coming over with *'his team'*. It was obviously something to do with the list of volunteers that Gaetano had provided. Speculation was futile. A further read of the document took them no further. The Wardroom door opened and in walked Hewey.

"Is that the list Bill Ward has been on about?" the Intelligence Officer asked.

Taken by surprise, both Norman and Enzo nodded in the affirmative, while greeting the honeymooner with a brief embrace.

"You are not due back until tomorrow!" Enzo said.

"Bill Ward did not know that! As Intelligence Officer for Operation Valletta, he contacted me first then you two. He thought that it was me who had sent the list to him. I just bluffed it out so I'd better take a look at it now and you can both brief me before he gets here."

Hewey, took up the list and read it.

"When did you arrive back?" Norman asked.

"Last night, late. Me and Patti hitched a ride back here on one of the Royal Navy Supply Craft that stopped off at Procida en route to Ischia. We stayed here last night aboard the Valletta in our quarters," Hewey explained, as he further scrutinised the subject list provided by Mayor Gaetano.

"There is no-one named on this list that means anything to me. Like you both I have no idea what this is all about!" Hewey declared.

The chugg-chugg of the landing craft ferry carrying Bill Ward and his team grew louder as it came into the port. Within a few minutes it was tied up dockside, Ward and other officers disembarked. Hewey went down to meet the visitors and escorted them to the Wardroom.

"Morning," Bill Ward said loudly to Norman and Enzo who were standing at the doorway as the General entered. "Let's get everyone in. I will do the intros and then get straight to the point!"

Two new faces had entered the Wardroom, one a US Captain in the newly formed OSS and the second, a British Captain in the Royal Signals. After the formal handshakes, Bill Ward made his introductions.

Captain Mike Nelson, formerly US Marines out of San Diego, now with the Office of Strategic Service (OSS), from Laguna Beach, California. Captain Ian Oliver, British Special Operations Executive (SOE) from County Durham, England. As of today, these officers will be joining 'Operation Valletta Stage Two', under your command, Hewey!"

Hewey intervened, "Sir, am I not scheduled to fly back when the Valletta leaves?"

"All changed, Hewey, you are now to stay with the Valletta. The men on the list I was sent will be signed on today. Once at sea each will be interrogated by Nelson and Oliver in the context of orders that they have been given. Between now and the Valletta's departure both will fully brief you, Enzo and Norman."

"What's so special about these volunteers named on the list the mayor provided?" Enzo asked the General who then deferred to Nelson to respond.

"Sir, what the General has been told is on a *'need to know'* basis. Namely that there are some names in that list that may be considered intelligence and / or operational assets. To what extent will be determined by Major Hewitson, Captain Oliver and myself from our interrogation."

Oliver added, "By the time we reach Gibraltar we will have a much better picture, Colonel."

Norman as the Master of a hospital ship had concerns. "General, this is a Hospital Ship not a floating interrogation facility. Are these men dangerous? What do I tell the Medics about Nelson, Oliver and the *'volunteers'* joining the Valletta?"

Bill Ward explained, "The men do not pose any threat. Anything said in this meeting can be shared with the Medics in confidence. Further briefings will be given at sea."

Norman checked his watch and as he did so the ship's duty officer knocked at the Wardroom door and was told to enter. Addressing his Captain, he advised, "Sir, all the Volunteers have arrived. I have them assembled in the main mess."

On that cue, Norman and the others followed the duty officer to where the men were gathered. A motley array of Italian men, some dressed in civvies, some in their old POW uniforms, some in a compendium of anything that remotely fit; exchanging war stories in animated groups.

Instinctively, they all went silent, stood to attention, and faced the officer group who had entered the room.

Enzo took command. In Italian he introduced himself, Norman and Hewey, General Ward, the two new Captains and the officer medics who had joined the group on entering the Mess. As BMG he thanked them all on behalf of the Allies and the Italian people for volunteering. After satisfactory medicals they would all be given uniforms, kit and assigned beds aboard the Valletta. Further instructions and orders would be given by the duty officer. Departure was in five days, on Monday morning. Enzo closed by repeating his thanks and handing over command to the duty officer. Norman then ushered all the officers back to the Wardroom where the stewards awaited with coffee and tea.

"There is one final matter!" Bill Ward remarked. "We have a wounded captured German Officer. He was being driven back to Rome when his retreating convoy was attacked by the RAF two days ago. This officer was one of the prisoners taken by ground forces and brought back to Naples. He has been identified as Colonel Karl von Prout the former German Military Commander of Ischia, he has shrapnel wounds in his chest, arms, and head. He was barely conscious when he was found. He will be ferried here later this afternoon and stay aboard the Valletta for treatment and transportation to England. When deemed fit enough he will be formally interviewed in accordance with the Geneva Convention by Hewey, Nelson and Oliver."

Oliver volunteered further details, "The convoy was specifically targeted. We had intelligence that the German High Command were trying to get von Prout back to join Rommel who had overall command of the German defences on the Western Front. Like the 'Desert Rat', von Prout is a professional soldier and not a Nazi. He was a major on Rommel's general staff in North Africa, was promoted to Lieutenant-Colonel and went with Rommel in November '43 to oversee and set up defences in Normandy and Brittany. Promoted to Colonel, German High Command transferred von Prout to Ischia. He is believed to be one of an increasing number of German officers that want to overthrow Hitler and seek peace with the Allies. Even though he is now a Prisoner of War, he will be given the full status of his rank whilst aboard the Valletta."

"Does he speak English?" enquired Hewey.

"Fluently. His Italian and French are also good," answered Nelson. He also explained that he and Oliver had spoken to von Prout at the field hospital to which he had been ambulanced.

As the officers drank their respective teas and coffees, a brief silence ensued while they digested the new orders.

Chapter 52

New Faces

Bill Ward left for his base after lunch in the Officer's Mess on the Valletta, Betty, Roger, Patti and Angela had all joined the visiting group. When Hewey gave his new wife the news that he would be staying on the Valletta, she went over to the unsuspecting General sitting at lunch and kissed him on his balding head. Enzo introduced Ian Oliver and Mike Nelson to the Medics. Betty was puzzled when Oliver was introduced as SOE but was wearing the uniform of a Royal Signals Captain. He saw her puzzled look and pre-empted her inquiry.

"Usually in civvies, but they commissioned me in the 'Signals' for this op! Joined the Foreign Office from Cambridge, then volunteered for SOE when it was formed!"

"Well, welcome aboard the Valletta, we are all very informal here, close, but at the same time very professional when we need to be," Betty commented.

Nelson and Oliver were beckoned from the post lunch group by the duty officer who took them to the Officer's Accommodation deck. There he introduced them to the Chief Deck Steward and left. The Chief then took the two captains to their allocated adjacent midship cabins, explaining as they went.

"Before the War this was the Italian Luxury Cruise Ship 'Principessa Emilia', and this deck was for First-Class passengers. There are six of us doing eight-hour shifts, twenty-

263

four/seven servicing this deck. You'll get the hang of it from the other officers," he added as he let them into their cabins and handed each their respective keys, "Commander Butler has requested you join him and the other officers for dinner at twenty-hundred hours in the Officer's Mess. Casual dress," the Chief advised, as he left.

"This German Officer will be our only patient aboard whilst we are sanitising and sterilising. We need to set up a *'side ward'* fully equipped and fitted for treatment. No medical records have been provided so Roger and I will have to wait until he comes to see what is needed," Betty explained to Norman and Enzo, when she and Roger were told about von Prout's arrival later that afternoon.

"Norman, are there any specific instructions about security?" Roger asked.

"Unlikely, but that will be for Hewey to decide. We are going to have to play this very much by ear!" Norman replied.

Enzo, who had been pensively considering Betty's concerns, added, "My father told me that when the Germans were here and von Prout was in command, our family villa was being considered by him to be used as his residence. The bishop (of Ischia) had met von Prout before the war and he suggested to my father to invite the German to join them for lunch at the Villa."

Betty, curious to know more, asked Enzo, "Is he a Nazi?"

"No, definitely not! My father says that he was very impressed with von Prout who he said was very well mannered and cultured. The epitome of a Prussian Army Officer. I do not expect that he will cause any problem."

Hewey, having listened to everything being discussed, stated, "I agree. I do not see von Prout as any real threat, but he is still the enemy. Betty put him in the *'secure unit'* away from everyone else. Until we are at sea, I will arrange to have a twenty-four-hour guard outside his room."

Colonel von Prout, pumped full of painkillers, bandaged, intravenous saline drip and barely conscious, arrived at Ischia around sunset. He was stretchered off the shuttle from the mainland by medical orderlies on to the Valletta. Received by Betty and the two nurses she had assigned to Von Prout's personal care, one male and one female, the stretcher detail was led to the prepared ward in the secure unit. All the manoeuvring and accompanying commotion involved getting von Prout to his room, had made him fully conscious. When the detail and their charge eventually arrived, von Prout insisted that he would get into the bed without any help. Betty signed the required paperwork while the stretcher was being collapsed and tied. She handed the forms back to the Orderly in charge, who in turn saluted Betty as he followed the others out of the room.

"I am Major Elizabeth Kirby of the Queen Alexandra's Royal Army Nursing Corp, together with Major Roger Hill we command Valletta's hospital facilities. I will have direct and overall authority as to your hospitalisation while you are aboard this vessel. Major Hewitson is the officer in charge of your detention. Commander Norman Butler is Master and Captain of the Valletta. Until we set sail, we are under the jurisdiction of the British Military Governor Colonel Falcone."

Betty then removed from her clipboard the paper she had just read out, handed it to von Prout with a list of rules, and said, "Here is a copy of what I have just said and hospital rules in German and English."

With a submissive smile, von Prout took the documents and laid them on the bedside cabinet.

"Thank you, Major Kirby," von Prout replied in a well

265

enunciated English accent, which surprised Betty.

She continued, "Matt and Joan will be your personal nurses."

Both nurses nodded at von Prout in acknowledgement. He smiled back with a reciprocating nod to each and thanked Betty.

Following Betty's direction, the two nurses helped the German get into bed.

"An evening meal will be brought to you in about an hour, after which you will be due for further analgesics. The surgical team will visit you in the morning," Betty announced.

"Thank you, Major."

Transfer of Colonel von Prout had been very low profile. As the sole patient aboard the Valletta his presence was not easily hidden but his identity was not to be disclosed until after the Valletta had left port. On Ischia, as in most of the South of Italy, the Germans were resented and subject to retaliation. Knowing that the island's former German Military Governor was a prisoner aboard the Valletta was something that might provoke the locals. Only those who needed to know were told the sole patient's identity. All others were simply told that he was a wounded high-ranking German POW being taken back to England.

Chapter 53

Arrivederci Ischia

The Valletta's last weekend in Ischia had arrived. Festivities that had been organised by Mayor Gaetano involved the municipal band and a contingent of Ischia's *'Dad's Army'* marching towards the adjacent quay. The Band would play *'Torna Sorriento'* as it departed. *'Dad's Army'* would stand to attention as it left the harbour together with a section of six Royal Marines and a Sergeant. More importantly a dinner was to be held in the town hall at which all the officers, crew, medics, and the new volunteers would be entertained and fed on the Saturday night. Enzo as BMG and Angela were to remain on the island. Both were saddened that they would soon be separated not only from the people who had become almost family, but the Valletta itself, which had brought them all together. In thanks for returning his son safely back to him and a new daughter-in-law, Il Cavaliere gifted from his vineyards two five-hundred litre barrels of wine, one white and the other red, to the Valletta for its journey. Gratefully accepted by Norman on behalf of the ship and the crew.

Sunday was to be occupied making final arrangements for departure, testing engines, refuelling, taking on supplies and carrying out final checks. It would also be the last time that Enzo and Angela would be aboard the Valletta. That evening all the original members of *'Operation Valletta'* that had left Liverpool plus the two newcomers, Mike Nelson and Ian Oliver, were guests of its Master in the Wardroom. War stories shared, the anticipated journey discussed, and the ship's next destination speculated. Based upon the recent arrival of von Prout, the unanimous consensus of those gathered was that the Western Front was likely to be the next *'theatre of battle'*. Probably Brittany or Normandy.

By the time Hewey and Patti had returned from their short *'honeymoon'* to Procida, in the guise of an official visit on behalf of the BMG, the *'married'* quarters previously occupied by Enzo and Angela had been vacated when they moved to the family villa. Believing that they would be separated when the Valletta departed, Norman had directed that their suite be prepared for the newlyweds. Now that Hewey was to remain with the ship, the accommodation was theirs for the duration of the current tour of duty. That final weekend the Hewitsons transferred their belongings and settled into their new quarters.

The Italian contingent of Operation Valletta, namely, Savino, Corso and De Cristofaro, were to continue working with Enzo, who as BMG was tasked to oversee the return of normal life after the war. They too had become attached to the Valletta and had come to Ischia for the weekend to reminisce with the others. Much had happened to their lives since their return and like Enzo and Angela this too would be their last time aboard the ship, which had brought Leo and Paolo back home to Naples.

Examination of von Prout by the surgical team under Betty's supervision found the German fit for surgery to remove the embedded shrapnel in his abdomen. This was to be done under general anaesthetic that morning rather than when the Valletta had put to sea. With the help of the administered analgesics, Von

Prout had slept well, spent a comfortable and good first night as the hospital ship's only patient. Despite being a prisoner, he was getting full service and the best medical treatment that could be provided to any VIP. For this German, the war was over, and he realised that his side was losing. The only thing he and others with like minds of the Wehrmacht could do, was to make peace and end the killing as soon as possible.

As a prisoner aboard the Valletta, von Prout was not under the direct authority of its Master until at sea. The BMG was the representative of his captors and Enzo had overall jurisdiction, he and Norman held the equivalent rank of the prisoner. Through Betty, von Prout had discovered that his old acquaintance the Bishop of Ischia was to say Mass in the ship's chapel that Sunday prior to departure and he requested that he be able to attend. Enzo, seeing that this would be an ideal opportunity for him to meet his German predecessor, granted von Prout his request. Hewey arranged for von Prout to be wheeled into the back of the congregation after all had entered the chapel, then taken out immediately after the last blessing. He was then to be wheeled to the Chapel's informal vestry where he could receive holy communion from the bishop. Enzo, Norman and Hewey would also be there.

The bishop welcomed his old acquaintance with a warm smile and blessed him in Latin. Alert but still weak from his wounds and surgery von Prout thanked him in English, "Thank you, Giovanni. For obvious reasons we should converse in English."

Hewey stepped forward to make the introductions. "May I present the British Military Governor, Colonel Vincenzo Falcone, Royal Army Medical Corps, and Commander Norman Butler, Master of the Valletta."

Hewey stood back. Von Prout spoke, "Thank you, Major!"

His tone was respectful, deferential, and dignified. It had the impact of softening any potential adversarial stance that his captors may have been contemplating.

"My father has told me of your meeting with him and acquaintance with the bishop when you were stationed in Rome as a young officer!" Enzo volunteered.

"That is correct. It was a very enjoyable lunch we had. High Command had put the Villa on a list of properties to be requisitioned. I removed it. Please send your parents my sincere regards, Colonel."

The sincerity of this response from von Prout disarmed all. A fellow officer who happened to be on the wrong side. Enzo remembered how he was treated in captivity, now he was the captor he expected no less treatment of this prisoner than what he had received. Norman and Hewey had already met von Prout and had briefed Enzo that the German would be given a degree of freedom aboard ship once at sea.

"Good luck, Colonel and bon voyage!"

Enzo shook von Prout's hand and exited the vestry.

Based on the tide that day, Norman planned to cast off at noon. Both he and Enzo would have preferred an inconspicuous and informal departure but HQ in Naples had requested a formal send off. This required uniforms, bands, parade, and the bishop's blessing for good measure.

'A show of the flag and who's in charge' was the rationale for it all. For Mayor Gaetano it demonstrated his link with the BMG and the chance to flout a little pomp and ceremony for his constituents. He stood next to the uniformed Enzo in his formal tailed black three-piece black suit, wing collar, white cravat with his tricolour sash of office. Side by side they both stood to attention as the band played the national anthems of both nations. The walkway from the Valletta was withdrawn, ropes untied, freeing the vessel from the quay. Engines already engaged, the ship's horns gave three blows which cued a three-shot salute from the royal Marine detail. As the Valletta edged away from its moorings the band played and the crowd cheered; Angela squeezed her husband's arm when, like her, the tears rolled down his face. Together with Mayor Gaetano they joined everyone else as they cheered.

"Addio Valletta buon viaggio e buona fortuna."